Intervention

Books by Terri Blackstock

If I Run Series
1 *If I Run*
2 *If I'm Found*
3 *If I Live*

The Moonlighters Series
1 *Truth Stained Lies*
2 *Distortion*
3 *Twisted Innocence*

The Restoration Series
1 *Last Light*
2 *Night Light*
3 *True Light*
4 *Dawn's Light*

The Intervention Series
1 *Intervention*
2 *Vicious Cycle*
3 *Downfall*

The Cape Refuge Series
1 *Cape Refuge*
2 *Southern Storm*
3 *River's Edge*
4 *Breaker's Reef*

Newpointe 911
1 *Private Justice*
2 *Shadow of Doubt*
3 *Word of Honor*
4 *Trial by Fire*
5 *Line of Duty*

The Sun Coast Chronicles
1 *Evidence of Mercy*
2 *Justifiable Means*
3 *Ulterior Motives*
4 *Presumption of Guilt*

Second Chances
1 *Never Again Good-Bye*
2 *When Dreams Cross*
3 *Blind Trust*
4 *Broken Wings*

With Beverly LaHaye
1 *Seasons Under Heaven*
2 *Showers in Season*
3 *Times and Seasons*
4 *Season of Blessing*

Novellas
Seaside
The Listener (formerly
The Heart Reader)
The Heart Reader of Franklin High
The Gifted
The Gifted Sophomores

Stand-Alone Novels
Smoke Screen
Catching Christmas
Shadow in Serenity
Predator
Double Minds
*Soul Restoration: Hope
for the Weary*
Emerald Windows
*Miracles (The Listener
/ The Gifted)*
Covenant Child
Sweet Delights
Chance of Loving You

Intervention

TERRI BLACKSTOCK

THOMAS NELSON
Since 1798

Intervention

Copyright © 2009, 2020 by Terri Blackstock

All rights reserved. No portion of this book may be reproduced, stored in a retrieval system, or transmitted in any form or by any means—electronic, mechanical, photocopy, recording, scanning, or other—except for brief quotations in critical reviews or articles, without the prior written permission of the publisher.

Published in Nashville, Tennessee, by Thomas Nelson. Thomas Nelson is a registered trademark of HarperCollins Christian Publishing, Inc.

Published in association with the literary agency of Alive Communications, Inc., 7680 Goddard Street, Suite 200, Colorado Springs, CO 80920. www.alivecommunications.com.

Interior design by Emily Ghattas

Thomas Nelson titles may be purchased in bulk for educational, business, fund-raising, or sales promotional use. For information, please email SpecialMarkets@ThomasNelson.com.

All Scripture quotations, unless otherwise indicated, are taken from the Holy Bible, New International Version®, NIV®. Copyright © 1973, 1978, 1984, 2011 by Biblica, Inc.® Used by permission of Zondervan. All rights reserved worldwide. www.zondervan.com. The "NIV" and "New International Version" are trademarks registered in the United States Patent and Trademark Office by Biblica, Inc.®

Publisher's Note: This novel is a work of fiction. Names, characters, places, and incidents are either products of the author's imagination or used fictitiously. All characters are fictional, and any similarity to people living or dead is purely coincidental.

ISBN: 978-0-7852-3740-2 (2020 repack)

Library of Congress Cataloging-in-Publication Data

Blackstock, Terri, 1957–.
Intervention: a novel / Terri Blackstock.
p. cm.
ISBN 978–0310–25065–4 (pbk.)
1. Parent and adult child—Fiction. 2. Drug addicts—Rehabilitation—Fiction. I. Title.
PS3552.L34285I58 2009
813'.54—dc22   2009018582

Printed in the United States of America

20 21 22 23 24 LSC 5 4 3 2 1

*This book is lovingly dedicated
to the Nazarene.*

one

The interventionist stood on the sidewalk at baggage claim, smoking a cigarette and chugging a Red Bull. What irony. The woman who'd promised to help rid Barbara's daughter of her addictions clearly had a few of her own. Barbara considered driving past her, leaving her to get back on the plane and return to the rehab she ran. She could work this out herself—lock Emily in her room and take away her car keys, force her to stay sober. But hadn't she already tried that? Despite Barbara's best efforts to turn their home into a lockdown, Emily still managed to sneak out and get high.

How had this happened?

That familiar knot burned in Barbara's stomach as she pulled to the curb and waved at the woman. It had to be her—the long red skirt, the white peasant blouse, just as she'd said. The outfit made her look more like a college student than someone who could escort a determined addict across the country. What if Emily put up a fight? How would this petite thing handle her?

Barbara stopped along the curb and popped her trunk. Forcing a welcoming smile, she got out of the car. "Hi, are you Trish?"

"Sure am." The woman dropped her cigarette on the concrete

and stomped it out with a sandaled foot, then thrust a hand out to Barbara. "Trish Massey."

"I'm Barbara Covington."

Barbara glanced at the small bag at the woman's feet. "Is this all you have?"

"Yeah, I won't be here long."

She picked up Trish's bag and set it on the back seat as Trish got into the car. Barbara slipped back into the driver's seat. The car that she'd freshened with Febreze suddenly smelled of smoke. "How was your trip?"

"Uneventful, which is always a good thing." Trish was all smiles. "So where did you tell Emily you were going?"

"To an Al-Anon meeting."

"And that's okay with her?"

Barbara breathed a laugh. "Oh, yeah. She likes it when I'm working on her problem. She would love it if everybody she knew were going to meetings and wringing their hands. She loves to keep us playing the What-To-Do-About-Emily game."

There she went again, letting her bitterness spill out to a stranger.

"Meetings are good," Trish said. "Have you really been to any?"

Barbara slipped the car into Drive and pulled away from baggage claim, heading to the loop that would take them out of the airport and into Jefferson City. "Plenty. I've done the workbooks and gone through the twelve steps, like I'm the one with the problem. I've done everything they've told me to do. But she's still using."

"Al-Anon meetings are to help *you* cope, not to give you some secret code to sober up your loved one."

Barbara knew that now. She'd gone to a few meetings, hoping to learn what would work with Emily. When she didn't get those answers, she'd lost interest. Her own sanity would return when her daughter was sane.

Strange that a woman who couldn't be more than thirty would

be counseling Barbara now. And who was Trish to counsel an eighteen-year-old? Emily would take one look at her and declare her dominance.

What was she doing? Maybe this was all wrong.

"You're doing the right thing," Trish said, as though she'd read Barbara's mind.

Barbara didn't want to cry in front of the stranger. For a moment she drove silently, staring at the taillights of the car in front of her. Finally, she spoke again. "When Emily was going into preschool, I personally visited fourteen schools. I interviewed teachers. I even spent a day with her at the one I liked, to see how she fit in."

"I don't blame you. I'd probably do the same thing if I had children."

"It's no easy thing, sending her to a place like this, halfway across the country. But I had to act quickly. There wasn't time for a careful, deliberate search. I should have been more prepared when things escalated."

"You mentioned on the phone that she'd stolen money?"

"Yes. Not the first time, but this was the most she'd taken. Four hundred dollars, right out of my account. She got my debit card out of my purse, went to the ATM. Spent every penny on drugs."

"How do you know?"

Barbara's fingers tightened over the steering wheel. "Because she didn't come home for three days. I found her strung out at a friend's house. I got her to come home, and while she was sleeping, I searched her things. Found some credit cards she'd taken out in her dad's name. John, my husband, died four years ago."

Barbara paused, expecting a gasp, but it didn't come. She supposed Trish had heard it all before. "You had to intervene," Trish said. "It sounds like her life has spun out of control."

Barbara's *own* life had spun out of control. First, John's cancer had disrupted their idyllic lives. When he died, she swam through grief so deep it almost drowned her. Being a forty-year-old widow with two children was the next mire she slogged through. But now, Emily's drug abuse was more than she could take.

"You won't be disappointed in our program," Trish said.

Barbara glanced at Trish. "She'll be locked in, right? Because if she isn't, she'll leave. I've tried treatment two other times—one time, she ran away after only a week. The second time, she smuggled drugs in and got kicked out."

"We don't lock them in, but she'll be monitored at all times. Don't worry, we do this all the time. She'll be very comfortable."

Comfort wasn't Barbara's main concern, though she didn't want Emily to be miserable. Barbara bit the inside of her cheek as she pulled onto the interstate, headed for the hotel she'd reserved for Trish. She was sinking thirty thousand dollars into Road Back Recovery Center, money that had come from a second mortgage on her house. But being expensive didn't guarantee that it was good. Even the best rehabs had underwhelming success rates.

She wished Trish inspired more confidence. "You seem very young. How did you come to own Road Back?"

Trish flicked her hair behind her ear. "I'm a recovering addict myself. I got clean at Road Back, and when I graduated, I stayed and worked there. I've been doing interventions for them for five years. A couple of years ago, the directors wanted to retire, so I decided to buy it. I couldn't stand the thought of it not being there anymore. That's how much I believe in the program."

That made Barbara feel somewhat better. She wished she could go to the facility herself to make sure it was all they advertised. But once she'd made up her mind to do the intervention, there hadn't been time to take a trip to check it out in person. Waiting could have resulted in Emily's arrest.

And Barbara knew she couldn't take Emily there herself. No, it would take a professional to convince Emily to go, and Trish had to be the one to escort her. Barbara was sending her daughter off to some unknown place with this woman she didn't know. Emily would pass this new threshold all alone . . . and be there for ninety days.

Emily had once been a fan of Hello Kitty and Amelia Bedelia. Now she collected pictures of her hero, Amy Winehouse, the famous addict with the hit song about avoiding rehab. Barbara still loved Emily with a love so painful that it ached through her at night, keeping her from sleep, but she didn't like this person who'd replaced her daughter. If only this rehab could exorcise the addiction within her, and return Emily home in her former condition . . .

It would be a miracle.

But what if this failed too? What if turmoil and madness were all the potential Emily would ever fulfill?

Blinking back tears, she took the exit near her home. The Hampton Inn sign loomed ahead. "I hope the room is okay. I went ahead and checked you in." Barbara handed Trish the key card.

"It'll be fine. You should see some of the places I've had to stay." As Barbara pulled into the parking lot, Trish shifted in her seat to look at her. "So, did you write the letters?"

"Yes." She parked and got the envelopes from her purse. "Here they are."

Trish took them and turned on the overhead light. "And who is Lance?"

"My son. He's fourteen. It's just us."

"Did Emily's problems start when her father died?"

"Not right away. But losing John was hard on all of us. Over the next year she got in with the wrong crowd." She paused and settled her gaze on Trish. "I want you to know, we're not like this. There was never even alcohol in our home. I've taken her to church every Sunday of her life . . ." Her voice faded. Trish had probably heard this same song and dance from every parent she dealt with.

"It's not your fault."

Then whose fault is it? Pursing her lips, Barbara let Trish read.

Finally, Trish looked up. "Will anyone else be at the intervention? Grandparents?"

"They're too far away, and not in good health. I've kept them in the dark about all this. It would kill them."

"Friends? A boss? Teachers?"

"Emily dropped out of school several months ago. Her senior year, six months before graduating, so there aren't teachers. Her friends are like her. They don't want her sober. And she lost her job three weeks ago. Hasn't been sober enough to get another one, so there's not a boss who can get through to her." Barbara glanced at Trish in the shadows of the car. "Is it a problem that it's only my son and me?"

"No, we can work with that." Trish handed the letters back. "You both did a good job with the letters. You told her what her addiction is doing to the family, how you see her destroying herself, and what you're asking her to do. The main thing is that you stick to your guns about what will happen if she refuses to go. To bring about change in her, you have to be willing to throw her out with no resources."

Barbara said nothing. She had grappled with that issue for months now and lain awake for the past three nights, begging God to give her a way out. Why couldn't he sweep down and deliver Emily, before Barbara had to send her away for help or throw her out on the street?

"Are you ready for that? Putting her out if she refuses to go?"

Barbara swallowed. "I don't know. I know it's what I should do, but it's like giving up. She'll die for sure."

"Or she might hit bottom and decide to get help."

Barbara wondered what hitting bottom really meant. The picture that always came to mind was of a body lying broken and bloody on the street after falling from a twenty-story building.

"I've tried tough love. The third time she got arrested for a DUI, they sentenced her to three weeks in the juvenile detention center. I didn't bail her out. It was the hardest three weeks of my life."

"But it still didn't scare her straight."

"No. She went back to drugs a week after she got out."

"Did you really think it would change her?"

"I'd hoped. What good was all that suffering while she sat in jail, if she didn't change?"

"Your suffering, or hers?"

Barbara looked at Trish. "Both."

"Again, you're doing the hard things *because* you expect them to change her. You need to shift your thinking. Tomorrow, if she refuses to go and you have to put her out, do it because you and your son refuse to keep participating in her destruction. Do it for the mental and emotional protection of you and Lance. And you have to convey that to her. Make her understand you've come to the end of your rope."

Barbara leaned her head back on the seat. "She has to go with you. That's all there is to it."

Trish reached over the back seat and got her bag. "Sometimes they want treatment," she said. "Sometimes they're more fed up than you know with the endless cycle they're caught in. Constantly trying to get enough money for another hit, thinking about it every waking moment, and never able to get that high they're looking for. Running on that horrible treadmill just to feel normal—or their version of normal. Do you think she's there yet?"

"I don't know. I really don't. I was hoping you were here to convince her, even if she doesn't want help."

"I can only do so much."

So what had this extra thirty-five-hundred-dollar fee paid for? A free vacation for this woman? "She *has* to go with you. If she doesn't, she'll wind up in jail."

"Or dead."

Dead. No, Barbara couldn't survive burying anyone else. "I can't let that happen. This has to work."

"I'll give it everything I've got. Maybe she's sick of her disease."

Barbara fought the urge to argue semantics. She hated the AA words like disease and relapse, like it was a virus Emily had caught somewhere. Yet she couldn't deny that Emily was sick.

Trish opened her car door. "What time will you pick me up?"

Barbara tried to think. The flight she'd booked for Trish and Emily was at three p.m. tomorrow, and this thing could take hours. They had to start early. "Eight a.m. I'll get her up while you're there."

"Tonight, you need to take her car to a friend's house. Park it there and hide the keys. If it's not in the driveway, she can't talk you into giving her the keys. If she leaves, it'll have to be without the car."

That wouldn't be hard. Emily could have one of her drug buddies there in minutes.

"Hopefully, her connection with you and her brother will be enough to make her go. And I'll do my part to make her see the possibilities." She got out her cigarettes, pulled one out. "It'll be okay. Most of the interventions I do are successful."

"But there's no guarantee."

"I'm afraid not."

She'd have to pay her whether Emily agreed to go or not. It had to work. Her resources were running out.

two

Morning was slow in coming. All night, Barbara's mind raced through possible outcomes. A year ago when she'd tried to force sobriety on her daughter, Emily had run out in a rage and called a cab, which took her to a place where she could use without censure. It had taken Barbara a week to locate her. Emily's network of drug-using friends was loyal and kept secrets well.

Barbara had taken pains to keep that from happening this time. She'd made certain Emily had no cash or credit cards in her wallet. Emily's car was parked in the driveway of Barbara's assistant who lived fifteen miles away, and the keys were well hidden. Barbara had taken Emily's cell phone out of her purse, and her laptop was hidden in Barbara's closet so Emily couldn't communicate with her friends during the intervention.

Still, her daughter's resourceful, conniving mind usually ran a few steps ahead of Barbara's. She had tried many times to guess what Emily might do in a given situation, but Emily almost always surprised her.

"Mom?"

Startled, Barbara sat up in bed and turned on her lamp. Her fourteen-year-old son, Lance, stood in her doorway, his dark hair tousled from his pillow. She glanced at the clock. It was five a.m. The sun hadn't begun to come up yet.

"What is it?"

He sat down on her bed. "I could tell you weren't sleeping. I listened at the door, and you weren't snoring."

"I don't snore!"

"You do, Mom. It's not the demonic, gargoyle kind of snore, like Jacob's dad does, but you definitely cut some Z's."

He looked like he'd had a rough night, as well. "So, you couldn't sleep, either?" she asked.

"No. I keep thinking about how Emily's gonna react when she sees that lady. She'll just freak. It's not gonna be fun. Mom, are you sure it's the right thing?"

Barbara had asked herself that question a million times. "Honey, what do you think will happen to her if we don't intervene?"

He considered that for a moment, his blue eyes soft in the lamplight. "I don't know. I guess she'll die."

"Then we have no choice, do we?"

"But maybe she'll come to her senses. I know a guy who had a brother who was heavy into cocaine or something, and one day he just got sick of it and quit."

"Emily's addiction has taken over her mind, Lance. She's not thinking clearly. I don't think she can quit without some help."

"But if we force her to go, don't you think she'll just wait to get out and go right back to it, like she did the other times?"

"My hope is that she'll get sober there, and then she'll be able to think clearly. If she gets back into her right mind, she'll *want* to get well, won't she? How could anybody in their right mind not want that?"

Lance lay down next to her, on the pillow where his dad once slept. "I don't know, Mom. Maybe her mind is wrecked so bad that she can't ever think like that again."

Barbara stared at the ceiling. "Then we'll keep her alive for the next few months. After that, we'll figure out another way to keep her alive."

Lance lay silently for a moment, staring up at the ceiling. "Can't we do it another day, and just go to the zoo or something?"

Barbara smiled. If only she could turn back time, to before Emily had her driver's license and all the freedom that entailed. If only she could have her as a bright-eyed kid again, happy and enthusiastic, with hopes and dreams as big as the universe.

"I wish the zoo was the answer," she whispered. "But this is big."

"You could ditch the rehab lady and take her yourself. At least then she wouldn't be so scared. I'd be scared if some stranger showed up to take me across the country."

"What do you think would happen if I did that? First of all, she'd never go. She'd flat-out refuse. And if I did get her on the plane, she'd spend the whole time trying to talk me out of it. By the time we got there, Lance, she'd have me so worn down that I'd give in for sure."

"Yeah, she would."

"We can't force her to go. All we can do is make her understand that if she won't go, she won't have our support anymore."

"That's forcing her, Mom."

"No, she still has a choice. Deep inside that brain of hers, maybe she really wants a way out of this bondage."

"I hope so. I'm sick of all the drama."

"Me too." She closed her eyes as painful memories flooded her mind. "Hey, Lance?"

"Yeah."

"Don't make me go through this again with you. Look at what drugs are doing to your sister, and decide never to use them."

"I won't. I like my teeth. Emily's look bad."

Just another casualty of Emily's drug use. After never having cavities as a child and wearing braces for a year, the drugs and nicotine were ruining her smile.

"I mean it," she said. "There'll come a day when you'll have the chance, and you'll think it's no big deal. That you can handle it. But that's a lie straight out of hell."

"I know. I've already had the chance, and I did say no."

She sat up and looked down at him. "You had the chance? You're only fourteen. Where did you have the chance?"

"Don't worry about it, Mom. The bottom line is that I didn't do it."

"Who offered it to you? One of your friends? Are they already using?"

"You can get it anywhere. If I wanted to do it I could. But I'm not a loser like Emily."

"Your sister is not a loser." Barbara dropped back down on the bed. The ceiling fan had a spider web trailing across the blades. There had been a time in her life when they were spit-polished. Everything was once nice and neat, organized and beautiful—like an advertisement for her interior design business. Now bedlam ruled her home. "I wish I could gather you both up and take you to some utopia where nothing bad could ever happen to you. I want you away from a culture that could do this to its young."

"It's not so bad, Mom." Lance's eyes were closed, and his voice was a whisper. "You did your job. You raised us right."

"Did I?" Barbara's mind did its familiar replay of all those critical moments in Emily's life when she'd done the wrong thing. She'd put her in the wrong high school, allowed her freedom too soon, failed to say *no* enough. There hadn't been enough consequences for her infractions, and the consequences Emily *had* faced had been too severe. Barbara had been overbearing and under-attentive. She'd yelled too much, let too much pass.

She heard Lance falling into a gentle sleep. The soft, rhythmic sound of his breathing told her she'd lost him.

Funny how a parent's goals could change. She had once dreamed of college and careers for her children, godly spouses and bouncing grandchildren. Though she still held that dream for Lance, she had only two goals for Emily—to keep her daughter from prison or death.

That had to be enough for now.

Tears burned as she thought of John, who'd died entrusting these children to her. She had done a terrible job with Emily. What would he think if he came back for a day and found that his daughter had given her life to drugs?

She wished he could be here to sit through this intervention with her. He would be able to convince Emily to go. But if he were here, her daughter never would have chosen to medicate away her grief.

Unable to sleep, Barbara got up to shower and get ready for this fateful day. She was a soldier going into battle, embarking on a fight for the soul of her child. Defeat was not an option.

three

Emily was hard to wake. Barbara stood over her bed, shaking her gently, pulling her from her sleep. Emily had slept fully dressed in a ragged pair of jeans that she'd worn for a week, and a Third Eye Blind T-shirt that reeked of odors Barbara couldn't name. Tangled hair strung into her eyes, unwashed and greasy, thinner than it was a month ago. Deep, dark circles hung like bruises under her eyes.

Barbara had left Lance in the living room making awkward conversation with Trish, who sipped black coffee, waiting to do what they'd paid her to do. Barbara's heart was heavy as she turned Emily over and shook her again. "Emily, wake up, honey."

Emily's eyes slit open. "What? I'm sleeping."

"I need you to get up."

"Leave me alone." She turned over again and pulled her pillow over her head.

"Emily, get up. Now."

"What time is it?"

"It's eight-thirty."

"Are you kidding me? I'm not getting up at eight!"

Losing her patience, Barbara threw back the covers and pulled

Emily up to a sitting position. "I want you to come into the living room. Somebody's here to see you."

Emily squinted up. "Who?"

"Come out and you'll see."

"No, tell me now. Is it the police?"

Barbara's heart sank. Did Emily know something Barbara didn't know? Were the police after her? Barbara crossed to the door, opened it. "Come on."

Emily slid out of bed. "Can I at least go to the bathroom?"

"Yes, but hurry." She watched as Emily dragged herself into the hall, to the bathroom next door. She followed her and waited outside the door. Emily was taking way too long. Was she using? How would they get through to her if she was high?

Barbara opened the door. Emily stood at the sink, pills in her hand.

"What is wrong with you?" Emily yelled, closing her hand. "Why can't you give me some privacy?"

This wasn't going well. Barbara's job was to get Emily to the living room quietly, in a non-threatening way. The introduction of her interventionist was supposed to be done calmly—not with yelling and anger. By the time Barbara got her in there, Emily would have her defenses up as high as the Wall of China.

"Someone needs to talk to you. It's an emergency."

"Are they arresting me? Because I didn't do anything."

The thought of the police was only making Emily drag her feet. "No, it's not the police. It's a family meeting."

"At the crack of dawn?" Emily's defenses lowered a bit. "Okay, fine, I'm coming."

Barbara wished Emily would take a moment to brush her teeth and hair. For some reason, she wanted Emily to make a good impression on the woman who dealt each day with those who'd ravaged their own bodies with poisons of every flavor.

Instead, Emily came out of the bathroom looking like she'd just been dragged from a crack house. Arms crossed over her chest, she followed Barbara into the living room. Her gaze landed on the strange woman sitting in her dad's recliner. She paused and hugged herself tighter. "Who are you?"

"Emily, this is Trish Massey."

Trish stood up. "I'm a counselor, Emily. Can we talk for a minute?"

Emily frowned and sat on the couch next to her brother. Lance couldn't meet her eyes. Barbara's heart hammered so hard that she feared Emily could see her blouse thumping as she sat down on the other side of her.

"Your family asked me to come here and talk to you about your drug problem."

Emily sprang up. "This is a setup! One of those stupid interventions. I should have known. I'm not sitting here for this."

"Emily, just hear me out."

Barbara stood and took Emily's hand, trying to keep her from walking away. She jerked back. Lance stuck out his legs and blocked her on the other side.

"I don't have a drug problem," she said. "I'm fine. Do I look like I'm on drugs?"

"Actually, yes," Trish said.

Emily turned on Barbara. "I knew I couldn't trust you! This is as bad as the cops."

"No, it isn't." Barbara tried to keep her voice calm. "We're trying to help you."

Calmly, Trish nodded to Lance and said, "Go ahead and read your letter."

"No, I'm not listening!" Emily cried. "This is garbage. I'm not doing this!"

She stepped over Lance's legs and moved around the couch,

headed for the front door. Barbara sprang up and blocked her at the foyer. "Emily, you can't leave. Your car isn't here. I moved it."

"You stole my car?"

"I own your car."

Emily let out a frustrated yell. "Forget it, I'll call somebody."

"Your mother hid the phones too," Trish said. "And your computer. You need to sit down and listen."

Emily looked like a trapped animal. "I'll walk, then."

"Emily," Trish said, "all we're asking is a few minutes. I know you don't want to be like this. Just hear us out."

Trish met Barbara's eyes. They'd talked about this. It would all have to be done in order, Trish had told her on the way to the house. If they let Emily leave the room, she would get the upper hand.

"I *know* what those stupid letters say! I've watched that show on TV, with those lame interventions. They're all about how much you love me and want to see me get help. But I don't need help."

Trish nodded to Lance to start reading. He looked like he'd rather be dragged behind a car.

"Dear Emily," he began. "We used to be closer, but in the last few years you've changed."

Emily turned back and jerked the letter out of his hand. She ripped it into little pieces and let it snow down onto the floor. "I'm not listening," she shouted into his face.

Lance sprang up, his cheeks blotched red. "You're gonna die, just like Dad. How fair is that, huh? He's probably watching from heaven and crying because you weren't supposed to be stupid!"

She flinched like she'd been slapped.

"He thought you were gonna be somebody!" Lance yelled.

"Shut up, Lance!" Emily cried. "I don't want to talk about Dad."

"He died proud of you!" Lance shouted. "You think he's proud now?"

Emily's face twisted, and tears muddied the mascara smudged

under her eyes. She turned to Barbara, who was still blocking her. "Get out of my way."

"Emily, I took your cash, your phone, your keys. You can't leave."

Trish's voice rose above the chaos. "Emily, I work at the Road Back Recovery Center. It's north of Atlanta, on twenty acres. It's a beautiful, peaceful place, and it changed my life when I was in your shoes."

"No! The last thing I want is to be around a bunch of dope-sick addicts. I'm not like them."

Lance's eyes were moist. "Emily, I saw the website. It's really pretty, on some river. They have boats and a pool."

Emily smeared her tears across her face. "I don't want to leave my friends and change my whole life. I need to at least say good-bye. I need a few days to pack and get my stuff together. Then maybe I'll go."

"No, honey," Barbara said. "We have an airline ticket for you today at three."

Emily grunted. "No way I'm getting on a plane today! And you're sending me off with somebody I don't even know? That's just like you, Mom. Dad would never hire some stranger to do his dirty work!"

That knocked the wind out of Barbara, and Emily took the opportunity to push past her into the hallway. Before Barbara could stop her, Emily had slammed herself into her room.

For the next hour, they stood at the door trying to coax her out. It had happened just as Trish warned. Emily had taken control of the intervention, and they were going to have a hard time getting it back.

On the other side of the door, things crashed as Emily screamed profanities, sometimes breaking into stage sobs. Barbara closed her eyes, imagining the state of Emily's room when they finally got through that door. Drawers emptied, clothes piled high on the floor, drink cans overturned . . .

Barbara's voice was hoarse from yelling, and she shivered as if she were cold. Maybe this wasn't going to work. Maybe all the effort was wasted. An hour had ticked by, and Emily still had the upper hand.

"The drugs are like a romance for her," Trish said in a low voice. "They're a lover that she doesn't want to leave."

Lance leaned against the wall. "She's probably in there using right now."

"Probably, if she has some," Trish admitted. "Does she smoke?"

Barbara's head was beginning to hurt. "She's not allowed to smoke at home, but I found cigarettes in her purse last night. I took them out and threw them away."

"Good," Trish said. "That gives me an opening." She knocked on the door. "Emily? This is Trish."

"Leave me alone! I don't know you!"

"Would you like to step outside with me and have a cigarette? We can talk alone out there."

Barbara's stomach tightened and her jaw clenched. She had never allowed Emily to smoke in her sight, and she didn't want to condone it now. But suddenly the door flew open.

Barbara held her breath.

Emily shot past her and out the back door. Trish got her cigarettes and followed. Barbara watched through the French doors, amazed as Trish gave Emily a cigarette. Her daughter lit up.

"Well, isn't this fun?" Lance gave Barbara a strained smile.

She laughed, thankful for a break in the tension. At least they weren't moving backward. "How does anybody do this for a living?" She wanted to collapse into a chair, but there was too much to do. "Pray. We've wasted a lot of time. I need to have them at the airport before two, so we need to leave here around one."

Emily's eyes were swollen, but she was talking now, and that look of defiance seemed to have melted away. Who would have thought Trish's smoking habit would turn out to be helpful?

"You could pack now, while she's busy."

He was right. Barbara went to her own closet to get a suitcase, then to Emily's room to inspect the fallout. Just as she'd suspected, Emily had trashed the place. Framed pictures of family and friends lay broken and torn on the floor. There was a hole in her closet door, and everything that had once been on her dresser lay spilling onto the carpet—perfume bottles and hair products and nail polish remover, her box of keepsakes, and the basket of barrettes and ribbons from years gone by. The only thing left on the dresser was the picture of Emily with her dad.

Barbara had done laundry yesterday and put the folded clothes on Emily's chest of drawers. They lay in a heap now, among her dirty clothes. She sifted through the pile and found the clean ones. What would make Emily comfortable for ninety days? What was northern Georgia like in October? She'd need sweatpants, warm sweaters in case it got cold at night, T-shirts, jeans. She dug for some socks, then went through Emily's drawers, searching for that pair of silky pajamas she'd given her last Christmas Eve.

Barbara heard the patio door open, Emily coming back in. Abandoning the suitcase, she returned to the living room.

"I'll go on one condition," Emily announced. "I need my cell phone and some cash."

"I'll give Trish some cash for your soft drinks and snacks, but I'm not giving you any."

Emily crossed her arms. "Then I'm not going."

It was a power struggle, as always. Barbara looked at Trish, gaining some strength from her nod. "Okay, I'll give you ten dollars so you can buy food at the airport."

"And the phone."

"You can't bring the phone," Trish cut in. "I'm sorry, but it's not allowed."

"That's ridiculous!"

Emily burst into tears, and Barbara thought it would all start up again. But finally her daughter threw up her hands. "All right, then, treat me like a prisoner. I can't go cold turkey, I hope you know. I have to take something before I leave."

"Go ahead," Trish said.

Appalled, Barbara shot Trish a look.

"It's okay," Trish said. "She'll be in detox for the first couple of weeks. We don't expect them to be clean when they get there."

Now Barbara wanted to scream. "I don't want her high on the plane. They won't even let her through security."

"I won't be high!" Emily shouted. "Don't you get it? I can't get a high anymore. I take more and more just to keep from feeling crummy."

It was the first time Emily had ever admitted her addiction. To Barbara, it felt like a huge step; she had to hand it to Trish.

"I've run out before and tried to stop cold turkey, and I get diarrhea and sick to my stomach and horrible headaches. Do you want me hurling on the plane?"

Barbara's heart softened. Emily had tried to stop on her own? It brought her a fragile hope, but at the same time she knew it could just be a con. Emily had known she could get help if she needed it, yet she had resisted it over and over.

"She told me what she's been taking," Trish cut in. "Withdrawals from some of those drugs can even cause seizures."

"Emily, you can't take drugs through airport security," Barbara said. "They'll arrest you."

Distraught, Emily turned her wet eyes to Trish. "Do you promise me they'll give me something when I get there? That I won't have to vomit my guts out?"

"We have a doctor who'll prescribe what you need to keep you comfortable through your withdrawals."

Emily sat on the couch, pulled her feet up, and hugged her knees. She looked so small. Barbara knew her daughter needed comforting, but time was running out. She stood helpless, not certain what to do next.

Lance sat next to Emily and touched her back. "Look at it as an adventure, Sis. You loved camp."

Emily shot him a disgusted look. "It's nothing like camp. You don't know what you're talking about."

Barbara sat on the other side of Emily and pulled her into a hug. Emily fell against her. Stroking her tangled hair, Barbara said, "You need to do this for yourself, honey. You need to get your life back on track and be the girl who could do or be anything she wanted."

Emily pulled away from Barbara then and sat stiffly, drawing in a long, deep breath. "All right, I'll go. What choice do I have?"

Warm, sweet relief washed through Barbara's heart, renewing her hope. "Okay, let's get you packed."

four

The ride to the airport was tense. Emily sat in the front passenger seat, crying, defiantly smoking out the window.

Lance sat rigid in the back seat next to Trish, as if his slightest move would frighten his sister into jumping out of the moving car.

"Will I be able to call my friends?" Emily asked.

Barbara glanced in the rearview mirror at Trish.

"You'll be allowed to make a ten-minute call once a week for the first two weeks," Trish said. "After that, you'll earn more privileges."

"Sounds like jail."

"It's nothing at all like jail."

"Do I have to share a room?"

"With one person."

"Is she my age?"

"Within a couple of years, if they put you with the girl I'm thinking of."

"Is she nice?"

The question caught Barbara by the heart.

"She's cool," Trish said. "You'll like her."

"What's her background? With drugs, I mean."

Trish hesitated. "I'm not allowed to discuss that. Confidentiality and all."

Barbara glanced over as Emily took a drag of her cigarette, staring out the window. Was she nervous about meeting new people, this child who slept in dope houses?

When they reached the airport, Barbara pulled into short-term parking and found an empty space near the front of the garage.

Emily put out her cigarette and lit up another as Barbara got her suitcase and carry-on out of the trunk. Lance took the bag, and Barbara rolled the suitcase. Trish carried her own bag.

Emily walked along detached from the group, refusing to help.

"We need to hurry, Emily," Barbara said. "There's no telling how long the line is at security. And I forgot to print out your boarding pass, so you'll have to go to the kiosk."

Emily walked in front of Barbara, her too-long jeans dragging the concrete, the dirty hem frayed and rolled. She had a peace sign bleached on the hip. She still wore the black Third Eye Blind T-shirt she had slept in. It made her skin look pallid and gray.

"Put the cigarette out, Emily. You can't take it in."

Emily located an ashtray over a trash can and stubbed her cigarette out.

They went inside and found the Delta kiosk, got the boarding passes, and checked Emily's bag. Lance took Emily's carry-on to security. Thankfully, the line was short.

Barbara reached out to hug her daughter. "It's going to be fine, honey. You'll get well and come back as good as new."

"Three months is a freakin' eternity."

She took Emily's face in her hands. "It'll pass before you know it. Work hard, okay? I'll be praying for you. And we'll come and visit as soon as you're allowed to have us."

Emily turned to Lance and took her bag, gave him a hug. She

held her brother a moment longer than she needed to. Finally, she kissed his cheek and let him go.

Barbara thanked Trish, who winked at her. Then she and Lance stood back and watched as the two sailed through security without a search. Emily didn't look back. As they disappeared from view, Barbara stood frozen, her throat tight. For a moment, she thought she would be sick.

"We better get out of here before she comes running back," Lance whispered.

Gathering herself, Barbara followed him out.

"You okay, Mom?"

She touched her chest. "Yeah, just a little light-headed."

"You're breathing like Grandma."

"I can't believe she went. I'm still shaking." They reached the car and got in.

"Let's wait until her plane leaves."

"Okay." She started the car. It would be a long wait, and they probably wouldn't be able to pick out her plane, but Lance didn't seem any more eager to leave the airport than she was. They needed to be here, in case she refused to get on the plane or caused trouble once she was on it.

"If she calls from Trish's phone, you can't wimp out, Mom."

"I won't answer."

They sat quietly in the car for a while, watching the planes coming and going. When it was about time for Emily's flight, they saw a Delta plane take off. She told herself that was it. Barbara whispered a prayer for Emily's safety.

As the plane vanished into the clouds, so did her heaviness. Her nightmare was almost over.

five

Instead of going home to tackle the mess Emily had left in her room, Barbara dropped Lance off at a friend's house and went to her office to work for a while, hoping Emily's departure would restore her creative energy.

It had been months—maybe years—since Barbara had felt creative. She'd learned to fake it well, to do her work as though she still had passion. Clients raved about her interior designs in their homes and businesses, but it took longer and longer to pull off those successes, which meant it took longer and longer to get paid.

Now business was slow and things were tight. If she wasn't able to win some new jobs soon, she would have to lay off her assistant, and she'd lose her construction crew. It had taken her years to develop trust and respect with the subcontractors who executed her designs—knocking down walls, restructuring floor plans, building and painting and installing flooring . . .

Their loyalty to her enabled her to get tough design projects completed in a shorter amount of time. She could call her trusty crew and have them at work within a matter of days, instead of waiting weeks for unreliable contractors. But when business was slow, her crew had no choice but to contract other jobs. The threat of losing them for good always hung over her.

The opportunity to renovate the governor's mansion had come just in time. It was exactly what she needed to breathe new life into her design studio. It would keep her and her crew busy for months, and net her enough to pay off the debts she'd accrued trying to save Emily. She had the skill and talent, but doubts had plagued her. Could she accomplish such a job with Emily's problems distracting her?

She had hope now. If Emily didn't run away or get thrown out, she would be at Road Back for three months—long enough for Barbara to get started on a knock-dead design for the governor and his wife. If Emily returned home whole, Barbara could give her business the attention it needed to survive, and even thrive.

The presentation was only days away. The mansion hadn't been updated in fifty years, and Barbara was honored to be among the designers being considered. In fact, she'd heard from her friend who worked for the governor's wife that she was the favorite going in. Barbara had decorated the home of the first lady's sister, so Mrs. Pearson had seen her work. If she got the bid, it would become her masterpiece and a huge draw for other clients who had money and prestige. It was what Barbara had worked her entire career for, and was probably the only thing that could pull her finances out of the tank.

Her big presentation was a week from Friday, and she had a ton of work to do to get ready. She had found dozens of choices of fabrics for each room and had completed the plans for the parlor, the living room, and the opulent dining room. With that base, she now had to find the new furnishings and accessories for fifteen other rooms, and display them in a compelling way on her design board. Getting ready would take every waking moment between now and the presentation.

She was just deciding on the style of window covering for the master bedroom when her cell phone rang. She checked the caller ID. It was Trish's number. They must be in Atlanta.

She clicked it on. "Hello?"

"Mom, we just landed." Emily sounded stopped up, as if she'd cried the whole trip.

"Hi, sweetie. How was the flight?"

"Okay. I didn't even have time to shower. I look awful."

"Where's Trish?"

"Right here."

"Did she sit by you on the plane?"

"No, they didn't give us seats together."

Barbara closed her eyes. Didn't Trish know better than to leave Emily unsupervised?

"Mom, please let me come home. I can quit without rehab," Emily said. "I know what to do. I just have to do it."

Barbara heard an announcement in the background, the voices of a crowd. She was glad she wasn't there. "You're not coming home, Emily. You want a future, don't you? I've tried for years to get you clean, and you're still using."

"Don't you understand? I'm scared!"

Barbara's defenses lowered a notch. She squeezed her eyes shut. "Let me talk to Trish."

She heard Emily sniffling and whispering, then Trish took the phone. "Barbara, she'll be fine. We're going to get our bags, and we'll be at Road Back in a couple of hours."

"She took something on the flight," Barbara said. "She sounds slurred."

"Don't worry about it. She's fine."

"You can't search her or something? Make sure she doesn't overdose because she's so upset?"

"We'll do a thorough shakedown once we get there. Everything's going according to plan."

Barbara sighed. Why had she chosen this woman? On the phone, she'd seemed completely anti-drugs. If Barbara had known Trish would shrug off Emily's use of drugs on the plane, she'd have found someone else. "Have her call me when you get to the center, okay? I'm really nervous about all this."

"Will do. Just relax. She'll be fine."

As Trish hung up, Barbara looked down at her phone. If this didn't work, what would? Covering her face with her hands, she prayed that God would lift Emily's misery and give her daughter a more positive outlook about her future. She tried to put herself in Emily's shoes. Was Trish right? Was Emily grieving a lover, plotting ways to save her romance with drugs? How could she romanticize something that would inflict a slow death? In no other circumstance would anyone cling to their murderer.

It was insanity, a self-inflicted sickness. Emily had summoned it, fed it, bowed to it, and now she was the only one who could turn away from it. Barbara couldn't do it for her.

She prayed that God would give Emily the strength and clarity to do just that. It would take his miracle to heal her now.

six

Barbara worked in blissful silence for the next two hours, until Lance called to tell her his friend's dad was bringing him home. Finally, she left her office and stopped by the grocery store to pick up a few things. As she went through the checkout, she glanced at her watch. Emily and Trish should have already made it to the center. Why hadn't they called her?

She tried calling Trish's cell phone, but got voice mail. Maybe they were out of range. Surely they'd call when they had service again.

When she got home, she found Lance playing a video game. "Heard from Emily?" he asked.

"I talked to her when they got to Atlanta. Nothing since."

"Good sign, I hope."

Barbara hoped so too. She picked up the phone and dialed Trish's number again. It rang four times, then voice mail came on. Trish's greeting sounded upbeat and lyrical. "Hi, this is Trish. I'm totally bummed about missing your call. Okay, not really, because I don't know you called yet, but when I find out I'm sure I'll be devastated. So leave a message so I can make things right. Talk atcha soon. Bye!"

Barbara hoped the woman's sunny disposition would rub off

on Emily. "Trish, this is Barbara Covington, just hoping for an update on Emily. Please call me when you get this." She hung up and checked her watch again.

"Don't worry, Mom. They've probably got the music turned up too loud to hear the phone."

That didn't make her feel any better. Heavy metal and sobriety weren't exactly soulmates, were they? She caught her mind heading down that negative trail and forced herself to rein it back in. Nothing in Trish's demeanor suggested that she listened to heavy metal. And even if she did, it didn't make her evil.

Lance dropped the controller. "Either that, or Emily bolted and Trish is trying to chase her down."

Barbara felt sick.

Lance grinned. "I'm just kidding, Mom. She doesn't even know anybody in Georgia. Not like she can get somebody to pick her up."

Barbara wasn't so sure. Emily had a huge network of "friends" through social media that sucked up so much of her daughter's time. She wouldn't be surprised if Emily had cyber-friends in northern Georgia. It would be just like Emily to call somebody she thought was a teenaged girl, only to find that it was some perverted middle-aged pedophile thrilled to "rescue" her.

"Mom, they're fine, okay? Maybe their luggage was lost and they're waiting to get it all worked out. Remember that time ours got lost? We had to wait in line for forty-five minutes, and then found out it was coming on the next plane. That's probably it. They're probably waiting for the next plane to bring it in."

If Lance hadn't been as concerned as Barbara was, he wouldn't be trying so hard to think of every possible scenario. But this was getting them nowhere. Deciding to give her anxiety a rest, she retrieved her design board out of her trunk. Lance went back to his game.

Barbara worked on her presentation for the governor's bedroom as the next half hour passed. Still no word. She called and left another message.

Too anxious now to concentrate, she called the rehab to see if Emily had checked in yet. She hadn't, and they hadn't heard from Trish.

Where could they be?

Another hour passed, and Lance fell asleep on the couch. Abandoning her work, Barbara began pacing. She called and left a third message. As she did, her phone beeped. An Atlanta number.

Quickly, she switched over to answer the call. "Hello?"

"Could I speak to Emily Covington, please?" It was a man's voice.

"Emily's not here. Who's calling?"

There was a pause. "This is Detective Kent Harlan from the Atlanta Police Department."

Her heart crashed like a crystal chandelier. "This is Emily's mother. What is it? Has something happened to my daughter?"

"I got this number from her Delta itinerary. Could you tell me how I could reach her?"

"Why are you looking for her?"

"I'm at the airport investigating a case."

She closed her eyes. What had Emily done now? "What kind of case?"

"I'm with the homicide division."

"Homicide? Who . . . who was killed?"

"A woman named Patricia Massey. Do you know her?"

Trish!

The room began to reel. Barbara reached out to steady herself. "Dear God, Trish is dead? What . . . How?"

"What is your relationship to Ms. Massey?"

"Emily was traveling with her!" she yelled. "Trish is an interventionist. She was escorting my daughter to rehab. What happened?"

"Ma'am, we're not sure. Have you heard from Emily at all since she left Jefferson City?"

"She called briefly, and I talked to Trish too. They were going to baggage claim. But nothing since then. I've been calling for hours, trying to get in touch with them." Perspiration dripped into her eyes, burning them. "Please . . . how was she murdered?"

"I'm afraid I can't give out that information. But your daughter isn't here. If you hear from her, I need you to call me. It's very important that we speak to her."

"You're sure she's not there at the airport?"

"No, we're not sure. We're looking for her."

"Well, didn't someone witness this? Didn't they notice Emily? She couldn't have just vanished!"

"We're still investigating, ma'am."

She looked frantically around the room, trying to think. "I'll be there on the next flight. But you have to find Emily. She's in that airport somewhere." Her mind made random connections. "If someone killed Trish, they might have hurt Emily. She's only eighteen and . . . she might be impaired."

"Impaired, how?"

Was this man deaf? "I told you she was on her way to rehab!"

"Oh, right. I see."

"No, you don't see. She was fragile and upset, and if she just witnessed a traumatic event, then she could be hiding somewhere, scared to death . . ."

"Mrs. Covington, is your daughter an IV drug user?"

Barbara hesitated. "I don't know. Maybe. I've found needles once before, but lately I think it was pills."

His pause made her regret her answer. "I think it's a good idea for you to catch the next flight, Mrs. Covington, and it would help if you could bring some current pictures of Emily. When you get here, call me back at this number."

She promised to call and said she would be there as soon as possible.

It was almost ten o'clock. Would there be any more flights out to Atlanta tonight?

She ran into the living room and shook Lance. "Get up!" she said. "Your sister's in trouble."

He sat up, groggy. "What did she do now?"

"She's vanished, and Trish is dead!"

He sprang off the sofa, suddenly awake. "No way!"

"The police just called. I have to take the next flight to Atlanta." She ran to the bedroom and grabbed an overnight bag from her closet, unzipped it, and threw it on her bed. "Call Jacob and see if you can stay with him."

His cheeks were mottled pink. "Mom, I want to go with you."

She ran to her closet but couldn't decide what she needed. She grabbed something off a hanger and threw it in. "You can't come. I don't know what's going to happen when I get there."

"She's my sister! I'll go crazy staying home."

"Lance, I don't have time for this!" Her ticket! She fell into the chair at her desk and, with shaking hands, began searching flights. "The last flight is at eleven, an hour from now. I'll never make it."

"See? You don't have time to drop me by Jacob's. But we can make it if we hurry. I'll go pack."

"Lance, call Jacob!" She dug her credit card out of her purse. If she made the reservation online, she could get her boarding pass and probably make it on time.

"Mom, if you leave me here, I'm liable to get into all sorts of trouble and wind up like Emily. Who knows how long you'll be gone?"

"Don't threaten me, Lance."

"I could help find her. I know how to think like her. Besides, this could be dangerous."

Her hands were shaking too badly. She couldn't do this.

"Here, let me," Lance said.

She surrendered the keyboard and tried not to cry. There wasn't time. "The eleven o'clock flight. Any seat. Whatever it costs."

He looked up at her. "Two seats?"

She threw up her hands. "Okay, two."

"Yes!" he whispered, and deftly entered the information. "Credit card?"

She tossed it to him, then ran back to her room and finished packing. By the time she was zipping her suitcase, he brought her the boarding passes. It took him two minutes to pack his own duffel bag, and they dashed out to the car.

On the way to the airport, Barbara prayed aloud that God would protect Emily from the forces of hell that stalked her.

seven

Detective Kent Harlan pocketed his cell phone and went back to the Lexus, where the body sat slumped in the driver's seat. Crime scene investigators stood at the doors, photographing the scene.

There was a handkerchief on the floor in the back seat, next to an empty syringe. They would send them both to forensics to identify what they contained. But he knew chloroform when he smelled it.

From the looks of things, someone had knocked Massey out with the chloroform . . . then injected her with something. Without touching the woman's body, he looked for an injection point. There was a small blood spot on her back. He'd wait for the Medical Examiner to confirm it, but it seemed likely that was where the needle had gone in. There had been no witnesses, but someone walking to his car had seen the woman slumped over her steering wheel and called 911. If the time of her arrival by plane was any indication, she had probably been dead for three hours by that time. Whoever did it had taken her wallet, since it wasn't in her purse.

The security video showed two women walking to the car, loading suitcases into the trunk. The deceased had gotten into the driver's side while the other one finished her cigarette. The second one—the girl that he assumed was Emily Covington—had gotten into the passenger side. She hadn't stayed there for more than a couple of seconds before she jumped out and ran. Clips from other cameras showed her running across the garage, then getting into a black sedan with an unidentifiable tag and a driver he couldn't see.

"Get anything?" Andy, his partner, asked.

Kent looked up at the man who'd just busted through thirty yesterday. He had bags under his eyes, testifying to his birthday celebration. Kent had passed on the party. At forty-five, he'd grown fonder of his sleep than boozing it up at bars. Besides, it always brought him down to see Andy's happy marriage and all his happy friends. It was sweet enough to give you cavities.

"Yeah." He glanced at the notes he'd taken while talking to Barbara Covington. "Emily Covington is an eighteen-year-old addict. According to her mother, she was being escorted to rehab by Patricia, nicknamed Trish, who was an interventionist."

Andy's chin came up. "Interesting."

"Isn't it, though?"

"So the girl was about to get the rug pulled out from under her. Took matters into her own hands."

Kent went back to his car and loaded the video from his thumb drive onto his laptop. The girl was a small, skinny kid. Not much taller than five-foot-two or three. If her mother hadn't just told him she was eighteen, he'd have sworn she was thirteen or fourteen.

Andy crossed the garage to Kent's car, leaned in. "So was the girl an IV drug user?"

"Her mother wasn't sure. Said she'd found needles once."

Andy shrugged. "What would the mother know, anyway? She probably knows about one percent of what the girl's been doing, and what she does know, she's probably in denial about."

"True, but if the girl had needles on her, you'd think security would have picked up on it before she flew."

"Addicts are really good at smuggling. And security guards miss stuff all the time."

Kent thought of Barbara Covington's voice. She didn't sound in denial, though she was clearly distraught. She also didn't sound like the foul-mouthed mothers of some of the drug addicts he'd encountered—meth moms who had babies and raised them to be methheads themselves. No, she sounded more like the members of his own family, who hadn't seen addiction coming until it crashed down on them like a crane load of bricks.

And then it was too late.

Barbara Covington's declaration that she was coming here meant she might actually be a decent person—someone clearly concerned about her child.

"So the girl has a motive," Andy said. "Didn't want to go to rehab, was probably jonesing for a fix. When we find her, she'll probably have the stolen wallet on her. Ready cash for a drug buy."

"Not to mention the credit cards," Kent muttered. "Get a list of the cards Massey was carrying and any charges made on them today. Hopefully, the girl will be sloppy and use them. Emily Covington's mother is coming here on the next flight out. I told her to bring pictures."

"Good. I'll get Emily's driver's license photo and check for priors, while I'm working on the credit cards," Andy said.

Kent looked around.

"I'll wait here. If she's in the airport somewhere, we'll find her. Maybe we can lock her up in time to get a few hours' sleep."

eight

Barbara and Lance reached the airport twenty minutes before departure time—ten minutes after everyone else had boarded. Thankfully, there wasn't a line at security, so they made their way through and reached the gate before the doors were shut.

"We're in 14A and B," Lance said as they boarded.

They greeted the flight attendant and walked down the aisle of the half-empty plane. Barbara found their seats and shoved their bags into the compartment above them, then dropped into the window seat.

Lance sat down next to her. "We made it."

She closed her eyes. She hadn't realized until now that she was drenched in sweat. The air conditioner on the plane made her shiver. She pulled her phone out of her purse and checked to see if Emily had called.

Of course she hadn't. She didn't have a phone. Barbara had sent her across the country without any means of communication.

Emily, where are you?

As the plane backed away from the gate, she closed her eyes and prayed again. Guard her, Lord. Protect her from others . . . and from herself.

And then she prayed for the family of that poor woman who lay dead at the Atlanta airport. Guilt surged through her that she'd been so judgmental about Trish. She'd judged her smoking, her drinking Red Bull, her plan for getting Emily from Point A to Point B. She'd even judged the amount of money Trish charged for her services, though Barbara had certainly been willing to pay it.

Now Trish was dead. It didn't even seem real. Her head throbbed, threatening to explode.

"Mom, do you think it could be a joke?"

She opened her eyes. "What do you mean?"

"Some kind of prank. Emily has a lot of sick friends. Maybe some crazy dude pretended to be a cop."

If only. "No, he sounded official. Older. Not a kid."

"There are a lot of older dopers. They could be getting a good laugh out of it right now."

"Then why hasn't Trish called? Why hasn't the rehab heard from her?"

"I don't know. Maybe Emily did get somebody to pick her up in Atlanta, and Trish is avoiding your calls because she doesn't want to get in trouble for losing her."

No, there would have to be too many people working together to pull that off. The idea made no sense. "Even if that were true, Emily's in danger. If she called some stranger to pick her up there, then God knows what kind of mess she's in." The plane accelerated down the runway, and she held her breath as they became airborne. "Nobody would play a prank like that."

"Emily's friends would."

Well, that was true. If Lance was right, they'd still have to find Emily, but at least Trish wouldn't be dead. As soon as they got to Atlanta, she'd call the police department and confirm that Kent Harlan really was a detective on the force.

Lance bent over and grabbed his backpack, fished out a notebook. Studying for school? She doubted it. She watched as he opened the cover and skimmed the first page. Emily's handwriting was unmistakable.

"What is that?"

He shrugged. "I grabbed her journals. You should read them. They're crazy. I brought two, and they're chock-full of her confessions."

"You read her journals?"

"Yeah." He said it like she was stupid to ask. "She leaves them out so any fool can read them. When she remembers to, she hides them in her bottom dresser drawer."

"So when she doesn't have them out, you just dig through her things?"

"Hey, I wanted to know what kind of stuff my sister was into. I wasn't just being nosy."

"Who do you think you're kidding, Lance? Give me that."

She took the journal and opened it, dreading what was inside. Emily's words hit her full force.

> If I were to write a story, my mother's disapproval would be a character all its own. It would be the villain pressing down on my miserable victim, time ticking as it grew closer to doing her in. Only, the miserable victim would be me.

Barbara almost closed the journal. How could she be the villain? Why was it always the mother's fault? Tears came to her eyes, but she gritted her teeth and read on.

> But I wouldn't be kidding anyone.
>
> I'm not a bad person; I make bad choices. I could have been a contender, as that wrestling guy in that old black and white flick says. Or was it boxing? I could have been a big shot, a person of substance, a woman of means. I could have called the shots. Now I just get high.

In my head, I'm like Anna Nicole Smith, that glamorous, misunderstood starlet, the version that danced and flirted with the cameras, before her drug-addled body lay decaying in some morgue because there was money on the line. In my head, I'm an unexpected heiress, a sappy-go-lucky clubber, a tragic talent who remains undiscovered.

But in the head of my disapproving mom, I'm the worst kind of failure. I'm the one all the scripture was written for. The one David was thinking of when he wrote about the wicked getting theirs.

My mother cries over those verses, because she hopes I won't get mine.

There was a time when I was younger, before I'd signed my own death warrant, when I gazed through the windshield each time my mother picked me up, assessing her expression. Her face was a color wheel on a silver Christmas tree. Yellow, happy; red, angry; blue, distracted. Sometimes as I got in the car I would see that evil twin of hers, Disapproval, and she'd pull up my neckline and threaten to toss my favorite shirt. Cleavage was a punishable offense.

So that's why I turned to drugs.

Just kidding. I know I can't pin my habit on my mother's transparency, though I've tried. You don't throw your life away because your mom has frown lines.

Barbara closed her eyes, sick that Emily had so clearly given up on life. She hoped her frown lines hadn't caused Emily's decline. But Barbara couldn't help rehashing every time she had peered at Emily through the car window, disapproving of what her daughter was wearing or who she was with or the way she hugged a boy good-bye.

But wasn't a mother supposed to chastise her child for disobedience? Of course she was.

Still, the journal entry left Barbara feeling like she was the villain, the one who'd caused it all.

She laid the journal in her lap and looked out the plane's window, trying to steady her breathing as she gazed into the night. After John died, Barbara had been so fragmented and distracted with her own grief that she'd allowed Emily too much freedom. Emily had gotten her driver's license a year later, and when she'd driven away from home, she drove herself right into trouble.

For years Barbara thought Emily was in denial about her own bondage. But this journal clearly showed she wasn't. Maybe Emily really did want to change. She knew she was driving her life off a cliff. She just had to be taught to care.

Barbara covered her face and begged God to help Emily, wherever she was. He knew what Emily was doing, thinking, smoking, ingesting . . .

God was the only father Emily had now. Barbara had to trust him to protect Emily as his own child, even if she wasn't turning to him.

nine

The moment the landing gear touched the runway, Barbara
checked her phone to see if Emily had called. No messages, and no
missed calls.

As they pulled up to their gate, she dialed information and got
the number for the police precinct closest to the Atlanta airport.
She pressed one to have it connect her.

"What are you doing?" Lance asked as it rang. "Didn't the cop
give you his number?"

"I'm just checking," she whispered. "Confirming that he really
works there before I call his cell."

"Airport Precinct."

She cleared her throat. "Yes, I was wondering if you could connect me to Detective Kent Harlan."

"With Homicide? He's not at this precinct. He works at the
main department. I'll transfer you." Just as she'd thought, it wasn't
a hoax. She held until it rang again.

"Atlanta Police Department."

She asked for Detective Harlan again.

"I'll have to take a message. He's not in right now."

"Um . . . that's all right. I have his cell phone number."

She hung up. Lance was staring at her. "There's a real guy?"

She nodded.

"So there's a real murder."

She couldn't answer. She waited until the airplane came to a halt, then unbuckled her seatbelt and stood. Lance slipped into the aisle and got their bags from the overhead bin. His cheeks were blotched red again, as if he'd been slapped. His emotions always registered on his cheeks.

Her heart pounded like she'd just run a marathon, and perspiration prickled her neck and her chest again. Her hair stuck to her aching forehead. She dialed the detective's number.

He answered after three rings. "Harlan."

"Detective, this is Barbara Covington. I'm in Atlanta. Where should I go?"

"Go to the long-term parking garage. You'll see where the police cars are. Come to the yellow tape and ask someone to grab me. Have you had any contact from your daughter?"

"No. Have you?"

"Unfortunately, no."

"We have to find her!"

"We plan to. I'll see you in a few minutes."

She didn't know what concourse they were in now, or how far they were from the parking garage. She waited as the other passengers took their time getting their bags from the overhead bins, oblivious to the mother and son with panic on their faces.

As she waited, she tried to think like Emily. If she was traumatized from witnessing the murder, she couldn't have gone far. She was probably right here in this huge airport, hiding in a bathroom somewhere.

"No word from her?" Lance asked quietly.

"Nope."

"We'll find her, Mom."

It was finally their turn to slip up the aisle, and as they bolted into the terminal, she saw that they were in Concourse C. She found the sign pointing them to baggage claim, which she knew should be across from the parking garage.

"This way," she said, and took off in a trot toward the underground Tram.

They rode the train two stops to baggage claim, then rushed out. Hurrying past the people slowing to collect their bags, Barbara found the exit door. Across several lanes of traffic, she saw the parking garage. There was a police car blocking the entrance. That must be it.

She pulled her carry-on behind her as she ran to the crosswalk. When she reached the garage, she gave the policeman Kent's name. He let her in. Deeper into the dim, muggy garage, she saw the crime scene tape.

"Is this where she died?" Lance asked. "In here?"

"Must be." She waited at the tape, trying to see what was in the car the police clustered around.

"Mrs. Covington?"

She saw him walking toward her, a tall man, probably six feet. He had light-brown hair with a receding hairline, and a tanned, leathery face. He made it to her and shook her hand. "Thanks for coming. I'm Kent Harlan."

She nodded. "This is my son, Lance."

"Nice to meet you." He shook Lance's hand. "Did you bring pictures of Emily?"

She unzipped her bag and pulled out the framed pictures she'd thrown in. "Here they are."

He took them and studied Emily's image. "Does she still look like this? Hair's the same?"

"Yes, just the same. Except she . . . she doesn't look as healthy now. Her skin is pale, her hair's thinner . . ."

He handed the pictures to an officer and whispered something to him.

"Will I get those back?"

"Remind us."

"What are you going to do with them?"

"We're going to make copies and give them to the press."

"The press? Please, she's probably here in the airport. She couldn't call because I didn't let her bring her phone, and she doesn't have more than ten dollars. Detective, what happened to Trish?"

"Let's go talk." He lifted the tape, and they ducked under it. He led them to a bench near the elevator and offered them a seat. She was too nervous to sit.

"Mrs. Covington, does Emily have any friends here?"

"I don't think so. But it's possible, with social media. I guess she has friends all over."

"You said she was on her way to rehab. What were her drugs of choice?"

Barbara didn't know how specific to be. He was a cop, after all. "Pills, mostly. Painkillers and anxiety medications."

"Are you in the medical field? Pharmaceuticals? Chemicals?"

"No, I'm an interior designer. Detective, how did Trish die?"

He seemed to consider how much to disclose. "I'd rather not discuss that right now. What exactly did Emily have with her?"

"Clothes, underwear, toiletries, her purse . . ."

"Did you watch her pack?"

"I packed her bags myself," she said.

"She left her suitcases in the trunk of Miss Massey's car. Did you search her purse before she left?"

Barbara felt that invisible foot on her chest. "No. Things were crazy, and I was trying to get her packed."

"Crazy how?"

"Just . . . busy. We convinced her to go, and I was trying to get her to the airport on time."

He scribbled something in his notebook. "Mrs. Covington, tell us what you know about Trish."

"Not much. I only met her last night, and had a few minutes to talk to her then. She works for the Road Back Recovery Center. She's been sober for five years, and two years ago she bought the rehab where she worked." Her eyes strayed back to that car. Was Trish's body still there? She glanced at Lance. His gaze was fixed on the crime scene.

The detective was still making notes.

"Detective, what's being done to find my daughter?"

He looked up, met her eyes. "We have a BOLO out on her."

"A Bolo?"

"Be On the Lookout. Could you tell me what she was wearing? I saw her on the security tape, but it's black and white. Looked like she was wearing a dark-colored T-shirt. Was it black?"

Barbara caught her breath. "You saw her? Then she was alive?"

"Yes. She left the car of her own accord."

"Oh, thank God." She touched her chest and blew out her relief. "Yes, her T-shirt was black. It was one of those bands . . . Three Eyes . . ."

"Third Eye Blind," Lance interjected.

"Yes. So the security camera must have shown where she went."

"We saw her get into a car on the other side of the garage. A dark Infiniti sedan. Do you know anyone who drives one?"

Her relief faded. "No. But you must have seen where they went. Which way they drove."

"They left the airport; that's all we know."

Barbara looked at Lance, her mouth open. He shook his head and muttered, "Unbelievable."

"Can you show me the video?" she asked. "Maybe it wasn't even Emily who got into the Infiniti."

"I'll show you a picture I printed out." He walked over to a case sitting across the garage and came back with a grainy black-and-white image.

Barbara took it and saw the girl getting into the black car. "It's not clear. It could be her, I guess, but it doesn't show her face."

"You said she was an IV drug user. Do you think it's possible that she could have gotten needles past security?"

"I didn't say that! I said I found needles once, but not recently. They weren't even hers." She knew that sounded ridiculous. She hadn't believed Emily when she claimed her friend had left the needles in her car, that she would never do anything so stupid. Clearly, the detective didn't believe it, either. "Why do you keep asking that? Did Trish's death have something to do with needles?"

He didn't answer, so she made a guess. "So it was an overdose? Trish really wasn't sober after all?"

"Trish wasn't shooting drugs, Mrs. Covington. That's not what I said." He got up. "The fact is, Miss Massey's wallet is missing. Your daughter was seen running from the crime scene."

For the first time, it hit her. He thought Emily did it. "Wait a minute. You can't seriously be wondering if my daughter is the killer!"

Detective Harlan just stared at her.

"Well, you're wrong. Emily is not a murderer!"

"Mrs. Covington, how desperate was she to keep from going to treatment?"

"Not that desperate. We didn't chain her up and make her go. She agreed to it."

"Why didn't you take her yourself?"

She spoke before she thought. "Because I knew she would spend the whole time begging and pleading for me not to take her. I thought an objective third party would make it easier." She saw the

I-told-you-so on his face. "She wasn't thrilled about going, but she wasn't desperate enough to kill. I didn't raise a killer."

"But you did raise an addict."

Her face flushed with heat as she got to her feet. "I want my pictures back."

"Mrs. Covington, you can't keep us from using Emily's image. If you stand in the way of our finding her, you could be charged with delaying the investigation."

"What?" Tears stung her eyes. "Are you kidding me?"

"Drugs are a powerful force. Some of them incite violence." The detective rubbed his face. "Did you know that most of the murders in this country are committed by people desperate for drugs?"

Barbara grabbed her bag. "Come on, Lance."

"Where are you going, Mrs. Covington?"

She swung around. "To find my daughter! And if you waste your time trying to paint her as the killer, you're going to miss the one who really did this. Maybe he's lurking around in this very garage, waiting for his next victim. He could have Emily right now. While you're being misled by your assumption that Emily did this, she could be in the hands of the killer. Her life could be in danger!"

"I don't think that's the case, Mrs. Covington."

She stormed back to the tape, looking for the officer who'd taken Emily's pictures. But he was gone. Harlan had ordered him to get copies made for the press. Within hours, her daughter's picture would be on every news station across the US. Since the murder had happened in a major airport, it would be of national interest. Besides all the other things Emily would have to overcome, she'd have to deal with this.

Oh, God, we need your help!

Lance's voice shook her out of her thoughts. "Mom, where do we start?"

Her head was killing her. "We don't even know if it was her who got into that car. She could still be here, hiding in the airport. The bathrooms are the most obvious place. We'll just walk through the terminals from restroom to restroom, looking for every possible place our Emily could hide. We can't get past security without a boarding pass, but neither could she after she left that area, so we'll comb the places she has access to."

They reached the baggage claim area, dodging people as they hurried by.

"I know my sister, Mom. She's not a killer. Not even on drugs."

"I know she's not. But she's in a terrible mess. And I don't know if we can clean this one up."

ten

"We have to think like Emily would," Barbara said. "Where would she go? What would she do? She only had ten stinking dollars."

"That's it," Lance said. "She hadn't eaten, so she probably got food when she got off the plane. Let's take her picture around to the people who work at the fast-food places."

"We can't," she said. "It's almost three a.m. They're all closed."

She saw a woman mopping the floor, so she hurried over and showed her Emily's picture. She hadn't seen her. Neither had any of the other employees they found, or the few passengers still walking through the airport.

They searched for the next two hours. Where had she gone?

Emily had never traveled alone. She had probably never taken an Uber, and she had no experience with cabs, shuttles, or trains. If she'd tried to leave the airport, wouldn't she have seen how difficult it was and decided to stay? Then again, if she really was the one who got into that Infiniti . . . Barbara shook off the thought. It couldn't be true. Emily couldn't have set up a ride, and she would never have committed murder.

Barbara thought of buying tickets to anywhere so they could

get back into the secure areas, but the Atlanta airport was so massive. The police were probably combing the place, and they had the benefit of security cameras. If they hadn't found Emily, how would she?

As Barbara talked with a janitor, Lance sat down on one of the vinyl seats, among others waiting for loved ones to come off red-eye flights. He closed his eyes, and she saw him drifting into sleep. She couldn't force Lance to walk like a zombie through the airport anymore. It was five a.m., and they really were getting nowhere.

Not knowing what else to do, Barbara took Lance and caught a shuttle to the nearest hotel. She showed Emily's picture to the man working the desk and asked if she'd come here, but he hadn't seen her. She rented a room, and wearily, they rode the elevator up.

Lance looked wiped out as he dropped his duffel bag on one of the beds. "Mom, what if we called her friends and asked if they've heard from her? Maybe she called them. Maybe they know if she has friends here."

"I don't have any of their numbers. I don't even know most of their last names. The people she's been hanging with aren't the kind who come for Sunday lunch."

Lance unzipped his bag and reached in. "Well, here they are, right here, on her phone."

Barbara's eyebrows shot up. "You brought her cell phone?"

"Yeah. Somebody had to think things through. You were freaking out. I figured we might need it."

"Good thinking." She reached for it, but he held it out of her grasp.

"Say, 'Lance is da man. I'm glad I brought him because he's such a big help.'"

"Don't make me kill you." She snatched the phone from him. "Did you bring the charger?"

He winced. "No, forgot that. I didn't even remember mine."

"Me neither."

"But it still has enough battery to copy the names and numbers down."

Lance bounced down on the bed and soon fell asleep. Barbara sat on the other bed and wrote down all of the numbers in Emily's contacts list. Taking out her own phone, she started dialing.

Most of them didn't answer. It was four-thirty a.m. in Jefferson City.

She decided to leave vague messages to make them call her back. "Zack, this is Barbara Covington, Emily Covington's mother. I need to talk to you as soon as you get this. Something has happened to Emily and I need to let you know."

There. Hopefully his curiosity would be piqued enough to call her back. She went through the list, leaving similar messages. Only one person answered—Emily's best friend, Paige.

"Hello?" Loud music blared in the background.

"Paige, can you hear me?"

"Yeah, who is this?"

"Emily's mother. Could you turn the music down, Paige? I need to talk to you."

The girl cursed, then the music cut off, and Paige came back to the phone. "Okay, what is it?"

"Have you heard what's happened to Emily?"

"No, what?"

"She's missing. We can't locate her anywhere."

Her irritated voice softened. "I wondered why she didn't call me back. Missing, like how? We were supposed to hang out tonight, but she bailed on me and didn't show up."

Barbara thought of telling her it was already morning, but it didn't matter.

"Who was she with?"

Barbara wanted to be vague, but any minute now those pictures would be flashed across CNN. She told Paige about the intervention and Trish's death.

The girl listened with a series of Oh-my-Gods.

"Does she have any friends in Atlanta?" Barbara asked.

"Not that I know of. You gotta find her, Ms. Covington. She's not like that. She's the nicest person I know, even when she's high or dope-sick."

Her words were small comfort. "Do me a favor, and don't screen your calls for the next couple of days. Answer every one you get, even if you don't know who it's from. It could be Emily from a pay phone or someone else's phone. And let me know the minute you hear from her."

"Okay, I'll call you. Let me know what's going on. She's my best friend."

Resentment welled in Barbara's heart as she hung up. Some friend. Paige was probably the one who had introduced Emily to her latest drugs. She might even be the dealer who provided them.

She lay down for a moment, holding Emily's journal against her. Her daughter was not a killer. Yes, she'd committed crimes. She had stolen from her mother, gotten credit cards in John's name, hocked jewelry and keepsakes John had given Barbara for birthdays and anniversaries.

Could a person go from being capable of stealing to support her habit to killing to keep it going?

It was possible for some addicts, Barbara told herself. The news was rife with reports of drug killings. But not for Emily. Emily's brain may be messed up from all the drugs, but she hadn't been turned into a killer.

Sleep pulled at her and her head was bursting, but she fought it, unwilling to give in. She had to read the journals to find names of friends and connections who might lead Barbara to her daughter.

Even as she picked up the journal, her head thronged with desperate urgency. The real killer may have found Emily already.

eleven

Aching all over, Barbara moved to the club chair by the window. She checked on Lance as she turned on the lamp; he didn't seem disturbed. She opened Emily's journal and saw her daughter's perfect script. She'd won handwriting awards in elementary school, and in high school she'd won contests for creative writing. Before she'd turned to other pastimes, Emily had been a voracious reader, and it was evident in her writing. Her prose, which was sometimes flamboyant and pushed a little too hard at sophistication, was still moving. But Emily only wrote when she was miserable.

She read past pages of blame-throwing, wincing at each blow, then came to a section where Emily reflected on that blame.

> Fault is a funny thing. My friends are always blaming their parents for things they do, and in some cases, I can see it. Their parents use, or they drink a lot, or they abused them as children. But how do I blame my parents when one is dead and the other is a teetotaler who never lifted a finger to hurt me? What could I say? That I skinned my knee when she was dragging me to church?
>
> I could say that all the church-going screwed me up in the head, but not many people would buy that. It's hard to get away with that

when your best friend was locked in a closet for days at a time and raped by her own father.

So my latest beef about my mother is that she didn't give me a better excuse for the choices I've made. Kidding again. I know that would be really sick.

When I've been in therapy, they've encouraged me not to admit that anything was my fault. I didn't lose my job because I couldn't get out of bed. I lost it because my boss had no compassion. I didn't lose my boyfriend because I cheated on him. I lost him because he's a jerk. My mother is on the flip side of the fault debate. She rages, sometimes, when we have this discussion, and tells me that things happened to me because I did certain things, took certain risks, put myself in certain places. Places she's spent her entire life trying to keep me out of.

She can be cold sometimes, so I guess I can pin that on her. That she doesn't cry when I cry. She doesn't grieve over the things that grieve me. She's like a statue sometimes, with this pinched look that says, "I'm ready for whatever she throws at me next." An ice statue.

She's cold, all right.

Barbara stopped reading and looked up at the wall, feeling a chill stiffening her spine. She'd never thought of herself as cold. Just numb.

She had felt warm when she rocked Emily to sleep way too many nights when she was young and refused to stay in bed. She had spoiled her with tighter hugs and more kisses.

All wasted effort. Now Emily saw her as cold. Barbara blinked back the tears burning her eyes and read some more.

I try to remember the time before Dad died, whether my mom was cold then. But I can't remember what Mom's face looked like before my dad got sick. I don't remember whether it was pinched then.

Sometimes I stay awake nights, trying to remember Dad's smile, and the way his laugh lines wrinkled when he joked. I'll never forgive God for forcing me to strain my brain for a memory.

Then I'll get his picture, study it, and say, "Yes, now I remember. He had that glint in his eyes. He smiled out of one side of his mouth." My mom was always behind the camera, so I don't have that many pictures of her. I can't remember her pre-cancer, pre-death, pre-drugs expressions.

I guess if blame is going to be placed, she places it on me. I've turned her well-organized, well-designed, well-decorated life upside-down. She keeps her office so pretty and coordinated, smelling like vanilla. At home, while our house is neat as a pin, there's chaos rippling.

I guess that's what I bring to our nicely set table.

Barbara closed the journal and leaned her head back, self-indictments and recriminations battering at her psyche like metal blades of a fan . . . knocking her, knocking her, knocking her. Closing her eyes, she wondered if Emily ever would have imagined that her addictions would take her to where she was now.

Lord, show me where that is.

twelve

Lance woke some time later and got up to go to the bathroom, startling Barbara awake. Rubbing her eyes, she realized she'd dozed off in the chair.

Why had she wasted time sleeping? What was wrong with her? Now it was eight-thirty.

Lance came back into the room. "Sorry I cratered on you, Mom."

"No problem. I cratered a little too."

"Did you talk to her friends?"

"Only Paige. The rest of them haven't called me back."

"Word'll get around."

She rubbed her face, then slid her fingers down to her chin. "Do you think any of them will help us?"

"Doubtful. They'll figure Emily doesn't want to be found."

"Even to save her life?"

"Those people are selfish, Mom. If one of them ODs, they'll let them die and take the body somewhere else to be found, because they don't want to get in trouble."

The foot on her chest grew heavier. "How do you know this?"

"Hey, I know some of those losers. Remember Mike Cramer, dude who used to play third base on my baseball team?"

"Yes."

"Well, he's heavy into drugs now. And when he's high, he likes to talk about the drug culture, like it's some really cool club he's in."

"Why were you around him when he was high?"

"Because I sit next to him in science. He comes to school high. Gets wasted in the bathroom."

"What? Do the teachers and principal know?"

"They know he's hopped up on something, unless they're blind. They've searched his locker and stuff, but they never find anything. He's been suspended three times this year, but they haven't expelled him yet."

Acid burned Barbara's stomach.

"What we need is a computer," Lance said. "You should have brought your laptop."

"Why?"

"Because we can look on Instagram and Snapchat with her phone, but it would be faster if we had a laptop. You've got those old lady eyes . . ."

"Excuse me?"

"What? You complain all the time about how hard it is to read on your phone. The point is, we have to see what her friends are saying and whether she's been in touch with them."

"Yeah, that would help."

"Maybe some of her friends are helping her. And that interventionist lady probably has social media accounts too. We could find out who her friends and enemies are."

Lance had a point. But she couldn't fly back home to get her laptop. That would cost as much as buying a new one. And there was no time to get a friend to ship it.

"All right," she said. "We're going shopping."

"For what?"

"For a new laptop."

"For real? Sweet! Can I have your old one?"

She sighed. "I don't know, Lance. Just go change clothes. We've been in these since yesterday. Hurry. I'll change after you."

While he was in the bathroom, she Googled the nearest Best Buy.

But they needed a car. She could ask at the front desk where the nearest rental agency was. But it would probably be faster to take the shuttle back to the airport and rent one.

And when they got to the store, she'd have to buy a charger and car adapter for their phones. Their batteries were low, and she couldn't risk having Emily unable to reach her.

She had left town totally unprepared.

At the airport, the rental car agency was out of compacts, so she agreed to pay for a Navigator and gave them her American Express card. Her bill this month would be astronomical.

Would Road Back return her thirty thousand dollars since Emily never made it there? Did a dead interventionist warrant a refund?

She got Lance some breakfast from McDonald's and tried to choke down an Egg McMuffin herself, even though her stomach churned. On their way to Best Buy, she stopped at Kinko's and ordered some posters with Emily's picture. The sales guy said they would be ready that afternoon.

At Best Buy there were at least twenty different laptop brands and models available.

"Find the cheapest one," she told Lance.

He zeroed in on a popular brand. "You don't want the cheapest one, Mom. You want one that's better than the dinosaur you have at home. This one is hot. Jacob's dad has one. If I were you, I'd go with it. Look at the storage. The hard drive is primo. And it's fast. You want fast, don't you?"

This model was almost a thousand dollars more than the cheapest ones, but she did need fast. She had even looked at this one online a few weeks ago but decided she couldn't afford it.

If she was going to invest in one, she might as well get one she liked. Maybe she could make up the difference by selling her old one.

She grabbed the chargers they needed, then made the purchase as quickly as possible and headed back to the hotel. She hoped the new laptop didn't have any bells and whistles she'd have to learn to use. All she needed right now was the Internet so she could browse Emily's social media pages. Then maybe she would be able to get inside her daughter's head. And, perhaps more importantly, Trish's.

Lance grabbed a newspaper as they made their way back into the hotel. "Mom, check this out."

The headline read, "Woman Murdered in Airport Garage."

"It's already started." She began reading in the elevator. The reporter hadn't gotten any more information than she had. The police had probably released Trish's name right before deadline, and they hadn't had time to dig into her life. Barbara read quickly through the article, looking for anything about Emily.

"Here it is," she said. "Ms. Massey, a drug interventionist, was accompanying a woman to Road Back Recovery Center in Emerson. Emily Covington, 18, fled the scene. Police would not comment on whether Miss Covington is a person of interest in the murder."

"Oh, man," Lance said. "If the newspapers are reporting it, it'll be on TV too. Everybody who ever knew us is gonna think Emily killed her."

Yes, even people who had known them only as acquaintances would be coming out of the woodwork to get on television, to comment about Emily and her problems. All of those who grew up with Emily, the very ones who used to drink and party with her, then turned against her when her drinking and drugging got out of control, would suddenly claim they were her best friends.

She could just hear it now. *We knew she'd gotten into some pretty dark stuff, but we never thought she was capable of this. But there were times when she talked about wanting to kill her mother. We thought that was just talk, but maybe she did have murder in her all along.*

Barbara had tried to keep Emily's addictions secret, but it was difficult when her daughter wrote about them online where they could be read internationally. To Barbara, it was like a banner waving, advertising her failures as a parent.

But what did it matter? Long ago she'd given up her pride and gotten over the humiliation. Police cars in front of her house when Emily had been brought home high had cured her of that. And if that hadn't done it, standing in line at the jail to bail her out after a DUI had hardened her to embarrassment.

It just never ended. Clearly, Barbara had a little pride left in her, because God seemed to think she needed more refining as she descended deeper into public exposure.

They got off the elevator and went up the hall to their room. As she stuck the key card in, her phone rang, startling her. Her heart stopped, and she grabbed it out of her purse pocket to see if it was Emily. She didn't recognize the number, so she clicked it on. "Hello?"

It was a man's voice. "Mrs. Covington? This is Randall Ainsley from FOX News. I was wondering if I could talk with you for a minute."

Panicked, she hung up. "It's FOX News."

"No way," Lance said, setting the computer box down. "How'd they get your cell number? Why'd you hang up?"

"Because I don't know what to say. I don't want to get Emily in more trouble. I need to think about this."

"Next time, let me talk to them," he said. "I know what to say."

"No! You don't say a word to them, do you hear me? I'm serious. If we say one wrong word, we could get Emily into a ton of trouble."

"Like she needs our help getting into trouble."

"I'm serious, Lance. Someone has given them my number, so it's just a matter of time before they have yours too."

He grabbed the remote from the bed and turned on the television. He flipped around to the news channels. CNN was talking politics, and MSNBC was doing a segment about a Supreme Court case. He got to FOX and saw Emily's picture on the screen.

"There she is!" Lance yelled.

Barbara's throat closed as she listened to the details of the crime.

We have with us Ronald Miller, director of operations at Hartfield-Jackson Atlanta International Airport. Mr. Miller, how was Miss Massey killed?"

"My understanding is that the murder was committed inside her car."

"Airport parking garages are usually crowded after a flight has landed. Weren't there witnesses?"

"Not to my knowledge."

"She was an interventionist traveling with eighteen-year-old Emily Covington, the drug addict who fled the scene. How is it that anyone could flee the scene of a crime like this, with all the security around the airport?"

"That's a question we're trying to answer, but I assure you, we have stepped up security today. However, I hope travelers will keep in mind that this wasn't a terrorist attack, and despite all our security measures, there's not a lot we can do about personal violence among our passengers. If we see it, we make an immediate arrest. In this case, it was done outside our terminals in the privacy of the car."

"Man, she's wrecking my life!" Lance cried.

"Your life?"

"Look at this mess! How'm I gonna go back to school with people calling my sister a murderer? Junkie was bad enough!"

"They call her a junkie?"

"She calls herself a junkie. Wait till you see her Instagram posts."

The phone rang again. Barbara didn't recognize the number, but she answered anyway. "Hello?"

"Is this Barbara?"

"Who's this?"

"I'm Bret Pendergrass from CNN . . ."

Barbara hung up. "CNN."

"Mom, come on!"

"I don't want to keep the phone tied up. How will Emily's friends get through to us if we're on it? Or Emily herself?"

"Heard of call waiting?"

"It doesn't always work. I can't take the chance."

Lance grunted and took the phone. "That's not it. You're just afraid of the press. At least we can add them to your contacts, so you know it's CNN and NBC when they call back." She watched him add the phone numbers, then he tossed the phone back to her. Turning back to the computer, he opened the box, pulled out the laptop, and plugged it in. He turned it on, and the Welcome screen popped up.

Quickly, he navigated his way through it, typing in the info to register. As he did, she flipped over to CNN. A similar story was already coming up, complete with file footage of the long-term parking area where the murder took place.

She never should have given them pictures of Emily.

No one seemed to care that her daughter was missing. Why didn't they even consider that Emily could have been kidnapped by the killer? She'd heard of human trafficking operations. They loved blue-eyed blondes, and the fact that Emily was an addict was a plus for them. They might be able to manipulate her as long as they kept her high.

Why weren't the networks reporting on the beautiful teenager who'd gone missing, instead of the drug addict who may have committed murder?

Maybe she did need to talk to the media, to make them understand the truth: that Emily was an innocent bystander, that she was fragile and frightened, and that she could be in the hands of a killer crazed enough to murder a woman in a public place.

"Got it up, Mom. Here's her Instagram account."

Barbara went to sit beside him in front of the laptop. Snapshots of Emily wearing too little clothing and looking like someone on a three-day drunk filled the screen. "This is public? For anyone to see?"

"It's set to private so you won't see it. But she accepts almost everyone who friends her, strangers and all, so it might as well be public. I got accepted with a fake account, and she didn't even ask who I was."

Barbara studied the statistics on the page. "She has four thousand followers."

"Yeah, see? That's the problem."

"Can you see if she has any private messages?"

"No, I'm reading it through my account. I can break into hers, though. I know her password."

Barbara frowned. "How do you know her password?"

"She wrote it in the back of her journal."

Barbara grabbed the journal. Just as he said, it was right there.

"It worked," he said. He was quiet for a few minutes as he read the messages. "Love this laptop. Please, can I have it?"

"No. Has she messaged anybody?"

"No. Nothing since a couple of days ago."

Barbara sighed. "I don't know what to do. I just hope the media doesn't read her accounts."

"They will."

"But not unless she's on to friend them, right?"

"Technically, yeah."

"Let's see if Trish has an Instagram account."

He typed in Trish's name. There was her page on Instagram, full of comments from grieving friends who'd heard about her death.

"How do I get to her posts?"

Lance showed her. Barbara started to read.

"I'm going to take a shower while you read, Mom, in case we wind up on national television. You got a razor?"

She shot him a look. "You don't shave."

He rubbed his jaw, offended. "Sometimes I do. I want to look nice for the camera so they'll know we're not total losers."

"Just go shower."

He picked up his duffel bag and took it into the bathroom with him. "Try not to mess anything up on the laptop."

Barbara ignored him and quickly scanned Trish's blogs. There wasn't time to read every word, but they gave her a feel for the dead woman's life. Some spoke of her past addictions and the fact that, even though she wasn't using now, her family still accused her of addictive behaviors.

She studied the comments from friends before her murder, searching for anyone who displayed mental illness or anger.

When there were no red flags on Trish's posts, she went back to Emily's, which were much longer than others' posts. Her words cut like knives.

I hated my mother when my father died. She got over it so quickly. The Saturday morning after we buried him she made pancakes. She hosted people in our house for days afterward. It was like Christmas.

People came and went, laughing and talking, like we cared that their daughters were getting married and their sons had graduated. They brought casseroles that made me want to puke, and Mom gushed in gratitude, inviting them to come and share them with us.

Didn't she care that Dad was gone? I heard her telling people she was sad for herself and us, but thrilled for him. That he was out of pain and romping around heaven somewhere.

But I didn't even believe that anymore. I'd prayed for him to get well and he didn't, so I figured if there wasn't a healing, there wasn't a heaven, either. That heaven was just something we told ourselves about so we'd feel better. Mom was in the worst denial of all. I wondered, then, if she even loved my dad. If she even cared that he was dead.

Barbara stopped reading and looked at the ceiling, horrified at her daughter's perception of the whole thing.

Those days following John's death were a blur of suffering, worse even than the days preceding his death, when she'd gone days without sleep as she tried to help him with his pain, while he valiantly fought the disease eating away at him.

In the aftermath, she'd felt such a void. If her purpose before was to keep John from suffering, what was it now? Her head told her that her children needed her, that she had to go on and not fold into herself. Emily was fourteen, and Lance was only ten. She didn't have the luxury of grief.

So she saved her tears and anguish for those long, lonely nights in the bed he'd died in. Then when morning came, she forced herself up and went through the motions of living. She tried to keep her children distracted and happy . . . tried to be cheerful and calm.

She remembered the pancake morning. She'd cried so hard the night before that she had to go into her closet and cover her face with a pillow, so her children wouldn't hear. She hadn't slept a wink, and had showered at dawn in the hope of cleaning up her face and looking like a person who wasn't battered and abused by the anguish of life and death. She'd used ice packs to battle the swelling in her eyes.

She had washed a load of clothes before her children got up, because that was what mothers did, and she dressed in freshly ironed jeans and a crisp white blouse, determined that her children would have normalcy that day. After pancakes, she took them swimming at the neighborhood pool. Lance splashed around with his friend while she sat in a chair, fully dressed, staring into space. Emily had only gone along because Barbara insisted, but her daughter glued herself to a book.

All that time, Emily was thinking how cold and heartless Barbara was?

Lance came out of the shower, steam bursting into the room. Quickly, Barbara wiped her face. But he saw her tears. "You okay, Mom?"

"Yeah, I'm fine."

"She's gonna be okay. We'll find her."

"I know."

He stared at her a few seconds longer. "Find out anything reading her stuff?"

"Not really." But that was a lie. She'd found out plenty about what her daughter thought of her, and the mistakes she'd made. She would, no doubt, learn of many more before their nightmare was over.

thirteen

Kent sat at his desk rubbing his eyes, wishing he'd taken an hour or two to sleep. But the case had kept him working all night. He flipped through the notes he'd already taken, compared them to the medical examiner's notes. Trish had been injected just where he'd suspected—in her back, where he'd seen the blood spot.

His phone rang, and he picked it up. "Harlan."

"Kent, Rick Graves."

Kent sighed, glad the toxicologist had gotten back to him so quickly. "Rick, you know what was in the syringe yet?"

"It was Tubarine."

"What's that?"

"A paralytic drug used in surgery to stop convulsions."

Kent frowned. "How did that kill her?"

"It would have paralyzed her to the point that she couldn't breathe. She would have asphyxiated. Interesting drug, that one. Pharmaceutical companies get it from a few plants in South America, used to make arrow poison."

"Arrow poison? How would an eighteen-year-old girl get her hands on that?"

"I don't know. Maybe she had a friend in the medical profession, who got it from a hospital."

He thought that over for a minute. "So let me get this straight. The killer would have knocked her out with the chloroform, so she wouldn't struggle. Then injected her with the paralytic."

"Looks like it. They didn't even need a vein. It could be done pretty quickly."

When Kent hung up, he stared at his notes again. He could see a teenaged drug addict injecting the woman with heroin or something, but Tubarine? It wasn't like it was sold on the streets. And where would she have gotten chloroform? Surely she hadn't gotten through security with that. There was a strict limit on liquids.

He opened his laptop and found the security video he'd watched at least a hundred times. He played it again, checking out Emily's purse, hanging on her shoulder. It wasn't very big, and as she stood smoking outside the car, she didn't dig into it at all. Her hands were empty after she dropped the cigarette.

Besides that, she was only in the car for a couple of seconds. There hadn't been time for her to pour chloroform into a rag, knock Trish out with it, then inject her. Even if she'd had it all in her hands before she got into the car—which she hadn't—it seemed like too much to do that quickly.

And the girl didn't have to kill to escape going to treatment. She could have walked away at any point, and Trish couldn't have stopped her.

He played the video in slow motion during the moments that the murder must have occurred, and focused on other areas of the car. He could see nothing through the windows, so he watched the other side of the Lexus—the side hidden from the cameras—trying to see if there was a reflection in the car next to them, something that showed what was going on in the Lexus.

Emily got out then and ran. He slowed it even more, squinting, watching for some sign that the woman inside was fighting for her life, or that there was someone else there with her.

Then he saw it—something moving on Trish's side of the car. Was it the back door opening? He zoomed in as much as he could, circled that area, then blew it up even more.

"Hey, Kent, I just heard back—"

Kent cut Andy off as he came up behind him. "Look at this," he said. "This is the area over Trish Massey's back door. Is the door opening?"

Andy bent down and looked at it. "It's too grainy, but I don't think so."

Something white came into view. "What's that?" Kent asked, pointing.

Andy took over the laptop and blew that up even more. "I don't know. Maybe a child was walking by or something. Could be a baseball cap."

"Or a hand opening that back door." Kent used every tool he had to bring it into clearer view, but it was still blurred, grainy. He wasn't going to get the picture any clearer. He'd need the video lab to enhance it.

He picked up the phone, called the video tech he trusted the most. "Jack, I need you to enhance the clip I'm sending over. Tell me if somebody is getting out of the back seat on the driver's side, or what it is we're seeing there. I'll come over in a little while and see what you've come up with. Call me if you find anything conclusive."

Kent hung up and looked at his partner. "If that's someone getting out of the car . . ."

"It's not," Andy said. "I just got Trish Massey's credit card company to fax me her activity. Looks like our little runaway used Trish's Visa card right after she ran off last night." Andy handed him the credit card report.

Kent checked the times on yesterday's purchases, saw the one that must have happened after the murder. "Capital Cab Company."

"I just got off the phone with them, and they say the passenger caught the cab at the airport. I was able to talk to the driver, and he says it was a couple—man and woman. The girl was a blonde."

Kent stood up. "So where did he take them?"

"To the Day-Nite Motel. Right in the middle of the worst part of town."

He read the report again. The cab company was the last purchase made, and it was definitely after the time of death. "So how did Emily wind up in a cab after she got into the black Infiniti?"

"Got me. Maybe she had the Infiniti drop her off at the taxi line."

"So who was with her in the cab?" Kent asked. "Her mother says it was just her and the interventionist."

"Maybe she met somebody on the plane."

Kent frowned and sorted through the facts, wishing they made sense. "I guess the Infiniti driver could have parked and gone in the cab with her. If he was in cahoots with her, maybe he realized his car could have been seen." He got his coat. "I'll get somebody to look for that car. It could be still at the airport. And I'll have security pull the footage for the cameras around the taxi line. Maybe we can see her getting in. But first, this motel is a lead we need to check out. Let's go. Maybe they're still there."

fourteen

Barbara left Lance in the room and took the laptop down to the business center to print out several pages of Emily's and Trish's pictures, posts, and comments. It took much more time than she could afford, but it was necessary. She didn't want to be glued to the computer all day, when she could be looking for Emily.

Too many things needed to be done, and she didn't know where to begin.

How had this happened? How had her precious daughter gone from being a debutante-in-training to a drug addict? How had she wound up on the run for a murder charge?

As the pages printed, Barbara rubbed her face wearily. She had a crick in her neck, and pain down her spine urged her to lie down. It wasn't unusual. She'd lived in a constant state of stress, going from one emergency to another, for the last few years. Though she'd read all the books on codependency and knew everything there was to know about tough love, her stomach still had a perpetual acidic knot and her temples always ached.

Doctors told her she needed to find a way to lower the stress in her life. She'd paid for that advice, while her symptoms persisted. One physician suggested she had a form of post-traumatic stress disorder. "How can it be post when I'm still in it?" she'd asked him.

She was a soldier on the front lines of the drug war. And her daughter had been captured by an enemy without a face. If she had to walk into oncoming bullets, she would. She'd go anywhere . . . do anything.

Her mind rolled to Ephesians 6, where Paul the Apostle spoke of wearing the shield of faith, to "extinguish all the flaming arrows of the evil one." If that wasn't written for her, she didn't know what was. The arrows were deadly and aimed right at her forehead, where her thoughts originated.

How many times in the past few years had Barbara wanted to run away screaming? When Emily was high, she chattered nonstop and practically bounced off the walls, trailing a mess from room to room. Besides dealing with that, Barbara busied herself locking up jewelry and pharmaceuticals and financial records in her house. When Emily wasn't home, Barbara spent her time searching for her car, drilling boyfriends, racing to Emily's friends' houses to drag her home. Barbara had grown way too familiar with bail bondsmen and their function, attorneys and judges and jail guards. The whole ordeal was a day-to-day drain, one that seemed to have no end.

She was still laboring to solve Emily's problems. If things didn't change, there would come a time when Barbara would have to lock down her own maternal emotions and turn her back on her daughter.

But today wasn't that day. Today she believed this emergency wasn't Emily's fault, that this crime had been done to her and not by her.

She pulled the blogs out of the printer and closed her laptop. Fatigue was catching up with her. She wondered if Emily had slept . . .

Emily was alive, wasn't she? Wouldn't Barbara feel it in her burning gut if she weren't? Wasn't that something a mother would know?

Please, God. You'd tell me, wouldn't you?

She rode the elevator up to her floor, and as she stepped off, she saw that her door was ajar. Hadn't she told Lance to keep it locked?

She broke into a trot and burst through the door. "Lance?"

"In here, Mom."

Lance was sitting on his unmade bed. A man sat across from him in the chair. He'd made himself comfortable.

"Mom, this is Richard Gray. He's a reporter."

She caught her breath and opened her mouth to yell at her son, but for a moment nothing came out. Finally, words bellowed forth. "I told you to lock the door, Lance! You can't let strangers into the room!" She turned to the reporter. "What's the matter with you, taking advantage of a fourteen-year-old kid?"

Richard What's-His-Name got to his feet. "Mrs. Covington, I'm sorry to surprise you. Lance invited me in to wait for you—"

Heat pounded in her face. "I don't have anything to say to you. Get out before I call the police!" She went to the phone, snatched it up.

"Are you sure? Because if you came on my network and made an appeal for Emily, chances are that public opinion would sway in her favor and she'd be found."

"Public opinion? I don't care about public opinion! My daughter is in trouble."

"Then don't you think going on television would be a great way to help her?"

Tears came to her eyes. She hated herself for crying in front of this pushy man. How dare he? "Please leave."

"Don't you even want to give us a statement?"

"Get out, I said!"

Lance sprang up. "Mom, we need the publicity. It would help a lot."

She pointed to Lance and ground her teeth. "You! Quiet!"

"But someone might have seen her. Someone might know where she is! This guy can help us get the word out. That's a whole heck of a lot better than pinning up a bunch of posters."

The reporter dared to speak again. "I can see you're a private person. But this is a public matter, ma'am. It's already on the news, whether you like it or not."

"Mom, they think she's a killer. If you could go on and tell them she's not, that she's just some messed-up kid, maybe people would try harder to find her."

She couldn't think. She turned away, sliding her fingers through the roots of her hair. Her empty suitcase sat against the wall. She kicked it, and it toppled onto the floor.

The reporter wouldn't quit. "I know you're angry at me for coming in here and talking to Lance. I'm sorry about that. But I sincerely want to help you find Emily."

She swung back around. "Don't pretend you care about her! You want ratings. You all do."

"Okay, I admit it. But you should use that. Who cares why we're interested in Emily, if it helps you find her?"

He was right. She had to do this. She drew in a deep breath. "All right. Then help me set up a press conference."

"There's no need for that. I can put you on camera now. My cameraman is downstairs."

"No, I'll talk to you all together at a press conference."

He sighed. "Fair enough. I'll set it up. Tell me when and where."

Her brain raced. "I don't know. I don't want them here at our hotel. How did you find us, anyway?"

"I was checking the hotels in the airport area, asking if they'd seen Emily. One of the clerks let it slip that you'd checked in."

"Great."

"I won't tell anyone. You could do it on the steps of the police headquarters, if you want. Or outside the airport."

Airport security would surely run her off. But the police department might be the best option. Would the police do more if they knew she was talking to the press?

She missed her husband, and his clear head, and his wise insight. Why couldn't he have been here to help her through this? What would he do?

Of course he would want her to do the interview. The more people looking for Emily, the better. And Lance was right. If they could humanize Emily, make people understand that she wasn't a cold killer . . .

"Okay, I'll do it. Let's go now."

"You have to give me time to notify the rest of the media. If we give them two hours, it'll be a better turnout."

Two hours for him to exclusively report whatever Lance had told him. But it was too late to do anything about that. "Okay, whatever. Two hours."

"Maybe we can get the detectives involved to make a statement too."

She wasn't sure that would be a good thing.

The man backed out of the room. "All right, then. I'll see you at the police department on Ponce de Leon in two hours." He thrust her a business card. "Call me if you need me before then."

She took the card and closed the door behind him. Then she turned back to her son. "Lance, what did you tell him?"

"Just that she's not a killer. He'll help us, Mom. She's my sister. I want her to be all right."

"But letting strangers into our room when your sister is already in danger is more than I can handle."

"I know, but he was from ABC News. He told me through the door, so I thought it would be okay."

"No, you didn't. You knew it wasn't okay. I can't ground you here. I can't turn you over my knee." She gave in to her tears.

"I won't do it again, Mom."

She wiped the tears. "I can't lose another child."

"You haven't lost Emily."

She collapsed on the bed. "He wouldn't have left, volunteering to set up the press conference, if he didn't get some juicy, exclusive bit of news to report first. Tell me what it was."

"Nothing. I just told him she was a nice girl. That she'd been a cheerleader in middle school. That she was raised in church and Sunday school and that she was a cool sister sometimes. That she was a victim—not the killer—and that we're really, really worried about her."

If that was all, it didn't sound harmful. Maybe he really hadn't done any damage. If he had, she would know soon enough.

As if reading her mind, Lance turned on the TV and changed the channel to ABC. That knot in Barbara's gut tightened yet again.

Her mind was fogged with fatigue and frustration, but she had to pull herself together and figure out what she was going to say on national television.

fifteen

The Day-Nite Motel wasn't new to Kent Harlan. He'd been there before to investigate shootings. Occasionally, drug dealers turned on scheming clients who didn't have money, and people here wound up dead.

The manager, who sat in the front office, claimed no one fitting the couple's description had checked in last night. So he and Andy went from door to door, showing Emily's picture and asking the hookers and addicts if they'd seen her. No one admitted to it.

He'd called ahead and on their way back to the office, they stopped by the cab company and showed Emily's picture to the driver. "Is this the girl you picked up at the airport the other night?"

"Let me see." The driver, a Jamaican named Bastian, studied it way too long.

Kent had little patience. "Either it is or it isn't. Which is it?"

"It look a little like her. Blonde. But I didn't look at her dat hard."

"What about the guy she was with?" Andy asked.

"Brown hair. Five ten or eleven, maybe. Skinny."

"Did they call each other by name?"

"I don't remember, mon."

"Did they ask to go to the Day-Nite specifically?"

"De man did. Dey wanted to score some dope."

Kent studied him for a moment. Could he be involved in the case too? "What did you do after you dropped them off?"

"Went back to de airport and worked until tree a.m."

That was true. Kent had already reviewed the dispatch records for the night. Bastian had many more fares after taking the couple to the motel, so it was doubtful that he'd committed foul play.

When they'd gotten all they could out of him, they headed back to the office. On the way, Kent swung through a Krispy Kreme to get coffee. His lack of sleep was catching up with him, but he had to keep going. As he idled in the drive-thru line, he looked over at Andy, who looked just as weary. "So we can't confirm for sure that Emily was even the one in the cab?"

Andy yawned. "We can confirm that the person in the cab had Trish's credit card. Why are you having trouble believing that this is a simple, cut-and-dried case? That Emily Covington killed Trish Massey and ran away with her credit card to buy drugs?"

"Because it's too crazy that she'd have a syringe with Tubarine on her. And where would she have hidden the chloroform? Besides, she's small and skinny. She didn't look strong enough to fight Trish enough to get the chloroform rag over her mouth."

"She could have just taken her by surprise. You know as well as I do that some drugs do incite violence. In her fried mind, she may have thought murder was her only option. Despite what her mother said about the intervention being a surprise, she could have found out and prepared to kill her way out."

"All she had to do was refuse to go. She's eighteen. Her mother couldn't force her."

"I'm just saying . . . Her brain was toxic. She wasn't thinking clearly."

That, Kent knew, was certainly plausible, even if it was a

stretch. His own brother sat in prison now, after holding a loaded gun to a convenience store clerk's head and demanding cash. Drugs had set the course for the rest of his life. An intoxicated brain might have led the girl to the same insanity.

The only way to know for sure was to find Emily Covington.

sixteen

A mob of reporters stood in front of the police station as Barbara
and Lance arrived in their Navigator.

Lance grinned. "No way. All this for us?"

Barbara thought she might throw up. Her chest felt suddenly
tight, her breath trapped in little cages in her lungs.

"Wait till my friends see us!" he said. "I'll be getting texts all
day."

Last night he'd been worried what his friends would think when
they heard the news. Today he was flattered by his own celeb-
rity. She tried to draw in enough breath to keep from fainting. She
needed to stay conscious at least long enough to find a parking place.

But with all the news vans, she had no idea where she would
put her car.

Suddenly Richard Gray, the reporter who'd finagled his way
into their room, stepped out to the curb and waved them down. She
slowed long enough to see him pointing to a spot around the corner.
He trotted alongside the car as she drove toward it.

"See? I told you he was a nice guy."

She saw him as the one who'd opened her vein and was now
trying to catch the blood with a bucket. She reached the space and

saw that he'd stationed two cameramen there. They stepped out of the way and allowed her to pull in.

The cameras were already rolling. She tried to get a breath and turned to her son. "So help me, if you say one word when we get out of this car, I'm sending you home. Got that?"

"You mean I can't talk at the press conference?"

"No! Your sister is suspected of murder, and one wrong sibling anecdote could put her away for life."

"I wouldn't do that."

Richard knocked on the window.

She ignored him. "I'm serious, Lance. Not one word or we'll go straight to the airport after the press conference. You'll be on the next flight home."

"Okay, I get it!"

She opened the door and stepped out of the car. The blood flow hadn't returned to her head. She was even more certain she would pass out. Heat prickled her underarms, her chest, her back. Her mouth was like cotton.

"I told you it'd be a great turnout, Mrs. Covington," Richard said, thrusting his microphone toward her. "Do you have anything you want to say to our cameras before you get started?"

She went around the car as Lance got out. "Thank you for setting this up," she muttered.

Others realized she had arrived, but none of the cameras flew toward her as they would have if it were, say, Emily walking up. She had to be thankful for that. Richard escorted her as though he were her publicist, but a police officer stepped through the reporters and met her halfway.

"Mrs. Covington, I'm Clyde Purvis, the chief of police here in Atlanta. Are you sure you want to do this?"

His challenge energized her, and she flung her chin up. "I have to find my daughter."

"But if you could postpone this until a little later in the day, we were going to make a statement, anyway."

She stopped and looked up at the man in his uniform. "Do you have some new information? Have you found Emily?"

"No, ma'am, I'm afraid not."

"Where is Kent Harlan?"

"He's busy investigating the crime."

"Is he looking for the real killer, or still trying to pin this on my daughter?"

"He's trying to bring resolution. May I at least read your statement?"

She glanced back at the camera following her. "I didn't write it down. I was going to speak from my heart. You'll have to hear it with everyone else."

He leaned down and said into her ear, "Mrs. Covington, please don't disclose any details of the case. That could seriously hamper the investigation, and even cause your daughter harm."

She looked at the crowd, second-guessing her decision.

"I won't." She pushed past him and reached the steps, and a flurry of activity buzzed around her. Battling reporters spoke into their own cameras, prepping for her statement. She got to the jumble of microphones and looked back to see where Lance was. He was right behind her.

She took his sweaty hand, pulled him next to her, and clung with all her might. She cleared her throat.

Everyone grew quiet, but she was aware of the cars passing on the street and the helicopter flying overhead, the hum of the air conditioner on the lawn of the police station. How would anyone hear?

She cleared her throat, and realized the microphones did nothing to amplify her voice. She spoke as loudly as she could. "My name is Barbara Covington, and this is my son Lance. My daughter is Emily Covington, age eighteen. Emily is a beautiful young lady, as I'm sure you all know from her pictures. She's very precious to me." The words broke off in her throat, and she felt her lips trembling.

Forcing herself, she went on. "As many of you have already reported, we hired Trish Massey this week to come to our home and escort my daughter to treatment for some . . . some problems she was having." She looked out into the flashing cameras. What would she tell them about the nature of Emily's addictions? Wouldn't the truth make her sound like she could be a crazed killer?

She decided that the less she said, the better. "My daughter went with Trish willingly. She went through security willingly and got on the plane willingly, and had every intention of arriving at their destination at the Road Back Recovery Center in Emerson, Georgia, north of Atlanta.

"I heard from my daughter when they landed. They were on their way to baggage claim. I spoke to Trish, and she told me that they were fine, and that the flight had been uneventful. They were going to call me when they arrived at Road Back." She tried to swallow. "Something terrible happened after that."

She stopped and tried to keep from breaking down in front of them all. "Sometime after that, Trish was murdered, and my daughter Emily vanished. I'm here to plead with all of you to help me find Emily and bring her home. She didn't kill Trish. She's not violent and never has been."

Cameras clicked and she glanced back at Lance again. He was doing just as he'd been told. Staying quiet.

She leaned into the bank of microphones. "I believe that whoever killed Trish Massey has my daughter. She's naive and young and not in good health, and she doesn't have the resources she needs to fight a violent killer who may have abducted her. Please . . . if anyone has any information . . ."

She stopped again and realized that she didn't have a phone

number to give them. Should she give out her cell number on national television? What if she was barraged with calls from reporters and Emily couldn't get through?

She decided to give them Lance's number. "If you have information . . . please call me at 573-555-3232. Thank you."

She tried to step away, but the reporters called out to her like rabid fans at a hockey game.

"Mrs. Covington, is your daughter a drug addict?"

She paused, knowing this had to be addressed. "She . . . uh . . . has had some recent problems with substance abuse, but she was ready to get help."

"Have you had any communication from her?"

"No. She doesn't have her cell phone and only had ten dollars."

"Mrs. Covington, where is her father?"

Her stomach roiled. "My husband died of cancer a few years ago."

"Did Emily have friends here in Atlanta?"

"None that we know of. She doesn't know her way around Atlanta, and if she's been abducted by whoever did this, then her life could be in danger too. Please, if any of you know where she is, I'm begging you to come forward. Or if there were witnesses who saw her in the Atlanta airport yesterday, if you could tell us if you saw anyone with her and Trish . . . or if you know of anyone who had reason to hurt Trish, please, call me or the Atlanta police. One life has already been lost, and I'm begging you not to let my daughter's life be taken too."

They were like vultures, pecking at her with their questions. She turned and tried to step away again, but she'd been closed in from behind.

"Tell us about your daughter, Mrs. Covington," a voice called above the noise. "Give us a feel for what she's like."

It was Richard, their tormenter/savior. She wanted to ignore him, but then she realized that the question might be just what she needed. Sighing, she turned back to the microphones.

Trying to steady her trembling mouth, she said, "Emily has been a precious child since she was born. She was very sensitive, and writes and paints and dances ballet . . . She was a cheerleader in middle school, and was elected Class Favorite her freshman year. She has a lot of promise."

What could she tell them that would make them understand? "She took her father's death very hard, as we all did. But she never quite bounced back from it. She's been depressed for the last four years. I believe that's why she wound up with a substance abuse problem. We did stage an intervention for her yesterday, and I believe she truly wants to get better."

She picked one of the cameras and looked into it. "Emily, if you can hear me, please do whatever you can to get to a phone and call me. I'm worried about you. I need to know you're okay. Please. We love you and are praying for you, and I'm doing everything I can to find you."

She couldn't say more. She turned to go again.

"Was your daughter desperate, Mrs. Covington?"

She couldn't step away with that hanging in the air. "She wasn't what I'd call desperate. She was nervous about what to expect in rehab, as anyone would be."

"What was her drug of choice?"

"I don't want to get into that right now. It has no bearing on what happened yesterday."

"Doesn't meth make people violent and combative? Doesn't it give them more strength than they normally would have? Paranoia?"

"It wasn't meth."

"Even cocaine—"

"I'm not commenting on my daughter's drugs!" she bit out.

"Why didn't you take her yourself?" someone asked.

There was no escaping this. She should have listened to the police chief. "I thought she would talk me out of it on the way. I thought with a professional interventionist, her fears might be calmed and things might go better."

"Then you clearly knew that she might balk and run."

Now she was in a mess. Her mind raced for an answer. "She was traveling with Trish in good faith because I sent her, and something horrible happened. Rather than focusing on what my daughter's addictions were, or why I hired Trish to help her, you should focus on helping me find her."

That was when the police chief took over. He parted the crowd and stepped up to the mike, allowing her to escape inside the building. She pulled Lance with her. Behind her, she heard the chief announcing another press conference at three that afternoon, at which time they would share what they could about the murder.

As Barbara pushed through the glass doors, she realized she was soaked with sweat. She dropped into a folding chair. A woman in uniform offered her a glass of water.

She drank it, her hands shaking.

"Good job, Mom. You okay?"

She looked up at Lance, who was looking out the window at the crowd. Her forehead still throbbed. "Yeah. I didn't say anything to make it worse, did I?"

"I don't think so."

She wiped her face. "I just hope Emily heard it." She pulled her cell phone out of her purse. No calls.

But Lance's had already started ringing. He pulled it out of his pocket. "Since you gave them my phone number, does that mean I can talk to reporters?"

"Give me that." She took the phone out of his hand and dropped it into her purse. "We'll let voice mail get it, then return the calls that are important."

"But how will I talk to my friends?"

"We're not going to worry about your social life right now, son."

"They'll be calling to tell me they saw me on TV. What a trip, huh? And now Emily's famous, like Lindsay Lohan. It's what she's always wanted."

Her dream come true. Barbara closed her eyes and prayed.

seventeen

Kent Harlan's melancholy sank its claws in a little deeper as he sat outside the intake office of the Road Back Recovery Center. He hadn't been home since seven a.m. yesterday, and his shoulders ached. He desperately needed a shave. It had been important to work this case while it was still hot. But his fatigue wasn't helping his spirits. The dark-colored décor of the rehab's hallway, green paint with deep wood for wainscoting, was meant to relax anxious and irritable clients fighting their dragons. But he needed caffeine instead of soothing colors.

As he waited, he checked his phone to make sure he hadn't missed a call. Andy was meeting with the video tech who was enhancing the security footage. Kent hoped the tech could tell them if the movement he'd seen in the video was someone else getting out of Trish's car, after Emily ran away. If that was the case, it would change everything.

This afternoon they'd managed to reach the passengers who'd been seated near Emily on the plane. The woman who had the seat next to her, an eighty-year-old who was hard of hearing, said Emily had slept for most of the flight. Others around them hadn't spoken to her. The only person she was seen talking to was Trish after she got off the plane.

And the Infiniti sedan wasn't in the airport parking lot now. So much for the theory that its driver had ditched the car and ridden away in the cab with Emily. Nothing quite added up.

From his seat in the hallway, Kent's gaze strayed to the classroom where some of the Road Back residents sat in various stages of attention, listening to a counselor talk about the third step of Alcoholics Anonymous.

He was familiar with step three. His brother had spent years in AA and quoted the steps as often as children quoted the Pledge of Allegiance.

Made a decision to turn our will and our lives over to the care of God as we understood Him.

As they understood him. That left a lot of wiggle room, he supposed. He was glad he didn't have a problem with addictions, because he'd never get past step three. He could never turn his will or his life over to a God he didn't believe in.

He heard voices down the hall, as a group of men and women filed out of a classroom, laughing and flirting their way up the hall. His brother had come from every rehab with a new relationship, so he knew how it all worked. When they let go of drugs, many of them transferred their addictions to people. He watched as they passed him, headed for the front door. Were they leaving?

"Detective?"

He turned and saw a young man in the office doorway. He got to his feet and stuck out his hand. "Yes. Detective Kent Harlan, how are you?"

"I've had better days. I'm Sean Morris, the director here." He led Kent into his office. There was a box of stuff on one of the chairs, and two boxes of personal items that Kent supposed had been confiscated from some new resident who'd tried to smuggle them in. A pair of earbuds, an iPod touch, a cell phone, a laptop . . .

Kent wondered if Road Back sold the items, or if they held them until they released the residents. If the latter, they must have several warehouses full of bags and boxes. He was glad it wasn't his problem.

"Those people that were leaving. Are they residents?"

"Yes," Morris said.

"Where were they going?"

"We let them take a walk down to the convenience store every day."

Kent's old frustration with lax rules at rehabs feathered through him. "Without supervision?"

"There's a staff member with them. It's only six blocks. Gives them a chance to get some exercise."

Kent sat down, frowning. "There's a liquor store a block down. Isn't that tempting for them?"

"Either they want to get well or they don't."

"Yeah, but isn't the idea to keep them sober long enough that they start having some clarity?" He thought of his own brother's schemes when they'd gotten him into treatment. If he'd been allowed to roam the streets, he would have had dealers meeting him at the convenience store or waiting at a corner as he walked by.

The director sat down at his desk and slid a stack of AA books out of his way. "People won't choose Road Back if it's too restrictive, and we really want them to come so they can get help. Besides, they'll be back in the real world at some point. They might as well build some self-control now."

Self-control was out of reach for most serious addicts. Did these people expect new residents to sprout it just because they were in treatment?

He shook off thoughts of his brother and focused on the young director. Sean Morris seemed distracted, authentically troubled.

"We're still in shock about Trish. I have the other staff members joining us in here to talk to you as soon as their classes let out."

Kent glanced through the door again. "Are the counselors here recovering addicts?"

"Most are. We sometimes hire the ones who work hard and keep their sobriety. Addicts and alcoholics can relate to others who've been down the road they're on. That's why Trish is so good at what she does. I mean . . . did." He looked around as if he'd misplaced something, then frowned down at the floor. Trish's death clearly rattled him.

"So did Trish have much interaction with the residents, after she brought them in?"

"She taught two classes a day and counseled some of them. They loved her. Our minds are blown by this. Everybody's been crying. Some of the residents have threatened to leave."

Yet they hadn't looked all that depressed as they headed to the convenience store. Clearly, thoughts of a few blocks of relative freedom had lifted their spirits. "How many of the residents did she bring here?"

He had to think for a minute. "Maybe ten. The rest came on their own, or were brought by family members. We have beds for fifty."

"Where was her office?"

"Right next door." He pointed with his thumb. "Cops were here this morning and sealed it up. Thankfully, they didn't shut us down. There are some folks here that would wind up in a world of trouble if we had to send them home."

Kent nodded. "I had them seal it. I'll go in and have a look around after we talk."

"You'll probably find a lot. Trish was on her computer all the time. Has a pretty extensive contacts list, a calendar, notes on all her calls . . ."

"Any idea who did this?"

"None at all. I mean, there are times when we have to kick people out, and they get hot under the collar. But she hasn't personally kicked them out. I'm the one who generally does that."

"You kick them out on what grounds? If they have so much freedom . . ."

"If they have a hot drug test, they're out. If they break rules, or leave the premises without checking out, or go in each other's rooms, or disrupt class, all these things are grounds for dismissal."

"Anyone kicked out recently?"

"No. A few have left on their own, but we haven't dismissed anyone in a couple of months."

"Did Trish have any boyfriends?"

He shook his head. "No, not lately."

The woman he'd seen teaching the class across the hall bolted into the room. Her eyes were red, swollen. She took one look at him and burst into tears.

"Sharon, this is Detective Harlan, from Atlanta."

"How did she die?" she blurted. "I heard it was in the parking garage, but what happened?"

"I can't discuss that."

"Well, how could anybody be murdered in an airport?"

He ignored the question. "How well did you know her?"

She grabbed a tissue out of the box on Sean's desk and blew her nose. "We were best friends. Why would anyone want Trish dead?"

He spent the next hour questioning Sharon, but got little useful information. Then he talked to the other counselors, taking copious notes in case something proved useful later.

Finally, he went into Trish's office, saw the clutter of busyness, the expectation of her return. Before touching anything, he took a visual inventory. Her desk had Post-it notes stuck all over it. He saw one with Emily Covington's name at the top. Pulling his rubber gloves out of his pocket, he slipped them on and read.

> Emily Covington, 18
> Mother, Barbara
> Addictions: X, H, C, and others
> Crisis point—needs me Monday
> Payment wired

At the bottom, in a different-colored ink, she'd written, Paid.

He logged that in, photographed and bagged it, then spent several hours going through her things. He logged her laptop as evidence, along with some of the papers on her desk, using a suitcase to collect it all.

Finally, he locked her office up again, in case he had to come back. When he came out, he thanked the staff and saw the residents crowded around a television.

Barbara Covington was on the screen, talking to the press. She was crying, and she looked very small and delicate as she made an appeal for her daughter. A sudden, protective urge welled in his chest—an emotion he'd thought was long buried.

He hoped he didn't find the girl dead. He'd hate to have to break it to this woman and her son.

He would hate it almost as much if he had to tell her he'd arrested the girl for murder. But that was probably exactly what would happen.

His phone rang as he was taking the suitcase of evidence out to his car. He put it to his ear. "Whatcha got, Andy?"

"I've been with the video tech," Andy said. "There's definitely something in the video, but we haven't been able to enhance it enough to figure out what it is."

"Did you see the door opening? Could anyone be getting out?"

"The perspective of the camera makes it hard to see that side of the car."

Since Trish had parked her own car, he couldn't say that was by design. But if someone other than Emily was involved, they had chosen the door that couldn't be seen by the cameras. "So is he giving up?"

"No, he's taking it over to the state police to see if their equipment might do a better job."

"How long will that take?"

"He said he'd go this afternoon."

"Did you stress the urgency? We need to know how many people we're looking for."

"I did. He knows. I'll call you as soon as he gets back to me."

As Kent drove back to Atlanta, he thought of that mother who looked so fragile. Her determination suggested a strength that he couldn't help admiring. He suspected there was more to Barbara Covington than brokenness and fear . . . and the picture the social media posts painted of her.

He hoped Emily saw the press conference. It would do her good to see how hard Barbara was fighting. Maybe that would penetrate that ironclad head of hers.

eighteen

Barbara and Lance stopped at Kinko's on the way back to the hotel to get the posters they'd ordered. She went through a drive-thru for hamburgers, but she couldn't choke down more than a few bites. While Lance ate, Barbara read Emily's printed posts.

Therapy started today. My mother hired some big-ticket shrink to look inside my psyche, and I managed to convince him that I was majorly anxious, which meant more downers, and that I was depressed, which meant more uppers. I also did a little homework on ADD to explain my bad grades. I've always wanted to try some of those ADD meds.

But it wasn't like I was running the show. He started asking me all these questions about my dad's death, and whether I saw his body or not after he passed. How I felt when I saw him lying in the coffin. Whether I dreamed of him.

It got really hot in that room and I wanted to bag the

whole thing and leave. If a person has to feed some doctor's morbid curiosity, they should at least cool the place down ahead of time.

I don't like talking about my dad's death. Why do people have to focus on that? I want to remember him the way he was before he died, the way he was on Christmas mornings. The way he was when he'd say, "Hey, Em, wanna go with me to the hardware store?" And then he'd show me three choices of hammers he wanted to buy, and let me pick. He valued my opinion, even when I was six.

My mother chooses her own hammers.

Today Mommy-o worked up a couple of tears and said she didn't know why I keep hurling myself into oncoming traffic. I admit I was a little . . . compromised . . . at the time. Okay, a lot compromised. I'd just scored a fresh bottle of pills, with the name of some old lady on the bottle. Dealers used to stand on street corners, but Mom would never guess that they're now just normal-looking people who befriend the elderly in hopes of getting their medications. I like to think they pay them for the stash, but if they don't, I guess it'll catch up with them. All I do is buy them.

Barbara closed her eyes. She had spent so many nights picturing her daughter in the worst part of town, buying from evil men in the dead of night. This was new.

Anyway, when Mom said that about oncoming traffic, I had no idea what she was talking about, because I'm not stupid enough to run out into traffic, no matter how high I am.

She screamed that she wasn't talking about real traffic. It was a metaphor. Okay, so I know what a metaphor is. I'm not stupid. But I still don't get the traffic thing.

Besides, it wasn't even her that taught me not to run out into traffic. My dad taught me to ride a bike, and he was extra-careful to make me understand about oncoming cars. If it had been up to my mom, I never would have even owned a bike.

Sometimes I curse my dad for not being here to teach me to drive. Mom had a meltdown the first two times I tried. She forbade me to use the words "I know" when we drove, and after a few aborted attempts, where I had to pull over and let her drive, she finally hired a substitute to teach me. It went much better, but it wasn't fun. Dad would have made it fun, and he never would have turned it over to someone else.

My dinged and dented bumper tells lots of stories that would curdle my driving teacher's blood. Mom screams about revoking my driving privileges, but I know her hiding places. I always find the keys.

Barbara set down the pages and looked at her son, who had mustard on his mouth. "She really hates me. Am I so horrible?"

"No," he said, turning on the TV. "You're awesome."

"She just says such terrible things."

He grabbed his napkin and wiped his mouth. "She hates anybody that comes between her and her dope."

"But even through the haze, can't she see that I love her?"

"All she can see is that she loves herself."

"Then why is she trying to destroy herself?"

He shrugged and took another bite of burger, got mustard on his mouth again. Thumbing the remote, he landed on a sci-fi movie that snagged his attention.

She forced herself to read another post.

> My friend Christopher just got out of rehab. He says it
> wasn't so bad. That it was tough at first, but after a few
> days he got into the routine and made friends, and
> then it was kind of like camp. Seriously, he said that.
> I don't think it would be much like camp, especially
> when he's twenty-two years old. If I'm going to drug
> camp at twenty-two, you can just go ahead and
> shoot me.

So that was where Lance got the "drug camp" idea, Barbara thought—from reading these posts. Thankfully, Emily hadn't noticed when he brought it up at the intervention.

> It worked for him, though. He got religion and got
> sober, and made up his mind to go back to school and
> change his life. But then he came back home, and
> his parents, who drink every night, refused to get rid of
> their booze. They said that just because he's an addict,
> that doesn't mean they should give up alcohol. That
> he needs to learn to get along sober even when others
> around him aren't.

> Within three days, he was drinking their booze. The next
> thing he knew, he was right back with us, doing what
> we do.

I was glad to have him back, because he's a walking party when he's using, but I admit part of me was a little let down. I guess I was hoping he could do it, so I'd know someone could.

There was a moment when I went from being a party girl to a real, hardcore addict. I remember that exact moment, when I told myself that I could stop now and be all right. That if I got that next supply, there would be no turning back.

I chose to go on. Now my hair's falling out and my teeth are rotting, and I don't recognize myself in the mirror. If I could turn back time . . .

Mom likes to talk about generational blessings and curses. She quotes that verse that says the sins of the father are visited upon his sons to the third and fourth generations, but the blessings of those who love him go to the children for a thousand generations. Or something like that.

Christopher's family has those generational curses. Mine doesn't. But I wonder if I've messed up those blessings that should have belonged to my family because my mom loves God. My dad loved him too. Maybe I've undone all that, and brought curses on us all.

I don't believe in God, I don't think. But I do believe in demons. I see them at night, when I'm high. I see their shadowy forms looking in my windows and feel them breathing against my neck. I see hinges shaking and doorknobs jiggling, and know they're coming for me.

Even when I can't get my high, they come into my

dreams. I hate them. I hope it's true that someday they'll boil in the Lake of Fire.

I guess for that to be true, there would have to be a God who actually practices justice. But that's pretty scary, because then he'd have to practice it on me.

Maybe I do believe in him, after all.

My mother used to preach to Lance and me that alcohol and drugs are gateways for Satan to get a foothold in your life. She doesn't know how right she is. I feel like I have demons hanging off of me, strangling me, mumbling in my ear.

I don't know why I keep doing what they say. But I can't seem to stop myself anymore.

Barbara stopped reading as the horror of Emily's condition slammed into her heart. Dissolving into tears, she rushed into the bathroom and grabbed a folded towel. Closing the door, she pressed her face into it to muffle her sobs. She had to be strong for Lance. It would do him no good to see her falling apart.

nineteen

When Barbara had pulled herself together, she decided it was time for action. She and Lance went back to the airport and asked all the fast-food workers in the nonsecure areas if they'd seen Emily last night. No one had.

Then they rode the MARTA train to some of its main stops during rush hour and handed out five hundred posters of Emily, enlisting strangers to pass stacks of them around their offices. Wielding a hammer, they nailed them to posts everywhere they went. When they ran out, she called Kinko's to put in another order.

Weariness weighed on them both as they returned to the hotel room around eight o'clock that night. Lance flopped down on his bed and turned the television on, while Barbara began to sift through the interview requests on Lance's phone. As Lance changed channels, he found Emily's picture.

"Mom, look."

She held her breath as they reported Emily's part in the situation, then showed a clip of the press conference. Barbara couldn't watch herself. She looked awful.

Then they cut back to the anchor, who happened to be a lawyer. She pontificated on whether Emily had committed the murder.

"It's amazing that there aren't witnesses, Kirk. I've parked at the Atlanta airport many times myself, and it's not that private. People coming and going, security people driving around in golf carts, cameras everywhere . . ."

"Not necessarily, Marney. There are times when it's pretty quiet. But she was killed in her car, so if someone got in and waited for her, they could have killed her without being seen."

"Or the girl with her, this Emily Covington, could have done it. I don't know, Kirk. To me, the simplest explanation is usually the most likely."

"But her mother's plea was very moving—that Emily is just a kid who was headed off to get help. She could have simply walked away without killing her escort. It isn't like interventionists take their charges at gunpoint."

"This is true," Marney said. "But maybe she felt trapped."

Lance turned the TV off and flung the remote onto the bed. "Why do they get to do this? Just sit on TV and accuse somebody of something they didn't do? They don't get to decide if Emily's a killer or not."

That pain behind Barbara's eye returned. "Why don't they care that she's missing? If she weren't an addict, they'd have reporters searching for her, and people would be praying and volunteering to help. But because she has problems, they're content to just call her a murderer. *That's* a more interesting story." She went to the window, looked back toward the airport. Tears burned her eyes. "What if she's dead?"

"She's not, Mom."

Unable to stand it anymore, she curled her hands into fists and let out a yell that shook the walls. "Why didn't I give Emily her phone? Some money? Anything? She's out there with nothing.

If she did run, or if someone has her and she gets away, what can she do?"

"She'll do what you said in the press conference, Mom. She'll get to a phone. She's not stupid. She's been lying to you for years and doing a pretty good job of it. She doesn't have a job, but she's been smart enough to figure out how to pay for her drugs. She'll figure out how to reach us."

"But she's never been in this much trouble, completely out of her element, with no one to turn to!"

Lance shook his head. "Then maybe it's good that the police think she did it. Maybe they'll find her sooner. At least then she'll be safe."

"She won't be safe in prison!" Barbara started to cry, unable to rein her hysteria back in. "All I've wanted is to keep the two of you safe. When I sent her off to rehab, that was the reason. I didn't want her to wind up dead or in jail. And right now, those might be the only two options." She threw up her hands. "How did I let this happen?"

"Mom, somebody will find her."

"Dead!"

"No, not dead."

Suddenly, she heard a chime on her phone, the sound she got when someone texted her. She dove for the phone, almost dropped it. Inside the small text box, it said:

mom help me

Her heart almost shot out of her chest. "Oh, dear God, it's Emily!"

Lance snatched the phone and read it. "Whose number is this?"

"I don't know. We've got to call it." She took the phone back, returned the call to the number on the text. It rang once. She heard it connect, then cut off as someone hung up. She tried again, but this time it just rang.

"Don't leave a message," Lance whispered. "It might be the killer's phone."

She didn't know what to do. She lowered the phone and studied the number. It had a Georgia area code. "I'm calling the police. Here, write the number down."

Lance took the phone, and she dug through her purse for the card Detective Harlan had given her. Unable to find it, she decided to call 911.

"911, may I help you?"

"Yes . . . this is Barbara Covington. Emily, my missing daughter, just contacted me. It's the Patricia Massey case. I need to talk to Detective Harlan . . ."

"I'm sorry, ma'am, this number is only for emergencies."

She screamed into the phone, "This is an emergency! My daughter needs help!"

"Okay, give me an address and I'll send someone."

"I don't have one. She texted me. I only have a phone number."

"I'll transfer you to the police department. You need to talk to the detectives on the case."

She waited on hold for what seemed forever. No wonder people died.

Her frantic call was finally routed to a detective named Andy Joiner, who said he was Detective Harlan's partner. Now maybe she'd get some help. "This is Barbara Covington, Emily's mother. I just got a text from my daughter that said, 'Mom, help me,' and I called the number back and someone hung up, and now it's only ringing . . ."

"Hey! Slow down."

She tried to steady her voice. "You have to tell me whose number this is *now*. I have to go help my daughter."

"Okay, give it to me."

She read out the number. "Can you find out who it belongs to now? I need a name. An address."

"Ma'am, we'll take care of it."

"No! Just look it up on your database. You can do it in two seconds!"

"Ma'am, I appreciate your calling with this information, and I know you're upset, but I can't give you the name."

Was he serious? "Where is Detective Harlan? I want to speak to him."

"He's out investigating this case."

Where was his number? She had it in her purse somewhere.

"What's his number? I need to call him."

"He's probably conducting an interview. I'll have him call you." He hung up. She let out another frustrated wail.

"Mom, chill. Sometimes you can Google a number and get the name and address."

"Okay, let's try." She grabbed the laptop and almost dropped it. She turned it on and waited as it booted up.

She went to Google and put in the phone number. A link came up for a name search. She clicked on it and entered the number again.

It told her that the name and address were available, but she'd have to pay a fee for that information. Quickly, she entered her credit card number.

It processed the fee, and she waited, fidgeting, as it searched the database. Please, God . . .

Finally, the results came up.

This is an unlisted cellular phone number from Georgia. We are unable to locate the name of the owner or the address.

"It's a scam," Lance said.

She let out a long breath and fell back on the bed.

"What do we do now?" Lance asked, almost in tears.

She got back up and grabbed her purse. "We're going to the police station to camp out at Detective Joiner's desk until they go get Emily."

twenty

Barbara couldn't imagine how anyone in Atlanta's Police Department got anything done. It was a madhouse tonight.

Big-shot Detective Andy Joiner was even worse than Kent Harlan. At least the older detective had made eye contact when he spoke to them. Joiner was rude and abrupt. He treated Barbara like her presence was an annoyance. All he had to do was give her the name and address of the person who owned the phone Emily had called from, and she would be on her way. But Joiner wasn't cooperating, and Barbara wasn't leaving without it.

"Ma'am, I told you, we're working the case as hard as we can. I didn't get the information I'd hoped for from that phone number."

"Why not? It's a working number! She just texted me an hour ago."

"The information that's coming up on the database is bogus."

"How do you know?"

"Because that address doesn't exist. It's one of those pre-paid phones you can buy in a convenience store. The owner lied about the address. Look, it's a lead, and it's something I can work with.

But if I have to sit here and keep explaining things to you, then I can't get on it."

"Give me the address," she said. "I'll go there myself."

"Did you hear what I just said?"

"Then a name. If I had a name . . ."

"Lady, you're in the way. Don't you get it?"

She slammed her hand on his desk. "My daughter needs help!"

"Mrs. Covington, I'm warning you—"

She wanted to turn his desk over. "Do you have children?"

"Yes, I do." He gestured to the family picture at the corner of his desk.

It faced away from her, so she turned the frame around and saw three happy faces.

"Funny, I have a family portrait just like this one. Same smiles and everything."

He didn't answer.

She wiped her eyes. "Imagine that you dropped dead, and your wife struggled to raise the kids alone. And this one," she pointed to the girl, "medicated away her grief with drugs. And just when you thought you were finally getting her some real help, she gets in a situation like Emily's. The person taking her for help gets murdered. She texts her mother for help . . ."

"I get the picture," he said. "You've done the right thing. You brought it to us. We'll take care of it."

"How? Will you go there and get her?"

"We don't know where *there* is."

"But you know who owns that phone! Doesn't it have GPS or something?"

"No GPS. Not all phones have it."

"All right, you leave me no choice." She got to her feet. Lance, who sat in a chair at the empty desk behind the detective's, threw a questioning look up at her. "Come on, Lance. I feel a whole new speech coming on. Maybe we can call another press conference and give them this phone number. They'd know who owns it within minutes."

Now she had Andy's attention. "Ma'am, that's a real bad idea."

She swung back around and leaned over his desk, her eyes on fire. "Then give me a good one."

She heard footsteps behind her. Detective Joiner looked up and said, "Thank God."

She turned around and saw Detective Harlan.

"Mrs. Covington?"

"She's all yours," Andy said. "Get her off my back before I have to arrest her. I haven't slept in two days, and I don't need this."

"Arrest me?" Barbara cried. "Oh, that'll look good to the press. A terrified mother goes to the police with the phone number of someone who kidnapped her daughter and murdered another woman, and they *arrest* her?"

"Hold on, now," Kent said. "Detective Joiner called me. You heard from Emily?"

Using her name was a good sign. Maybe that meant he hadn't tried and convicted Emily in his mind, relegating her to a case number. "Yes. She sent me this text." She showed him her phone.

Andy touched Kent's shoulder. "Kent, can I have a word with you?"

"Sure." He glanced at Barbara. "Excuse me a minute. I'll be right back."

Barbara wiped her eyes again and nodded. "Please hurry." She couldn't sit, so she paced the floor, arms crossed, and watched the two detectives discussing the text.

"Mom." Lance's voice was soft.

She glanced at him, rocking back and forth in his chair. "What?"

"Check this out." He nodded to Andy's computer.

She glanced back. The two detectives were deep in conversation. She walked around Andy's desk and saw the display. It had a name and an address.

> Ethan Horne, 52
> 2412 Alamega Street
> Atlanta, Georgia

Her heart stopped. The name and address of the killer?

"Give me my phone," Lance said.

"What? Why?"

"Camera," he whispered. "Watch out, they're looking."

She pulled Lance's phone out of her purse and gave it to him. She stepped away from the desk again, resuming her pacing. Lance looked like he was doing what teens do—texting. But hopefully he was using the camera to get a clear picture of the screen so they could find out more about the owner of that phone.

Emily was probably with him, whoever *he* was. They were wasting time. Barbara's chest felt as if a two-ton anvil rested on it.

The men finished talking, and Barbara glanced at Lance. He nodded. He'd gotten the picture of the computer screen. Even if it was a bogus address, it might lead her to the area where Emily was. The closer she could get, the better her chances of finding her daughter.

Barbara grabbed her purse and stepped toward the two detectives. "Look, I've been here long enough, and I'm clearly not getting anywhere. Please call me the minute you figure out who this is. Thank you for your time."

Kent looked surprised. "I'd like to talk to you a little more."

She hesitated then. She could talk to him, get stalled even longer, or she could go find her daughter. The burning in her stomach told her that Emily's time was running out.

"I'm sorry, I'm feeling a little sick. I need to go back to the hotel and lie down."

Kent frowned. "Mrs. Covington, I hope you don't plan to go do something stupid."

She tried to look indignant. "If I knew what to do, I would have done it. I'm getting out of your way so you can work. Apparently, my being here is a roadblock."

"All right. I'll call you in a little while, and you can fill me in on anything you've learned since we last spoke."

"Just please hurry, okay? Too much time has already passed since Emily texted."

She gestured for Lance to come and led him to the elevator. On their way out, she looked at the image on the phone. "I can't read it. The print's too small."

Lance tried to stretch the image, but it only blurred. "We can upload it to your computer and enlarge it," he said.

Thankful Lance was with her, Barbara drove quickly back to the hotel, determined to find that address and get her Emily back.

twenty-one

"So what changed in the last two minutes?" Kent's fatigue cut deep lines into his face. "I came in and she was all frantic, and now she can't get out of here fast enough."

"I don't know. Lady's crazy."

"Her daughter's missing. You'd be crazy too."

"What I would or wouldn't be in these circumstances has no bearing on the probability that her daughter murdered Trish Massey."

"Whatever her daughter did, her mother believes she's innocent."

"Too bad. It's not my job to babysit a hysterical mother. Now, back to what I was saying. Kid calls from a phone activated by Ethan Horne. The address he used to activate is bogus. He doesn't come up in the system at all. No social security number, no job . . ."

Kent tried to focus, but the face of the crying mother kept dragging his mind from its work. He followed Andy back to his desk and saw that Ethan Horne was already up on his display.

Suddenly, he remembered the kid sitting a few feet behind the desk, texting.

"Now I see. Real smart, Andy, leaving him up on the display so they could see it."

"They didn't see it."

"The kid had his phone. He could have taken a picture or gotten the address."

"I don't think that happened."

"Of course it did. That's why they ran out so quick."

Andy looked at the screen and the proximity of the chair where Lance had sat. "Okay, so they saw it. It won't do any good. The address doesn't exist. The numbers on Alamega Street only go up to 400, and this is 2412 Alamega."

"Doesn't matter. She's going to go there looking for him, and it's a horrible part of town."

"Well, she'll find out pretty fast that she's on a wild goose chase."

He studied the profile to see if there were any hints of who really owned the phone. It was an Atlanta area code.

He decided to try giving the person a call. Using his cell phone, which blocked his name on the caller ID, he dialed, waited, as it rang again and again. There was no voice mail. Finally, he hung up and called the phone company, asked if they could tell him where the phone had pinged at the times of his call, and the text sent from the phone a while ago. They said they would call him back with that information. He gave them Andy's name and number. Then, hanging up, he told Andy he was going home to change clothes. He hadn't showered in over twenty hours.

But he'd have to wait another few. He wasn't ready to go home just yet.

twenty-two

"Mom, don't take me to the hotel! I want to go with you."

Barbara had no intention of taking Lance with her to Ethan Horne's address. Her phone's GPS couldn't find the address, so she stopped at a convenience store and asked the clerk if she knew the street. The woman told her it was in an area known by the locals as Cabbage Town.

"You don't look like somebody who got business there. You goin' by your lonesome?"

Barbara's knees grew weak. "I might, why?"

"Because it ain't such a good area. Lot of crime there. Drive-by shootin's, dope dealers, hookers . . ."

Her throat constricted. "Could you help me find it on my GPS? Do you know any side streets?"

The woman took her phone and quickly found it. "You got relatives there or somethin'?"

"Yes."

"Then I'd call and tell 'em to meet you somewhere else."

That was all Barbara needed to hear. She may be walking into hell's playground, but Lance was not going with her.

His protests continued as they drove back to the hotel. When they got there, she saw a television news van out front, and several people with cameras waiting near the front door. "Oh, no. Don't tell me."

Lance's face lit up. "Sweet! They're here to talk to us."

She drove past the parking lot and went around the block to come in the side entrance. No one seemed to be waiting there. She got her key card out of her purse so she wouldn't waste any time. "When we get out of the car, don't make any noise. If they approach us, keep walking and don't talk."

"But why won't you talk to them?"

"Because I can't tell them what I know or it'll jeopardize the investigation. Now please, just do what I say for once."

They got out, and Lance slammed his door a little too hard. She rushed for the hotel's side door, stuck her key card in, and prayed they'd get in before the reporters found them out. The door unlocked and she pulled it open and let Lance in.

"I don't see why we couldn't walk through them. It wouldn't kill us to make one little statement, so they'd put us back on TV."

"I'm not interested in being on TV."

"Well, it might help Emily."

"I'm about to help Emily right now." She reached the elevator and pressed the button. It opened quickly. "You lock the deadbolt behind me and don't let a living soul in. That includes reporters, and even maid service. Got it?"

"Mom, I'm not some little kid. I could protect you."

"I don't need protecting. I need for at least one of my children to be safe."

"But what if you don't come back? What will I do then?"

She absorbed the pain of his fear. "Call Detective Harlan and tell him."

"Those guys won't help!"

"Maybe he will. He seems more compassionate. Maybe he's not as useless as his partner."

The elevator door opened, and she got off and hurried up the hall to their room. Lance lagged behind. She unlocked the door and waited for him to go in. "Hurry up!"

"Why don't you wait and let Detective Harlan go with you?"

"Because he wasn't going to go! They were dragging their feet. And if he did go, he'd do it so he could arrest Emily. He thinks she's just some dispensable addict who's committed a crime. He's not concerned with saving her life. Besides, he'd never let me go with him."

"And why do you think that is? Mom, this is stupid. Detective Joiner told you it was a fake address."

"I have to see for myself. Even if the house doesn't exist, she could be next door or somewhere on that street."

"If Dad were here, he wouldn't let you go by yourself, and you know it. I'm the man of the house now, so it's my responsibility to protect you."

Her heart softened, and she touched her son's face. "Son, this conversation is over."

"Man!"

"So help me, Lance, if you don't stay in this room, I'll kill you."

"Will you at least get me a drink out of the machine before you go?"

"No, I have to hurry. Emily's in danger. Lock the door, Lance."

He let out a long-suffering sigh. "I will."

"Now. Lock it as soon as it closes."

He let her out. She heard the bolt turning behind her.

She tried not to think of the danger she was going into as she went back to her car. If it weren't for the delay at the police station, she could have been there and back by now. It had long ago gotten dark. Where had the hours gone?

She hurried down the stairs, hoping to avoid any press who might be wandering around the hotel. What was she doing, leaving Lance alone here at night? Was it the right thing?

Lord, I can't keep both of my children safe. Please watch over them.

She made her way back out the side door and slipped into her car. She turned on the overhead light and studied the map on her phone. All she had to do was get on 401 going north.

She said another prayer for her own safety. As she pulled into traffic, clouds moved in, darkening the sky even more. "Hold on, Emily. I'm coming," she whispered.

Her eyes stung, blurring the oncoming headlights. She had to pull herself together or she'd never find her way. She navigated to the right exit, then pulled into the parking lot of a convenience store with bars on the windows. She typed Alamega Street into the phone without a house number, and this time it came up.

She glanced through the windshield and saw some rough-looking men walking toward her. She pulled away, skirting past them.

On a normal day, she would have been terrified of going deeper into enemy territory. But tonight, fear for her child and rage at the circumstances controlling her life sucked all the anxiety out of her. If she had to, she could kill Ethan Horne.

She turned onto a dark street, saw men lurking on the curbs. Some of them stepped into the street to approach her car as she drove by. They were clearly drug dealers, competing for her business. She kept moving. Her headlights swept over the faces of men hawking their goods and hookers displaying their wares.

Her rage unfurled, forcing her on. She checked the locks on her doors and turned onto Alamega Street. There were men on the street corner, men gathered on porches and standing in driveways. Women also walked the streets, clad in high heels and scant clothing.

Emily, where are you?

She checked the house numbers. 394, 396 . . . She drove a little faster, moving down the street, looking for the 2400 block. The thought that Emily could be hidden in one of these houses nauseated her. This wasn't a place where a young girl should be.

She prayed Emily hadn't succumbed to an offer of drugs. She could be in one of these houses, lying in a stupor on the floor, or bouncing high as a kite. She could be doing all manner of things to get her next hit. She could have texted from one of her drug buddies' phones.

Barbara wiped her eyes and reached the end of the road. It came out on Cullman Avenue. Where were the 2400s?

Something hit her car, and she jumped. A man who blended into the night, except for a white muscle shirt, banged a fist on her hood and yelled something at her. She jerked the gearshift into reverse and backed up, looking for a place to turn around. Another man hammered a fist on her windshield. She jumped and backed into a driveway, then jerked the car into Drive and screeched out.

She stepped on the accelerator, trying to get away from them, but she wouldn't turn off this street yet. Emily was here somewhere. The numbers must be out of order. Maybe the 2400 block was before the 400 block.

Gritting her teeth, she drove up the street again, searching for the right house. Maybe Emily was watching for her. Maybe she'd come running out.

Headlights came up behind her and a horn blasted, jolting her. She glanced in her rearview mirror and saw a blue light flashing.

Had she run a stop sign? She pulled over, praying that no more predators would come out of the darkness to torment her.

She watched as the cop got out of his car and strode toward her. She wiped her face and rolled her window down.

Kent Harlan leaned in. "Mrs. Covington, I had a feeling I'd find you here."

She leaned her head back on the seat and closed her eyes.

"My partner told you the address was bogus," he said in a soft voice.

"I know, but I didn't believe him."

"I know you didn't." His voice was deep, soothing, non-condemning.

She looked up at him. The blue light still flashed across his face, keeping evil somewhat at bay. "I have to find her. She needs me."

"I know."

"If she's not here, then where did she text from?"

"We're trying to figure that out. Mrs. Covington, if we could just go somewhere and talk."

She looked through the windshield, saw that the men were clearing off of the street. "Are you sure . . . that there's not a 2412 Alamega?"

"Positive."

"She asked me for help, and I don't know how to help her!" She covered her face, pressing her eyes. Veins in her neck and forehead strained.

His voice was soft. "There's a coffee shop not too far away. Why don't you follow me?"

She thought about Lance, back at the room. She couldn't be gone that long, if it wasn't absolutely necessary. She smeared the tears across her face, wiped her hands on her pants. "No, I have to get back to the hotel. Lance is alone."

"Where are you staying?"

"The Hampton Inn near the airport."

"Good. There's a coffee shop next door to it. You could let Lance know we're there, in case he has any problems. Sound okay?"

"Okay."

"I'll lead, you follow."

She kept an eye on the men as Kent went back to his car. As her fear subsided, disappointment overwhelmed her. She had been so close. But it was all a hoax. A cruel joke. Emily wasn't here. Maybe the text was just a prank.

But only a few people had her number. It had to have been Emily.

Why won't you help me, Lord? I'm begging you!

Detective Harlan turned off the blue strobe and pulled his unmarked car around her. She followed him up the street to a turn-off. There wasn't a dealer or loiterer to be found now. The police light on his dash had frightened them back.

She was glad something could.

Staying close to his car, she followed him several miles to the coffee shop next to her hotel. She pulled into the parking space beside him. Before she got out, she blew her nose and tried to pull herself together. She was tired . . . so tired. All her efforts hadn't helped.

Maybe Detective Harlan could.

twenty-three

If Kent weren't a sucker for tears and broken hearts, he would have gone home. He hadn't slept in two days. She probably hadn't, either. Dark circles hung under her eyes. Her skin looked paper-thin.

He figured a little sympathy might be in order, before he called it a day.

She was on the phone with her son when she got out of the car. Judging from her side of the conversation, it sounded as if the kid was safe. She didn't sound so sure he would stay in the hotel room and not let anyone in. There must be some history there.

He led her into the coffee shop as she gave a few more admonitions to the boy. He found a table in the back corner and slipped into the booth. She sat down as she hung up. "Sorry about that," she said.

"No need to be," he said. "He seems like a good kid."

"He is a good kid. So are you ready to compare notes with me?" she asked.

He leaned forward and crossed his hands in front of him. "Mrs. Covington—"

"Barbara," she said. "Call me Barbara."

He didn't delude himself into thinking she was letting her guard down. "All right. And you can call me Kent. Barbara, I know you think we haven't been working on the case. But I want you to know that I've done nothing but work on it since Trish's body was found. I haven't even been home, as you can probably smell."

Finally, the hint of a grin. "You smell fine."

"Normally I'm clean-shaven and good-looking as all get-out."

Now she laughed. He considered it a victory, but it was short-lived.

"The point is, I've been up to Emerson today, I've searched Trish's office and collected evidence, I've interviewed her friends, I've talked to residents in her program . . ."

Her eyes came up, locked hopefully on his. "Did they tell you who could have done this? Who would want her dead?"

"They didn't know. I got some leads, and I'm working them."

She swallowed and looked down at her hands. "If you've been questioning them, that must mean that you don't think Emily did it."

"I didn't say that. We haven't ruled her out, but I'd be a terrible cop if I didn't consider every possibility."

"So when you find her, you're going to arrest her for murder, right?"

He sighed. "Depends on what the DA wants to do. But there are worse things than jail."

"Are there?" Her brows furrowed. "Are you a Christian, Kent?"

That had come out of left field. He almost flinched. "Well, no. Not really."

"Either you are, or you're not."

She was right about that. "I guess I'm not, then. But I don't have anything against people who are."

"Then maybe you won't understand. I raised my child the way the Bible taught me to. I did the very best I could."

Her sad eyes were killing him. "I'm sure you did."

"I guess . . . it's just my pride talking," she said softly. "I just want you to know that Emily was raised in a good home. We had morals and rules and we sat down to dinner, and I taught her right from wrong."

"You don't have to convince me you did that, Barbara. I can tell from how you've responded to this crisis that you're a good mother."

"Thank you."

Why did he feel so exposed when she met his eyes?

"The thing is, the last thing I wanted for either of my children, the very worst thing I could think of, was for them to wind up in prison. It hardly ever even crossed my mind because it was so . . . out there. Not even a possibility."

"It's better than death."

"And that's the other thing. The thought of burying one of them . . ."

He waited as she covered her face, hiding her terror from him. Her pain hit him deep, and he wanted even more to help her. "I bet having a kid on drugs wasn't in your top three dreams, either."

She shook her head. "No, it's an absolute nightmare."

A waitress brought them some coffee, and he dumped a few spoonfuls of sugar in his. "I know that nightmare. I have a brother with a drug problem. He's in prison right now for armed robbery. It was all about drugs. You get used to the blows, after a while. Your threshold for pain rises as they do worse and worse things."

"She's innocent. I know my daughter. She brings home stray animals. She spent a year on the rampage about abortion clinics when she was twelve. She picketed every Saturday. She couldn't kill anyone."

The words hung in the air as the waitress came back to the table, her order pad poised. "Can I get y'all something to eat?"

Barbara shook her head, but kept her eyes on Kent. "Nothing for me, thanks."

"Have you eaten today?" he asked.

She looked like she couldn't remember. "I had a burger earlier . . ."

He glanced up at the waitress. "Got any nachos?"

"Sure, how many orders?"

"Three," he said. "One in a box . . . for Lance."

"Yes . . . he'd like that. Thanks."

When the waitress left, Barbara locked onto him again.

"I'm not going to quit looking for her," she said. "I'll knock on every door in Atlanta. I'll go on every talk show. They love missing girl stories, and Emily's pretty. Before you know it, she'll be as well-known as Natalee Holloway." Her voice cracked. "Except it'll turn out better for my Emily. It has to."

Just what he needed. A hundred reporters intruding on the investigation, publicizing every iota of evidence, giving the killer their best escape strategies. "You don't want to do that. Not if you want her found quickly."

"I'll do what I have to do."

He knew she would. If she'd go into the neighborhood he'd found her in tonight, the woman would walk through an inferno to get her daughter back.

"Look, I know you don't know me, Barbara," he said. "You don't think I care about your daughter. But I do care. Even if she's the one who killed Trish Massey—"

"She didn't."

"Even if she did, I worry about her out there somewhere. If I didn't care, I'd be at home asleep right now. If she's in some terrible place of her own choosing, she'll be better off in our custody."

She sighed. "I need to see the videos of Emily at the airport."

So . . . she had finally accepted that Emily was the girl in the video. "I showed you the picture of her."

"I want to see the whole thing. Her behavior, the look on her face—"

"So you can decide if she's acting like a killer?"

She set her chin. "I might see something . . . someone . . . that you don't see."

"Look, Barbara, I have the video experts in the state police lab going over the security video. Showing them to you wouldn't accomplish anything. I'm not making any deals with you. But if you have something to show me, something that would help us find Emily, then you need to give it to me."

Finally, she let out a long breath, pulled some papers out of her purse, slid them across the table. "I printed out all of Trish Massey's posts from Instagram."

He knew that if she'd printed out Trish's, she had Emily's too. She was holding back, but it didn't matter. Andy had already downloaded them.

He took the pages and flipped through them, skimming passages from Trish's account that Barbara had highlighted. He'd read more than this in her emails. "I'll read every word," he said.

She sat back then, her shoulders slumped with their burden.

"We both need to get some sleep," he said.

She rubbed her eyes. "I can't. My Emily texted me for help. How can I sleep when I know she's waiting?"

"At least you know she's alive. There's nothing you can do for the rest of the night, unless you hear from her again, so you might as well rest. Come on, I'll walk you to your room."

They got all the nachos in boxes, then crossed the parking lot to the hotel. If the press were there, they weren't visible.

He followed her in and they rode silently up on the elevator. When they reached the room, he hung back from the door as she stuck her key card in.

"Thank you for rescuing me," she said quietly.

"No problem."

"And for the walk home."

"Glad to do it."

She opened the door and heard the television. It was a news channel. "Lance?"

She stepped inside and saw him sleeping, fully clothed, on top of the bedspread. He stretched awake. "Hey."

"He okay?" Kent asked from the doorway.

"Yes, he's fine. Thanks again, Kent."

She started back to the door, but he heard Emily's name on the television. She stopped and turned to the screen. Kent took a step inside her door to see what they were saying.

The television anchor had clearly been talking about Emily for some time. *"Sources tell us that Emily Covington went from the airport parking garage to the taxi line, and left the airport in a cab belonging to Capital Cab Company. She allegedly paid with Trish Massey's credit card."*

"What?" Barbara shouted. "That's not true! She got into that Infiniti. Why would they say that?"

Kent closed his eyes, wishing he'd never come here. He waited as a reporter interviewed a cab driver.

"Are you the driver who took Emily Covington away from the airport last night?"

"No, but I talked to the guy who did. He works for Capital Cab, and he says he picked the girl up and dropped her off at a motel. Said a man was with her, and they used the dead woman's credit card."

Barbara sucked in a breath. "That's the first I've heard of that." She swung around to Kent. "Did you talk to the cab company?"

"Yes."

"Well, what did they say? Is it true that Emily got into a cab?"

"It's true that someone did. We haven't confirmed that it was Emily."

"But how could it be her, when you saw tape of her getting into that Infiniti?"

"The Infiniti could have gotten Emily safely out of the garage, then dropped her off by the cabs."

"No, that doesn't make sense. She would have wanted to go for help."

"Unless she did it."

"She didn't do it!" she yelled.

She paced the room, rubbing her temples. "Do you have footage from the cab-stand during that time frame? There must be a security camera in that area."

"We studied it, but didn't see Emily. We weren't able to isolate that specific cab. Barbara, I can't answer any more of your questions. There are things that we're not ready to disseminate to the public yet."

"I'm not the public. I am her mother!"

"And you're emotional right now, and the press may convince you that if you just spill it all to them, they'll help you investigate. And that could ruin everything."

"Well, maybe that's true. If they know the cab driver and he knows the motel, then we could find Emily. She could be there right now."

"We already went there and didn't find her. I'm doing my job, Barbara. And before you think of going there yourself, that place is a drug den, worse than where you were tonight."

"Oh, dear God." She turned back to Lance and their eyes locked, as if they didn't know what to believe. Clearly, stealing a credit card and going to a drug-infested motel sounded like something Emily could have done.

He started back to the door.

"Kent."

He turned back.

"Emily's trapped somewhere and needs help! By God, I'm going to find a way to get to her! With or without you."

The message to Kent was clear. He'd better find Emily before Barbara got herself killed.

twenty-four

It was midnight by the time Kent left. Barbara checked messages on Lance's cell phone, listening for any leads the press were hinting at to make her call them back.

"I've been on the computer almost the whole time you were gone," Lance said, eating the nachos. "Emily's friends are all over this, trying to figure out if she had any dealers mad at her."

She shot him a look. "Dealers? I hadn't even considered that."

"Well, sure. If she owed them money or something, bad things would happen. I've heard of dealers setting houses on fire for not being paid. Families almost getting killed."

"What? Where have you heard of that?" They lived in a white-collar neighborhood in a nice, clean community.

"People talk, okay? And I see it all the time on TV. You have to at least consider it, Mom."

"Do they sell drugs on credit? It seems like . . . wait, no. She was talking about these dealers being people who get medication from old ladies, not the kind who hang out on the street. Besides, how would they even know to find her in the Atlanta airport? We tried every way we knew to keep her from contacting her friends before she left."

"Yeah, but how do you know Trish didn't let her call someone after she called you? She let her sit alone on the plane, let her use on the way. Emily has her ways, Mom. She's smart . . . or stupid, however you want to look at it. Oh, and I made a list of her social media friends from Atlanta."

"You did?"

"Yep." He handed her the list he'd written on a sheet of the hotel stationery. "There are twelve of them, and about twenty more from areas around Atlanta. I was going to email them and ask them if they know where Emily is, but I thought they'd just lie. It might be better if we found out where they lived and showed up at their houses."

Barbara sat back down in front of the computer. "You have their addresses?"

"Um . . . well, no. That's the problem."

"So how will we know where to find them?"

"Easy, Mom. You read their posts, look at their pictures, and you can find out all sorts of things like what school they go to, what kind of car they drive, even their parents' names. It doesn't take much snooping. Once you get the parents' names, you can Google them."

"Have you done that?"

"I was just at the snooping stage. I took a lot of notes. Ariel Carter's mother has been married six times, so it's a little complicated, but she hates her stepdad and writes about him a lot. She calls him Pinhead most of the time, but I found one post with his normal name. Oh, and this other kid on there? She admitted that her dad is abusive and cracked her skull last month. There ought to be some kind of law."

"There is."

"Anyway, she mentioned his first name, so I think we can look them up. And some of Emily's Atlanta friends live on their own. Most of them probably use cell phones, so they're hard to look up."

They had their work cut out for them.

"Know what, Mom? I'm pretty good at this stuff. I just might be a cop when I grow up."

She knew he was baiting her. Swallowing the cotton in her throat, she said, "You're right, son. You are good at this. You're a big help."

"Glad you brought me?"

"Of course."

"Don't lie. You wouldn't be leaving me all by myself in this room if you were glad."

She sighed. "You really had no business going where I went tonight. I had no business going there. You were right. It was a big mistake. A wrong address in a very scary area. I'm thankful Kent showed up when he did."

"He seems pretty cool."

"I guess." She opened her browser on her phone.

"What are you looking for?"

"The Capital Cab Company. I've got to talk to the cab driver who picked Emily up. He can tell me where he took her . . . and if it was even her."

"Great idea, Mom. You're good at this stuff too."

He got the computer and lay on the bed, his sock feet against the wall where the headboard stood. Barbara dialed the number and waited as the dispatcher answered.

"Capital Cab."

"Hi, this is Barbara Covington. I have a problem, and I wondered if you could help me."

"Do you need a cab?"

"No, I just need to talk to someone about a passenger who rode in one of your cabs last night."

"I'm sorry, but this line is for dispatch. We're not talking to the press."

So they'd gotten other calls. "I'm not the press. I'm the mother of the missing girl."

"I recommend you talk to the police."

"I have. Can I speak to a supervisor, please?"

"Offices are closed."

Barbara refused to give up. "Were you working last night?"

The woman grunted. "Yes."

"I need to talk to the driver who took her. Can you give me his name and a way to reach him?"

"If you call back tomorrow . . ."

She snapped. "By tomorrow, my daughter may already be dead!"

Silence.

"Please, just tell me who picked her up. Can you radio the driver and tell him that if he won't talk to me, I can only conclude that maybe he hurt her?"

"Ma'am, that's ridiculous."

"Then why can't he talk to me? It might save her life, unless he has something to hide."

"Hold on."

She waited again, wanting to break something. Closing her eyes, she prayed that even now, the dispatcher was getting that info from the driver. *Please, God, give me something.*

Finally, the woman came back. "Okay, I found the driver. Says he picked up a couple who seemed to be in a big hurry. He wanted his name left out of it, but he did tell me where he took them."

She wanted to jump through the phone and get her hands around the woman's neck. "Where?"

"The Day-Nite Motel in an area they call Cabbage Town."

Her heart clenched like a fist in her chest. Just as Kent had said, it sounded like a dive, and it was in the area she'd just come from. She touched her throat. "Did . . . did he know why she wanted to go there?"

"He said they were talking about buying some dope."

That acid worked through her stomach again. "What about

the person with her? I need to know what he looked like. What he said."

"Lady, I'm getting more calls."

"Fine. Then just give me a number where I can talk to the cab driver. I won't drag him into this. He could help solve a murder and save a life. He'd be a hero. So would you."

The woman sighed. "I can't give you his, but I'll give him yours. Don't know that he'll call."

Barbara gave the woman her number and hung up the phone.

"What?" Lance asked.

Barbara felt the numbness of shock creeping through her. "It doesn't make sense. If she was in the Infiniti, why would she need a cab?"

"It could have happened like Detective Harlan said. The Infiniti dropped her off at the cabs."

"But that makes her look . . . guilty. Why wouldn't she call for help? Why would she go to some fleabag motel with some guy? And who was he?"

The phone rang, and she grabbed it up. A man with a Caribbean accent spoke. "Ma'am, dis is Bastian, de cab driver."

"Yes, thank you for calling." She couldn't catch her breath. "My daughter is eighteen, and she has long blonde hair. She's about five-three and is very pretty."

"Yes, I picked up a blonde girl and de man she was with."

"What state was she in?"

"Here, in Georgia."

"No, I mean, how did she act? Was she upset?"

"She and her boyfriend seemed anxious, in a hurry."

"What did he look like?"

"Brown hair, not too tall." That described half the people Emily knew.

"Why did you take her to the Day-Nite Motel?"

"Dey asked for it."

"Asked for that particular motel?"

"Yes. I tole dem dey should not go dere, but dey wanted to. So I took dem and dropped dem off."

So, if that was Emily, she had willingly gone to a drug den without knowing a soul. And this man had left her there. She would make sure Kent followed up with him to make sure he hadn't done something to Emily, himself. It would be easy enough to find out if he'd had another fare right after her, or if he'd called it a night.

Her stomach was sick. When she got off the phone, she muttered, "I need to buy a gun."

"Got that right," Lance said.

The thought that this search could take her to even worse places than she'd already been filled her with dread and despair. How could Emily be sending them on a wild goose chase that took them into these hellish places?

She caught her thoughts, pulled back. What was she doing? Blaming Emily? Emily hadn't done this. She couldn't have done this. She was a victim, wasn't she?

"I have to go to that motel. I have to go now."

"Mom, no! You can't! He said it's full of druggies and dealers."

"I have to. She's there!"

"I won't let you."

She grabbed her purse. "How would you stop me?"

"Call Detective Harlan."

She closed her eyes.

"Mom, he said he went there already."

"But he might not have talked to the right people. I need to see for myself."

"If you have to go, get him to go with you. You're just a walking target in a place like that."

She got her bag and started for the door. "Don't let anybody in."

"I will, Mom!" he yelled. "I'll let everybody in. I'll have a party for the reporters. I'll catch a cab myself and go there too, or get one of them to take me. I might bring a whole camera crew."

She swung back around. "Don't you dare!"

Tears glistened under his eyes. "You can't trust me, okay? If you leave here, I'm going too."

"Lance, this is serious."

His cheeks were flaming. "You're right, Mom. It's dead serious."

She dropped her purse on the floor and leaned back against the wall. "Why are you doing this?"

"Because I don't want to lose my dad, my sister, and my mother!" he bellowed. "What's gonna happen to me?"

Her heart softened, and she realized how insane she had become. She had no right to jeopardize her life. She was Lance's mother too. What good would she be for him or Emily if she gambled her own life—and lost?

John, why did you leave me alone like this?

Lance kicked the bed. "Call him, Mom. Call Detective Harlan. This is one thing you can't do yourself."

She sighed. "All right, we'll compromise. I'll call him, but I'm going there too. I want to talk to those people. Someone there knows where she is."

"If you go, I'm going too. Period."

Her mind whirled with confusion. Should she go alone or wait for Kent? Should she take Lance or leave him? She'd have to be crazy to drag her son to a place like that, when she'd spent her life trying to keep him safe. But she knew he meant what he said. He would follow her there if she left him.

Too spent to sort through it all, she decided to give in. "Okay, you can come."

There was no joy on his face. "Call him and we'll go."

She called Kent then. He answered quickly. She told him about the cab driver. "I'm on my way to the Day-Nite Motel, Kent. I'd like for you to meet me there if you're really interested in finding Emily."

"Barbara—"

"I'm going, Kent. That's all I have to say." Then she hung up and tossed her phone into her purse.

twenty-five

She was losing it. She must be, taking her fourteen-year-old son to a motel where people paid by the hour. The patrons who stood in the parking lot and lurked on the curb in front were the very types of people she'd tried to shelter her children from. As they pulled into the parking lot, she was glad she'd called Kent. But where was he? Was he calling her bluff, letting her go it alone?

"Mom, this is really scary. Do you really think Emily would come to a place like this?"

"Apparently, she did." She pulled into the parking lot, eyeing the lit windows.

Fear twisted her gut. Emily had been a child afraid of the dark. How was it that she could run so quickly into it now, choosing it over light?

She felt queasy and wished she'd eaten some of those nachos. Her hands were weak as she pulled up to the front office and shifted the car into Park.

"Those guys are giving us dirty looks," Lance said, nodding toward a group of men standing in the doorway of a room.

Her fear morphed into anger. Suddenly, they represented all the evil that had preyed on her daughter. *Just let them cross me.*

"Get out. We're going in."

Lance looked at her. "I thought we were waiting for Detective Harlan."

"We can't wait. We're already here, and I want to know if Emily's in one of these rooms before her kidnapper sees us."

Lance put his hand on the door handle. "Man, we are so dead."

"We're just going into the office."

Lance blew out a sigh and opened his door. Barbara got out and tried to assess the risk. At least they wouldn't have far to walk. She locked the car and waited for her son, wishing she had a gun. When Lance was beside her, she pushed into the front office.

The motel clerk sat behind a barred window, in what looked like a cage. The room was thick with cigarette smoke and body odor.

The once-white linoleum was rotted and peeling, and mold grew on walls that had once been a mint-green. Leak stains soiled the ceiling.

She stepped up to the window and peered through the dirty glass. "Excuse me."

The round, bald man looked at her like she was a nuisance. "We don't got no vacancies."

"I'm not looking for a room." She thrust a picture of Emily between the bars, through an opening in the glass. "I'm looking for my daughter. She's eighteen, blonde, pretty."

He took one look and shrugged. "Fits the bill of half our girls."

"She would have checked in last night."

"Didn't see her." He turned away from the window.

"Are you sure?"

"Yes."

"Can I see your guest registration?"

He laughed. "This ain't the Marriott, lady."

"Yes, I can see that."

"I don't have a guest registration. I don't ask questions. Rent the rooms out by the hour, day or week, and that's that. And there weren't no girls checking in last night. I was here, and I'd remember."

Lance stood stiff, his hands in his pockets. "Mom," he said in a quiet voice, "maybe she didn't check in. Maybe she just went straight to somebody's room with the guy she was with."

That could be a possibility, but how would she get to the bottom of that? "She was with a man. They may have come here for drugs."

He took the cigarette out of his mouth and gave a phlegmy laugh. "Oh, why didn't you say so? Yeah, the drug dealer, he's in room 2308." He threw his head back and guffawed. "You think I'm crazy, lady?"

She looked at Lance, who was staring at his feet as if afraid he'd make the guy mad. "Mom, let's go."

"I guess I'll have to go door-to-door," she said. "I've called the police to help me. I'm going to find my daughter if we have to question every person here."

He kept laughing, and she realized why he was sitting in a cage. Someone probably wanted to kill him three or four times a day.

She bolted out of the office. Thankfully, Kent was pulling up in his unmarked car. She let out a lungful of air. *"Thank you, God."*

"Ditto," Lance said.

Kent got out. "Barbara, what are you doing?"

"I've come to get my daughter," she said, walking past him and rounding the office. "I would appreciate your help."

He caught up to her. "You'll never find her, barging up to their doors like some narcotics agent."

She swung around, hair slapping her mouth. "Well, since you brought it up, why aren't the narcotics agents doing something about this place?" Tears of rage reddened her eyes, and she resumed her trek. "Don't tell me the cops don't know what goes on here. Why do they allow it? Why do they turn their heads to this kind of evil?"

"We do the best we can, Barbara."

"Well, the best you can *stinks*! I'll make them talk to me. I'll give them money for information. I have a little cash."

"You may not get out of here with your life, much less your cash. And bringing Lance with you? Barbara, please let us handle this."

"You're *not* handling it," she grated.

"Yes, we are. We've already been here."

"Did you interview everyone here? Did you show them her picture?"

"Yes."

She didn't want to hear it. Whatever they'd done, it wasn't enough. Emily could be in one of these rooms right now, held against her will. She pushed past him and headed for the cluster of men who'd frightened her earlier. "Excuse me, gentlemen. Can I have a word with you?"

"*Mom!*" Lance whispered.

"Barbara, I'm warning you—"

"I'm looking for my daughter." She thrust the picture at the first one she reached. He had tattoos covering both biceps, and a dirty sleeveless T-shirt with food stains on it. "She came here last night in a cab. Did any of you see her?"

The men looked deadly, but she didn't care. "Naw, we ain't seen nobody," one of them said. "I'd remember her."

The others snickered.

"There's a reward," she told them.

Kent stepped forward and flashed his badge. "Kent Harlan, Atlanta PD, Homicide Division," he said, getting between her and the thugs.

"There's a reward for any information that leads to our finding her," Barbara said again.

"A reward?" one of the men asked. "How much?"

She didn't even pause to think. "A thousand dollars."

"On the spot?"

She hesitated. "I don't have it in cash. I have two hundred dollars cash right now, and will pay you the rest after we find her."

"Give me the two hundred now, and I'll talk to you," a man with no teeth said.

"Information," she repeated. "Tell me where my daughter is."

The man cursed her and backed away, and the rest of the men scattered, some walking up the street, others going into rooms.

"I'll go talk to the desk clerk," Kent said, "but right now, I need for you to wait in the car."

"But I—"

"Barbara, they know you have cash. You're a sitting duck. Sit in the car with the doors locked."

His tone brooked no debate, so she did what he told her. She led Lance back to the car. When they were inside, she locked the doors and watched Kent go into the office.

Lance shook his head. "Way to go, Mom. Blazing up there like Jack Reacher. My mom, the terror of stoners everywhere."

She didn't find it funny.

"You think they have room service here?"

He was clearly trying to break the tension, but she couldn't find a smile within her.

"Pool looks nice."

Her gaze gravitated to the pool. There were no lights over it, but in the moonlight, she could see the black algae floating on it.

Kent came back out, his face grim, and knocked on her window. She unlocked the door, and he slipped into the back seat. "Okay, here's the deal," he said, leaning up on her seat. "When I got your hysterical phone call, I was on the phone with Trish's credit card company. Trish Massey's credit card was used to buy gas and some grocery items at the convenience store across the street, just this afternoon. Last night it was used to buy about a thousand dollars' worth of stuff at Kohl's."

She frowned. "What kind of stuff?"

"High-ticket items. Stuff that was probably pawned for cash."

Drug money, she thought. Or maybe Emily was just trying to raise cash for a place to sleep.

"We don't have the authority to bust into these rooms without a warrant. Now if you can wait until morning, I can get video of the person who used the credit card, and we can see if it's Emily."

The back door opened, and Barbara jumped. A woman slipped in. "If they see me, they'll kill me," she said. "So if you want to hear what I have to say, start driving."

Barbara started the car and glanced at Kent in the rearview mirror. He nodded. She pulled out of the parking lot. "Did you see my daughter?" she asked.

"You said something about a reward?"

Barbara stuck one hand in her purse and pulled out all the cash she had. "I have two hundred dollars. It's yours, if you give me some information I can use. Eight hundred more after the banks open, if your information leads us to her."

"I saw the two people who came in a cab yesterday," she said. "I didn't see them leave, but I saw them get here."

Barbara glanced back. Shadows kept the woman's features dark, and she couldn't see her eyes.

"Did you see what room they went in?"

"Yeah, they went in 4C. Give me the two hundred."

Barbara looked at Kent.

"Did they check in," Kent asked, "or was that someone else's room?"

"Somebody else's," the woman said. "Belongs to a dude named Free-Roy. He'll kill me if he knows I talked to you."

"Is he a dealer?" Lance asked.

She looked at him. "Yeah, and I ain't kiddin' about him killing me."

Barbara almost ran into the car in front of her. She pulled into a dark parking lot and handed the woman the cash. She looked at her fully now. She had black teased hair, like a fifties beehive, skimpy clothing, too much eye makeup. "If you see her again, call me, and there may be eight hundred more." She gave the woman a card with her phone number on it. "Do you want me to take you back?"

"No, I can't be seen with you. I'll walk back."

"But isn't it dangerous?"

"It's my hood," she said. "I'll be fine."

The woman got out of the car and took off up the street. Barbara imagined she would spend that two hundred within the hour. She looked back at Kent. "What now?"

"Back to the motel," Kent said. "I'll call for backup, and we'll see who's in that room."

twenty-six

Andy and four backup officers showed up with a search warrant that Andy had acquired by waking up a judge. Kent made Barbara and Lance wait in the locked car as they searched 4C. Even though the dealer had had plenty of time to dispose of his drugs, knowing a cop was sitting in the parking lot, they were still able to find enough to lock up everyone in that room.

Unfortunately, it was only three men. Emily was nowhere to be found. As Kent escorted them out in handcuffs, he glanced through Barbara's windshield and shook his head. She slammed her hands on the steering wheel.

Kent didn't like making deals with drug dealers, but sometimes it was necessary to get information about important cases. Tonight was one of those nights. He took the men outside and separated them in three police cars. He went to the man who seemed in charge and leaned inside the door.

"Tell me something about the girl, and I might lower your charge from distribution to possession."

"I don't even know their names, man! They come in last night and got some dope from somebody."

"You?"

"No, not me, man. I don't do that. They didn't have much money, so they left and raised some cash and come back again."

"How did they raise the cash?"

"Got a ride to Kohl's, bought a bunch of stuff with a credit card, then pawned it all. They come back a few hours ago, got what they wanted. Took off after that."

Kent went back to his car and got Emily's picture. Shining a flashlight on it, he said, "Is this the girl?"

The man studied it for a minute. "Naw, man, I don't think so."

That wasn't what he wanted to hear. "You sure?"

"Pretty sure. I seen that girl on the news. I'da recognized her. The girl I saw been here before. Dude with her too. Wasn't their first time."

Kent studied the man, not sure he was getting the truth. "After they got their drugs, how did they leave? Did they have a car?"

"I think they left with somebody, man. I didn't see 'em no more. But I'm tellin' you, that ain't her."

He questioned the others and got the same story. Finally, he left the cops to complete the bust and went back to Barbara's car.

"He says the girl who came here wasn't Emily."

Barbara slammed her hand on the steering wheel. "Give him a lie detector test or something."

"I don't have to. The girl and guy we're talking about went to Kohl's and used Trish's card. I'll get the time of the transaction and look at the security video. Hopefully, we'll get a clear picture tomorrow and know for sure."

The crushing disappointment on Barbara's face would haunt him tonight. He doubted she would sleep a wink with that un-answered text screaming out to her.

twenty-seven

When Kent's alarm clock went off at seven, he felt the lingering sleep deficit deep in his bones. He forced himself out of bed and stumbled to the coffeepot. The urgency of the missing girl kept him from wasting time, and he hurried to shower and shave.

At his office an hour later, he had a voice mail from Jack, the video tech who'd been working on the security footage. "Hey, Kent, give me a call. The state lab just got back to me. I have some info for you."

Kent called him right back. "Jack, what have you got?"

"Check your email," he said. "I just sent you the new, enhanced video. They identified what we saw next to the car. It was definitely the back door opening, and a hand with a tattoo."

"You're kidding."

"Nope."

"Could they identify the tattoo?"

"It's a rising phoenix."

"Perfect, thanks. I'll look at it right now."

He hung up and downloaded the picture. So this guy could be the one with Emily in the cab.

He checked his email and found the credit card report he'd

asked for last night. It showed the Kohl's purchase at eight o'clock the night of the murder. He checked his computer for the pawn shops open late. There was one in the area that was open until midnight. That had to be where they'd pawned the stuff they bought.

He grabbed a coffee on his way to Kohl's and found the manager, who took him to security. He studied each person on the screen who'd gone through the line in the few minutes around the time the transaction had been made.

There was a girl who looked a little like Emily, with a guy in a baseball cap. Kent paused the tape and squinted at it. Could this girl be Emily? He pulled out Emily's picture, compared it with the girl on the screen. The girl's hair was shoulder-length, instead of long like Emily's. And it was all one length. Emily's was layered. Of course, the picture he had of Emily was almost a year old, and drug use had a way of thinning hair. And she could have cut it. But Emily was small, and this girl looked taller, rougher . . . and older. But he couldn't be sure.

As for the guy . . . there it was. A tattoo on his right hand. The picture was too blurry to tell whether it was a phoenix, but the scale was certainly the same.

He emailed the video to himself so he could access it on his phone or computer and called Andy on his way back to the office.

"Okay, let's think this through," Andy said. "So this dude is the one who got out of Trish's car after the murder."

"Right," Kent said, "which means he could've been the one to kill Trish, instead of Emily."

"Or they were working together. So was robbery the motive?"

"Not the main one. It was too premeditated. The Tubarine, the chloroform."

"Maybe the robbery was an afterthought."

Kent thought back over the video of Emily jumping out of the car. She hadn't hung back to wait for the guy in the back seat. She'd launched out as if terrified. The guy had waited a few minutes before getting out. If he'd been with her, wouldn't he have run when she did?

"What if Emily really was an innocent bystander?" Kent asked. "What if this guy was waiting for Trish? She had her itinerary up on her Instagram account. But she didn't say that she had someone traveling with her. He could have expected Trish alone. Maybe Emily was a surprise."

"Wouldn't he have seen them walking up together?"

"Not if he was hiding in the back seat. And if he did see them coming, Emily was straggling behind Trish. Maybe he didn't realize they were together." Kent tried to imagine what the girl would have done if she wasn't involved. She'd stood outside the car to finish her cigarette. When she got in the car, what would she have seen?

"If Emily got into the car, saw her interventionist slumped over, and a killer in the back seat, of course she would have jumped back out and run for her life. Dude finishes the job, then slips out and disappears."

"But they wound up together."

"I'm not sure about that. The girl in the Kohl's video may not be Emily."

"So if she's an entirely different person, where was the Kohl's blonde while Tattoo-man was killing Trish?"

"Who knows?" Kent said. "Maybe waiting for him over in the taxi line."

Andy was quiet for a moment. "Or maybe she was the driver of the Infiniti. We never saw whether that was a man or a woman. Emily could still be part of a conspiracy."

"But then who got into the cab? No, that was a man and a woman. A woman who looked a little like Emily, but wasn't her."

"I don't know, man," Andy said. "There are still a lot of holes in this thing."

"You're right. I'm headed over to Barbara Covington's hotel to show her the Kohl's video. She'll know for sure if it's Emily. But this girl looks to be in her late twenties, not eighteen."

"Can you trust her mother to tell you the truth? You know, we haven't considered the possibility that drugs have really changed Emily's appearance. A year's a long time. A lot of damage can be done in a year."

"Still . . . a mother knows her daughter. I'll be able to tell if her reaction is authentic. And the kid brother will react. He'll tell me what I need to know."

He called Barbara from the hotel parking lot to see if she was awake. She answered on the first ring.

"Barbara, it's Kent. You got a minute? I'd like to come up and show you some video."

"All right. Come on up."

Within minutes he was in her room, pulling up the video from Kohl's, as she and Lance stood behind him, staring over his shoulders.

"Right here," he said. "This couple." He pointed to the man and woman in question and looked up at her.

Barbara's face fell. "That's not Emily."

Lance shook his head. "No way, man. She doesn't look anything like that. Emily's shorter."

"Are you sure this is the couple that had the credit card?" Barbara asked.

"Positive," he said. "We know which register it was, and what time, exactly. It was them."

Barbara groaned. "So does this mean we've been wasting our time? That we haven't even gotten close to Emily?"

"Don't lose hope," he said. "This is a great lead. We'll track these people down, find out what they know." He snapped the lid shut on his laptop and hurried back to the door. "We're making progress, Barbara. I'll be in touch."

twenty-eight

While Lance showered, Barbara lay down and stared at the ceiling. She needed more rest. For most of the night she'd lain awake, her mind racing with fear.

She held her cell phone in her hand, its charger attached to the wall. If Emily called or texted again, she'd know.

She replayed the Kohl's video in her mind. Could she be kidding herself? *Was* the girl in the video Emily?

Sometimes Emily straightened her hair, and she could have cut it. But the girl in the picture looked tired and older. Drugs dehydrated you, wrinkled your skin. She supposed if Emily's hair hadn't been washed since she'd left home, if Emily hadn't had on makeup, if the camera was just grainy enough, if she'd been wearing heels . . . it was possible that her daughter was the one in the video.

No. It was only now, with her brain tired and muddled, that she was second-guessing herself. Lance had looked at the video too, and agreed with her. It wasn't Emily.

But that still didn't make Barbara feel better. So the couple had wound up with Trish's credit card. That did nothing to help Emily.

How could Barbara even know for certain whether Emily

was capable of murder? Her daughter had changed so much that Barbara didn't even know who she was.

She mentally reviewed the legal offenses Emily had already committed: driving under the influence, possession of narcotics, identity theft . . . Would it be such a stretch for her to go from theft to murder? Was that demonic craving in her body so strong that she could kill to assuage it?

Barbara felt the same demons whispering in her ear, twisting her heart, her lungs, her stomach, like cold hands reaching into her, reminding her of impending death.

The only armor she had was Scripture, so she whispered the 23rd Psalm.

Yea, though I walk through the valley of the shadow of death, I will fear no evil . . .

Maybe if she said it enough times, it would be true. But she did fear evil. Evil had been boldly stalking and taunting her daughter for years, torturing her before Barbara's eyes. Now it was even worse.

Barbara closed her eyes and turned onto her stomach. Pushing her pillow away, she lay on her face, pleading with God to save her child. Maybe he was doing this in Emily's life to work out something that would change her. Maybe the terror of it would be enough to pull Emily back.

But what if she *had* committed this terrible crime? Guilt burned through Barbara's veins. Had Emily's drugs cost Trish her life?

No, that was stupid. Emily hadn't done anything to Trish. Trish was used to escorting addicts. It was something she was prepared for. She was a match for Emily, wasn't she?

But Barbara knew that even she, herself, was no match for her daughter. Emily was stronger, more determined, bolder, wilder. So far, she hadn't found anything that could stand between Emily and her drugs. Maybe Trish had been too much of an obstacle, and

Emily had to take matters into her own hands. After all, Barbara didn't know what had happened at the airport. If Emily had made another call on Trish's phone, the phone records would have shown it. The police would have followed up. But after she called home, she could have borrowed some stranger's cell phone and called a friend. Some guy could have met her there. It was all possible, wasn't it?

She didn't want to believe it.

Yea, though I walk through the valley of the shadow . . .

She prayed that she would stop fearing such evil . . . even from her own daughter.

When Lance came out of the bathroom, he gave her a long, troubled look. "That wasn't her, was it, Mom?"

Barbara closed her eyes. "I don't know anymore, honey. I really don't."

twenty-nine

The pawn shop closest to the Day-Nite Motel had bars on all the windows and an off-duty cop stationed in the parking lot. Kent didn't know him. He went inside and looked around. Flat screen TVs and laptops were stacked in shelves on the walls, and another wall was filled with iPhones and Samsung Galaxies still in their packaging, plus dozens of other electronics and gadgets. One long counter was filled with rings, with diamonds of every cut and carat.

The owner came out of the back room. "Can I help you?"

He looked like a wrestler, round and built, with more bulk than height. Kent showed him his badge and got his name—Harry Roe.

Roe confirmed that a couple had come in the night before to pawn some things. But when he saw Emily's picture, Roe shook his head. "I've seen this kid on the news. It wasn't her. The girl that came in is somebody I've seen a few other times. She's older."

Kent had printed out a blown-up picture of the couple at Kohl's, so he handed that to Roe. "Is this them?"

Roe took one look. "Yep, that's them."

"What are their names?"

"I don't remember."

Kent had expected that. Pawn shop owners generally did have

memory problems—at least with the police. "Who'd you write the check to?"

Roe hesitated. "I paid cash."

"Is that right?" Kent doubted that was true. Cash was dangerous, and it could get a guy killed. Most pawn shops kept little cash on hand. Instead, they often wrote checks that could be signed over to others or cashed at grocery stores if no banks were open.

He walked over to a television on a shelf, looked on the back. "Where's the serial number on this baby?"

The man stiffened. "Come on, man."

"You wouldn't be buying stolen goods in here, would you? I'm shocked. Maybe I need to get a crew in here to take a look around."

"All right, just a minute." Roe went to a back room and came back with his spiral checkbook. He opened it, flipped back a couple of pages. Sliding his finger along the register, he came to the entry in question. Turning the register around, he showed Kent. "Right here. Wrote it to a dude named Gerald Tredwell. And I'm not lying when I say I don't know the girl's name."

Kent made a note. Gerald Tredwell.

Back at the department, Kent checked the database, hoping the name wasn't an alias. Within minutes, a mug shot came up. Tredwell, who worked as a registered nurse at a local medical clinic, had some prior arrests—a couple of DUIs, a possession charge, and a felony distribution charge awaiting indictment. Currently, he was out on bond.

Kent had an address now, and he didn't think it was bogus. He called Andy, who was out following his own leads. "I've got the name of the guy who was in the Kohl's video. Pawn shop owner wrote him a check for a bunch of stuff last night. Name's Gerald Tredwell. Works as a nurse." He finished filling his partner in.

Andy returned the favor. "I just went through the list of credit card purchases, and called some of the online companies they ordered from. The items were ordered in Trish Massey's name, and shipped overnight to an address on Forest Avenue. Buyer left instructions for the delivery guys to leave the packages at the door. Whoever had the card must have picked them up there. My guess is they planned to pawn the stuff."

"Did you go to the address?"

"I'm here now. Vacant warehouse."

"Forest Avenue. That's only three blocks from where Tredwell lives."

"Want to meet me at his house?"

"How about an hour? First I want to go to the jail and see if any of the guards recognize the girl in the picture. The more we know when we show up at Tredwell's, the better off we'll be."

Taking the picture he'd printed from the Kohl's video, Kent drove back to the police department and crossed the street. He found some of the guards from the women's jail in the break room, feasting on birthday cake. He showed them the girl's picture. "You guys remember this girl ever coming through here?"

One of them took the picture, showed the others. They all agreed it was a repeat offender named Myra Marin. "She keeps this as her second address," she said. "Tries to vacation here for a few weeks every year, just to keep her life interesting."

He went through the database and found Myra's mug shot. Yep, same girl. She was out on bond, awaiting a court date that was a month away. The charge was possession of a controlled substance. He attached the mug shot and Kohl's video of the couple to an email, then sent it to the cab company and asked them to get the driver to identify her.

As he headed over to the warehouse, he got the call back from the driver. "Dat is de girl I drove dat night," he told him. "De man too."

So Kent had been wrong about Emily getting into the cab.

What else had he been wrong about? Maybe she wasn't a killer. She wasn't the one with Trish's credit card, and she wasn't the one who'd gotten in the cab and gone to buy drugs.

Could it be that she really was running for her life, after encountering Tredwell in Trish's car?

So who was Tredwell, and why had he chosen Trish? Was he one of her former residents? A drug dealer she'd messed with and failed to pay?

Whatever the reason, Kent felt certain he was closing in on Trish's killer . . . and it wasn't Emily Covington.

So where was Emily? The video suggested she'd gotten away from the killer in that Infiniti, but maybe he'd caught up to her. Or maybe she was so traumatized by what she'd seen, that she'd gotten her ride to drop her off somewhere to buy drugs. Maybe she was lying somewhere in an intoxicated stupor, oblivious to all the activity surrounding her.

Or Barbara was right, and she'd fallen into a kidnapper's clutches.

She could be dead already.

thirty

While Lance worked on getting the addresses for Emily's Atlanta social media friends, Barbara listened to the voice mails on Lance's phone. There were dozens from news sources all over the country. Several from friends back home, leaving their messages of encouragement and hope and their promises to pray.

As she listened, her own phone rang. Her heart jolted. Emily? She grabbed it off the bed table and looked at the caller ID. It was her assistant, Fran.

Her spirits flattened. Fran had left several other messages, and since she was holding down the fort at Barbara's design studio, Barbara supposed she needed to answer. She clicked the phone on. "Hi, Fran."

"Barbara! I can't believe I finally got you. I've called a million times!"

"I've been a little busy."

"Have they found Emily?"

"No, she's still lost."

There was a heavy sigh and a long pause. "Barbara, you need to come home. She's jerking your life around again. Can't you see that?"

Fran had never had a child on drugs. Her understanding of the trials of a family racked with addiction was limited to what she'd seen on talk shows. But she had lots of opinions about the subject.

"Fran, I'm not coming home without Emily."

"So if you find her, you're not even gonna put her into treatment?"

"I don't know. One thing at a time."

Fran cleared her throat. "Barbara, I really hate to be the skeptic here, but you've got to face the fact that Emily probably killed that woman."

Barbara wished she'd ignored the call.

"Emily's a criminal, and until she sits in prison for a few years, she's not gonna turn around."

The muscles in Barbara's face went rigid, locking around her mouth, her lips.

"Even then she may not," Fran went on, "but it won't be your fault, Barbara. You've done everything you can."

"I have to go," Barbara managed to say.

"No, wait!"

Barbara hesitated, swallowing hard.

"I didn't call about this. I really didn't. I'm sorry I got off on it. I'm just trying to help."

"I don't want to talk about it anymore."

"Okay, fine. The real reason I called is to tell you that the governor's office has moved the presentation up two days. Instead of Friday, it's going to be Wednesday."

"No!" Barbara yelled. "We're not ready!"

"I tried to tell them."

"Do they know about Emily?"

"Sweetie, everybody knows about Emily."

She sighed. "I can't meet that deadline. Unless I find Emily in the next hour and work around the clock until then, it can't happen."

"Tell me what I can do to help," Fran said. "I don't exactly have your eyes, but I'm creative. Is there a list somewhere of furniture I can photograph for the board? Do you have the swatches you're planning to use for the other rooms? And where is the board for the master bedroom?"

"It's at my house. You can go over there and get it. There's a key in my top desk drawer. But it's not finished. We're talking eighteen rooms. I can't do them all on the boards. I have to be there."

"All the more reason to come home. You deserve this, Barbara. This is your big break. If it doesn't work out, we're both out of a job. I don't think I have to remind you of that."

Barbara wondered why she did anyway. "I'm fully aware."

"I just want to be able to help you in the best way I can, but you've got to tell me what to do."

"I don't have time to think about it right now. I'm in a crisis."

"You'll be in a worse crisis when you don't have an income and you're out having to interview for jobs with furniture stores. Emily's not going to care. She'll just keep milking you for everything you're worth. And it won't be much."

Maybe that was true, but she resented Fran for saying so. "All right, let me make some phone calls. I'll let them know that we need a few more days."

"They said they were sorry for your problems with Emily, and they knew this was bringing more hardship on you, but it couldn't be helped."

"Well, that's just great. They know I'm the best person for that job. The governor's wife loved the work I did for her sister. She told me if she had her way, it would be me."

"Maybe you should call her."

"I will."

"Okay, so what should I be doing in the meantime?"

She tried to focus her thoughts. "I was going to name the bedrooms after some of the past governors in Missouri. I was going to get in touch with their families and find out what their design styles were, and see if they'd donate any of their memorabilia. It would be interesting, kind of like in the White House, with the Lincoln bedroom . . ."

"I could make those phone calls."

"Yes, good," Barbara said. "Then get back to me. And pull out every design board I've got in my studio. Email me pictures of them. I can use some of the models from those boards to save time. If I can, I'll look online for the furnishings that would work for each room. If I can get pictures online, maybe we can use them on the board. Maybe it'll be close enough."

Even as she said the words, she closed her eyes. It wasn't good enough. She wanted it to be knock-dead professional, something that went beyond what everyone else was doing. Presidents had different, distinctive styles, but governors? There wasn't time to collect antique pieces from their collections in time for the presentation.

Besides getting the boards together, she needed time to practice her presentation so that it would be polished and fluid. She couldn't just direct their eyes to pictures, colors, and swatches. She needed to sell them a concept . . . and build their confidence in her skills and her aesthetic.

How in the world could she focus on that, when her daughter was lost out there?

There was no power in her voice when she said, "I'll let you know what they say."

"All right, Barbara. I'll get right on it. Oh, and one other thing."

"Yeah?"

"My paycheck?"

Barbara touched her forehead. How could she have forgotten? It wasn't Fran's fault any of this had happened. The single mom needed to feed her kids. "I'm sorry, Fran. I totally forgot."

"It's okay. Can you send it to me through PayPal?"

"Yes, I'll do it today. I promise."

"No biggie." Fran paused again. "I'm praying for you, Barbara. Praying for Emily to do the right thing and turn herself in. And for you to let her sink or swim. Practice tough love. That's what the experts say."

Barbara wondered how many of the talk show "experts" had children they were willing to watch run off a cliff. "There's a killer involved, and a dead woman. Emily was seen running for her life."

"Of course she was. She didn't want to get caught," Fran said.

Anger fired through Barbara again. "Sorry, I have to go now." She clicked off the phone, wishing people would offer her kindness instead of advice. Their wisdom and judgment were like razors slicing through open wounds. They had no clue what they would do in her shoes.

They'd probably do as many wrong things as she had.

She tossed the phone onto the bed and dug into her purse for her checkbook. She'd have to go looking for that bank.

thirty-one

The neighborhood where Tredwell lived was run-down, in a part of town that got a lot of police calls. Kent had been to this area at least twice to investigate domestic homicides. Tredwell had a yard full of trash, and his grass was a foot tall. As they approached the house, Kent scanned the unkempt bushes, the dirty windows, the houses on either side and across the street.

"Looks quiet," Andy said.

"Maybe they're sleeping." It was always good to catch someone asleep. They'd be groggy and their guard would be down, and they wouldn't have their act together enough to plot an escape. On the other hand, if the man and woman were still riding the high of the large amount of drugs they'd bought with all their pawned goods, this could prove difficult.

A cruiser came up behind them as they pulled to the curb, and two other backup officers came from the other direction. As they got out of the cars, they fanned out and surrounded the house to keep anyone from escaping.

As Kent and Andy got to the door, Kent's heart pounded. They just might find Emily right now, held here against her will. Not wanting to alarm Tredwell, he knocked gently.

They heard footsteps across a creaky floor, then the door cracked open. The house was dark, and they could barely make out a woman's eye and nose peeking suspiciously out. "Yeah?"

"Are you Myra?"

"What do you want?"

"I'm Detective Harlan from the Atlanta Police Department, and this is my partner Detective Joiner."

She flinched. "I didn't do nothing wrong."

"We're looking for Gerald Tredwell."

She looked back into the house, then stepped outside and closed the door behind her. She was wearing the same outfit she'd had on yesterday at Kohl's. A raggedy T-shirt and jeans. "He ain't here."

"Where is he?"

"I don't know. He went out for a while."

"Can we come in and talk to you for a minute?" Kent asked.

"No, we can talk right here." She looked like she was crashing from a meth high. If she did what most addicts did and loaded up with Xanax to cushion her fall, then her brain was sluggish. Dark circles were etched under her bloodshot eyes, and she looked even rougher than she'd looked in the videos. Her pupils were dilated and her lids were heavy. But it was definitely the same girl.

"We're investigating a homicide and wondered if you could tell us your whereabouts on Tuesday evening."

She stiffened out of her slump. "I was at work."

"Is there anyone who saw you there that night?" Andy asked. "Someone we could talk to?"

She crossed her arms. "No, I was by myself."

"Where do you work?"

"At the Quick Dry Laundromat. I do people's laundry."

"So those people could tell us if you were there Tuesday night?"

She stared at them for a long moment, as if she didn't understand the question. "Actually, no. I mean, there were people, but I don't know their names."

Success pulsed through Kent's veins. They were getting somewhere. Her alibi was collapsing. "Doesn't sound good. A woman was murdered, we know you were in the area, and you don't have an alibi that we can confirm?"

"And the funny thing is," Andy added, "you were in possession of the dead woman's credit card after the murder."

"I don't know what you're talking about."

"You're out on bond, aren't you? Who's your bondsman? We might need to revoke your bond."

She stood at attention now. "No! I can't go back to jail."

Now they had her scared enough to talk. "Myra, we need to talk to Gerald Tredwell. Tell us where he is."

She blinked and lowered her voice. "I don't know. I ain't seen him."

"In how long?"

"Days. Weeks. I don't know. We broke up."

She was making it up as she went along. "No, Myra," Kent said. "We know that's not true. You still see each other. You're right here, in his house. You ride in cabs together, shop together, do drugs together."

She frowned. "Look . . . whatever he did, I didn't know. He had that credit card. I had nothing to do with that."

"Where did he get it?"

"At the airport. He was meeting somebody. He didn't tell me who. He left me in baggage claim. Came back with her credit card. I swear, I didn't have nothing to do with it."

"We understand that," Kent said. "That's why you're not under arrest, as long as you cooperate with us. Come on, Myra, we know he's in the house. Is he sleeping?"

She drew in a deep breath. "Yes."

"Why don't you let us in?"

She let out a long, despairing sigh and opened the door. They followed her into the putrid house. It smelled like the toilets had backed up. Filthy clothes lay on the floor in piles, and he saw cat feces and spilled cat litter in a corner. Dishes with dried, caked food lay molding on tables around the room.

And in the middle of it all, Tredwell lay sound asleep on the couch. The rising phoenix tattoo on his hand was clearly displayed.

"Wake up, Tredwell," Kent said, shoving him awake.

The man woke up, groggy, and squinted up at him. "What the—" He shot a look to Myra. "What did you do?"

"They're threatening to pull my bond," she muttered.

"Get up," Kent said. "We're taking you in for questioning in the murder of Patricia Massey."

Tredwell sat up, wobbly. "The what? I didn't murder anybody. I don't even know who that is."

"We'll talk about it at the station."

"Can I at least get dressed?"

He was already wearing jeans and a T-shirt, the same ones he'd been wearing in the video. "You're dressed fine. It's come as you are."

They escorted the dazed, sleepy man out to their car and put Myra in another car. It wouldn't pay to give them a chance to compare notes as they rode to the station.

Tredwell was silent as they drove him in.

thirty-two

"We're kind of under the gun here." Kelsey Anderson, Barbara's contact at the governor's mansion, didn't offer much hope for an extension. "We're trying to get this thing done in record time so the mansion will be ready for the governor's daughter's wedding in six months."

"Six months?"

"I know it's a lot to ask, but you can see now why we have to get the designer chosen as quickly as possible."

"Then just choose me and get it over with. You've seen my work."

Kelsey chuckled. "If only we could, Barbara. We know the problems you're having, so it was especially hard to have to notify you that we had to move the date up. We realize it may knock you out of the running."

She wanted to beg, to point out how hard she'd already worked on this, that the future of her business rode on this deal. But that would be unprofessional. "Who do I need to talk to get more time?"

Kelsey hesitated. "I guess you could talk to Mrs. Pearson."

The governor's wife. "All right. Will you transfer me to her?"

"Barbara, she has four speaking engagements today."

"Please, just ask her to call me." She swallowed the lump blocking her throat. Mrs. Pearson was a mother too. Surely she would understand.

Kelsey sighed. "All right, I'll give her your number. She'll probably call because she's been very concerned about you. But I don't know when it'll be."

"That's all I can ask," Barbara said.

"We're praying for you."

Barbara hung up as resentment coursed through her. She was grateful for their prayers; she needed all of them. But saying they were praying for her, then deliberately making her life harder . . . the irony amazed her.

She hung up and saw Lance looking at her, waiting for the verdict. "So you're gonna talk to the governor's wife? Isn't she, like, famous?"

"She's famous in our state."

"But you're famous too. You've been on national news."

She didn't want to be famous for having a notorious daughter. The phone rang, and the caller ID said State of Missouri. The governor's wife, already? She picked it up. "Hello?"

"Barbara, this is Olivia Pearson. As soon as Kelsey told me you'd called, I had to call back. We've been watching the news, and my heart just breaks for you. Is there anything we can do?"

"Thank you, Mrs. Pearson. Yes, actually. You could give me a few more days to get my presentation together. I have a great construction crew, and with the right budget I can hire a lot more. We can get it done by your daughter's wedding."

"But what if this drags on with your daughter? What if you can't come home and work on it? It's really risky right now."

She drew in a deep breath. "If I go under, I'll have a missing daughter and no job."

The moment she got the words out, she hated herself for it.

She didn't want Mrs. Pearson to give her the job because she was in financial trouble. How could she convince her that she was the best one for it?

She shook her head, trying to change gears. "You'll love my plans. I'm putting an elegant bathroom in each of the bedrooms, and giving each one some modern touches that fit with the architecture and style of the home. We're naming each of the bedrooms after a former governor who's made an important mark on our state. And wait until you see what I've done with the ballroom. The fabrics are unbelievable, and the layout will be much more versatile than you have now."

She wasn't sure if it was wise to tip her hand that way just yet, but the first lady seemed intrigued. "I can't wait to see them."

"I'm in the process of trying to acquire antiques and memorabilia from the family of each of the former governors we'll feature. I promise you'll love what you see. It's very classy and grand, yet it all has a modern touch that will make it much more comfortable than it is now. Mrs. Pearson, we can make the mansion gorgeous for the wedding, and build in accommodations for future events like that."

There was a long silence. "All right, Barbara. We'll go back to the original deadline. I do want you to have a shot. But no more time than that. My husband was very emphatic that we have to get this underway immediately."

Well, it was something. "Thank you. I really appreciate it."

"And Barbara, please let us know what we can do for you from our end. We can use whatever resources we have to help with your search."

"I'll remember that, Mrs. Pearson. Just for the record, my daughter isn't a killer."

"We didn't think she was, Barbara."

She knew that wasn't true, but she was glad she'd said it anyway. "Thank you for the extra time. I won't let you down."

When Barbara hung up, she almost wilted.

"She liked the idea?" Lance asked.

"I think so." But the thought only made her sadder. "Isn't it just like my life?"

"What?"

"To have an opportunity like this, knowing that I probably can't pull it off because of some crisis I can't control."

"Maybe it's God's way of keeping you humble."

She couldn't believe her son had said that.

He laughed as she stared at him. "Hey, you said that to me when I didn't make the baseball team."

"Did I? Would I really say something that stupid?"

"Oh, yeah. You would, and you did."

"Then please accept my apology, and don't ever say it to me again."

She sat down on the bed and looked out the window. There were dark clouds coming in from the west, and weather forecasters predicted a plunge in temperatures as autumn took hold. Were storms coming? Would Emily be dry . . . sheltered?

She looked back at her son, trapped with her in this dilemma. He should be in school, thinking about girls and friends and football games.

Not here, unveiling nightmares.

thirty-three

Tredwell clammed up when they got him to the police station, refusing to talk until he got a public defender. Kent called the judge and asked him to appoint one as soon as possible so they could interview their main suspect. The judge agreed to issue arrest and search warrants, so they could search Tredwell's home.

As he hung up, Andy came over with some papers in his hand. "For you," he said. "From AT&T."

Kent stood up and took the paper, read over it. "This is on the phone Emily's text came from. Says that call pinged on a cell tower in Dalton." Dalton was two hours north of Atlanta, up in the foothills of the Appalachians. "Emily was in Dalton when she sent the text."

"We need to find out what connection Tredwell has to Dalton," Andy said. "Parents, grandparents, siblings, old girlfriends . . . Any property he or his family might own up there."

"Can't talk to him until his attorney gets here. But we can go by the judge's office and pick up the warrant, then go search his house."

They headed out with crime scene investigators. It didn't take long to confirm that there was no sign of Emily in Tredwell's house. They spent the next three hours searching the place and found a bag of syringes and other paraphernalia, plus dozens of sample packs of anxiety medications.

Finally, Kent got word that Tredwell's attorney had shown up. While the CSIs kept working, he and Andy hurried back to the jail, pulled Tredwell out of the holding cell, and took him into the interview room. Kent gave him a few minutes to speak to the public defender. The judge had appointed a guy named Bud Allen, who had shoulder-length white hair and a handlebar mustache. As freewheeling as Allen appeared to be, he was a good lawyer who made things tough for the police.

Hoping Tredwell was feeling chatty now, they went in. Tredwell still seemed groggy; his hands were trembling, and misery dragged at his features.

"You gotta let me outta here. I have to go back to work Monday, and I'm already on thin ice. I have a good job, and I need to keep it."

"Where do you work?"

"At Southside Medical Clinic. I'm a registered nurse."

"No offense," Kent said, "but you don't strike me as someone who could get through nursing school, with all your drug charges."

"Okay, I admit I have a problem." The man slumped over. "But I didn't have it until I got out of school and started working."

"So how have you managed to hold that kind of job with all these problems?"

"I do good work, okay? I'm a model employee. You can call my boss and ask him."

"And that would be . . . ?"

"Dr. Greg Leigh. He's a general surgeon. Best one around. Gave me a chance when nobody else would."

Kent made a note of the name. "Did the murder of Trish Massey have something to do with drugs?"

Bud bristled. "Come on, Kent. Don't you want to rephrase that question?"

Kent looked up. "Did you kill Trish Massey?"

"Man, I didn't even know her. Never met her in my life."

Kent had already checked to see if Tredwell had ever been a resident at Road Back Recovery Center. He hadn't, and he had found no connection between any residents and Tredwell.

Tredwell was sweating now. "Okay, look, I stole her credit card. I'll admit to that. But I didn't kill her."

Kent sat back, hands behind his head. He glanced at Andy, who was taking it all down. "How did you get the card?"

Tredwell looked from Andy, to Kent, to his attorney. "I stole it at baggage claim. My girlfriend and I, we rode the MARTA train to the airport, since we don't have a car. Our plan was to hang around at baggage claim, because we could go in there without worrying about going through security. While people were waiting for their bags, we could look for an open purse and steal a wallet or two."

Kent let his hands down and sat up straighter. "So you're telling me you never got in her car?"

"No, I stole it right out of her wallet, right there at baggage claim."

"All right, tell me about Emily Covington."

"Who?"

"The girl who was traveling with Trish Massey. The girl you saw when she got into the car."

"I never saw her."

"He's wasting our time," Andy said, pushing back his chair and standing up.

"No, please. All I did was steal her credit card. Myra got some lady across the room at another conveyor belt. Then we met up and took a cab away from there. No big deal. Just a robbery, not a murder."

Kent wasn't buying it. He nodded at the tattoo on Tredwell's hand. "Interesting tattoo. What is that?"

Tredwell rubbed it, as though he could erase it. "It's a phoenix."

"Oh, yeah. I see that now. Funny thing. Dude we saw getting out of her car? Same tattoo."

Tredwell squinted at him. "You couldn't have seen that."

"Why? Because you thought you were blocked from the camera?"

He scratched his face. "No, because I wasn't there."

Kent tapped his pencil on the table in a staccato beat, and thought of that cell phone Emily had texted from. It had pinged in Dalton, Georgia. "Where are you from, Gerald?"

"From here, born and raised."

"Got any family anywhere else?"

"Some in Savannah. Some in Selma."

"Any in the Dalton area?"

He met his eyes. "No, I don't know anybody there."

"Ever been there?"

"I don't think so. I don't have a car, so I don't get out of this area much."

"I think that's enough," Bud said, checking his watch. "I'm advising my client not to say anything else until I've had more time to talk to him. Is he under arrest?"

"Yes, he is. We got our warrant a few hours ago."

"And the charge?"

"First-degree murder, for starters."

"What?" Tredwell said. "No way, man!"

"What have you got on him?" Bud asked.

Kent went over the facts of the arrest warrant, then left Bud with his client. He found the guard waiting outside the room. "Put him back in the cell when he's finished with Mr. Allen. And call me if he wants to change his statement."

Frustrated that they hadn't gotten more information, Kent bolted back upstairs, Andy behind him. "Andy, check to see if another robbery was reported at baggage claim that night at the airport."

"Sure thing."

Kent went back up to his desk and called one of the CSIs to see if they'd found anything else in Tredwell's house. They were still sifting through his junk, but hadn't made any important discoveries since the sample drugs. They said they'd be coming back soon to go over everything with him.

Kent's stomach growled, and he checked his watch. It was seven o'clock, and he hadn't had time to eat. He dug into his pocket for some coins, and walked down the hall to the vending machine. When he came back, Andy was hanging up the phone. "Did you get anything?"

Andy reached into Kent's potato chip bag and took one. "Sure enough, there was a stolen wallet reported at right around the time the murder occurred, just like Tredwell said. Some lady named Mrs. Alvarez, who was on Trish and Emily's flight, realized her wallet was gone when she tried to pay her way out of the parking garage. So that part of Tredwell's statement was true. We can't pinpoint the time since she's not absolutely certain where her wallet was stolen."

"Doesn't prove anything except that Myra was making use of her time while she waited for him. But the tattoo speaks volumes. That was him in the car."

"Definitely the same guy. I think we ought to go pay a visit to the doctor he works for and see what we can find out. Maybe Dr. Greg Leigh can help us establish a connection to Trish Massey, and tell us if Tredwell had access to Tubarine."

"Meanwhile, Emily's still out there." Kent opened his computer again, fast-forwarded to the footage he had of Emily getting into the black Infiniti. He watched it drive away again, wishing the state lab could have gotten the tag number. "If we could just identify who was in that car. What's the point of having these cameras if you can't even read a tag number?"

Andy took another chip, stuck the whole thing in his mouth. Crunching, he said, "You can read all the others on cars around them. That tag's got mud all over it."

"Yeah, but there's no mud on the rest of the car."

Andy squinted. "Maybe it was by design. The driver didn't want his tag read."

Kent studied it, then glanced up at Andy. "I'll give the doctor a call, see if he can shed any light. Maybe he can help us get to the bottom of this."

thirty-four

When Kent called, Dr. Leigh wasn't in. The receptionist told him Leigh had been out all week. When she asked if she could help him, Kent said, "I'm calling about one of your nurses, Gerald Tredwell."

"Sure. What about him?" She sounded young—early twenties, maybe.

"Can you verify that he works there?"

"Yes, though I don't know why they haven't fired him yet. If I pulled some of the stuff he's pulled, I'd be standing in the unemployment line."

He chuckled. "Oh yeah? What kind of stuff?"

She hesitated. "I shouldn't say. Are you someone thinking about hiring him? If he has a shot at another job, I don't want to mess that up."

"Anxious to get rid of him, are you?"

She laughed as if she'd been caught. "I didn't say that."

"Well, I really just need to talk to Dr. Leigh," Kent said. "Could you give me his cell phone number or a home number where I can reach him?"

There was a pause. He wondered if she would clam up now.

But he got lucky. He could hear her shuffling papers, then she came back to the phone. "It's 555–6243."

He jotted it down. "Is that cell or home?"

"His home number. In case you don't get him, I'll tell him you called."

"When do you expect him back in?"

"I'm not sure. Probably Monday."

Kent called the number but only reached voice mail. The voice sounded clear and deep. "Hi, you've reached Dr. Greg Leigh. I'm not in right now, but leave a message."

He waited for the beep. "Dr. Leigh, this is Detective Harlan with the Atlanta Police Department. I'm calling about someone we have in custody. One of your nurses—Gerald Tredwell. I'd like to ask you a few questions about him. Give me a call back, please." He left his cell phone number.

As he hung up, one of the CSIs came in and got a cup of coffee. "Ready to come look at all the evidence we logged?"

"Was there a lot of it?"

"Yeah. We grabbed several bags of trash while we were there, so some garbage detail is in order."

Kent glanced back at Andy and smiled.

Andy sneered. "Sometimes I hate this job."

"Oh, you'll grow to love it." They followed the investigator to the evidence room, and Kent saw the bags of festering trash laid on a table. "Mmmm. Smells good."

Andy groaned. "Vintage waste. My favorite thing."

Kent pulled on his gloves. A host of things turned up in people's garbage, from credit card statements to pill bottles and doodles on notepads. If they could find any link to Emily at all, or to Trish Massey, they might be able to make this case stick . . . and find Emily.

Kent watched his partner dump the contents. As always, the

ooze of banana peels and discarded food stank up the place, but he got to work, looking for anything that would help their case.

An hour passed, and they hadn't found anything helpful, other than more evidence that he and Myra had been hard-core drug users. They found no connection to Emily at all.

When his cell phone rang, Kent stepped back from the garbage and pulled off his rubber gloves. He got his phone out of his pocket. The number was unfamiliar, but he answered it. "Detective Harlan."

"Yes, Dr. Greg Leigh here. I just got your message. I was surprised to hear that Gerald Tredwell is in custody. What did he do?"

"I can't go into all that just yet, but right now I'd like to verify that he's your employee and see what you can tell me about him."

"Yes, he's worked for me for four or five months."

"Good employee?"

"At times."

"And other times?"

"Other times, he comes in late or calls in sick. He can be unreliable."

He saw Andy wince as he peeled some receipts from a slimy brown banana peel. "Are you aware he has a drug problem?" Kent asked.

"I've suspected. I've been meaning to spring a drug test on him, but wanted to give him a chance to clean up his act."

"Really? Seems pretty risky having an addict working in a medical office."

"He'd had a lot of problems, gotten fired from other jobs. I don't use him in surgery, just in the office. This is probably his last chance to stay in this field. I have a soft spot for addicts." His pitch dropped. "I hoped he'd pull himself together. When I hired him he'd been sober for over a year."

"Has he ever been to treatment?"

"Not as far as I know. Is that what he was arrested for? A drug charge?"

"Among other things." Kent paused. "Would you happen to know if he had any connection to Road Back Recovery Center in Emerson?"

Leigh hesitated. "The place where that woman worked? The one killed at the airport?"

"Yes. Did he ever mention her or that rehab?"

"No. Do you think he was involved with that?"

"He may be."

"Wow. That's disturbing."

"We found a bunch of packs of sample medications in his home. Could he have gotten them from your office?"

"I don't know. We get tons of samples from pharmaceutical reps. But the samples are logged. I can get someone to do an inventory and get back to you."

"If you find he took them from your office, I'll need you to sign an affidavit. Also, could you tell me if he had access to a drug called Tubarine?"

There was a long pause. "Tubarine? I use that in surgery sometimes. I do keep some of it in the office."

"Check and see if he took any. We'll need an affidavit about that too."

"Will do."

When Kent hung up, he turned back to the trash heap.

Andy grabbed a syringe and put it on the edge of the table to log. "Anything?" he asked.

Kent looked down at the caller ID. "I don't know. Something's not adding up. Why would a doctor hire a guy like Tredwell and keep him around, even though he suspects he's using? He's checking to see if the pills or Tubarine were stolen from his office."

Kent added the number to his address book, and it prompted

him for the name. He typed in "Dr. Greg Leigh." There was something familiar about the phone number. He'd seen it before. "Hey, does this number mean anything to you?" he asked Andy.

Andy glanced at the readout on the phone. "I don't think so."

Kent shrugged it off and went back to sorting through the waste.

The garbage search did give them some information about the two people they had in custody, but nothing regarding Emily. Kent washed up and went back to his desk. That phone number kept playing through his mind, so he opened his notes and searched for it.

Finally, he found it, written in the top margin of a page devoted to all the paths they'd followed after Emily's text. He had seen that phone number before . . .

It was the phone Emily had used to text her mother.

thirty-five

The walls were concrete, cold and damp, and Emily had a cough that ripped at her lungs almost every time she exhaled. The withdrawals were catching up with her—the mucus in her lungs thickening, diarrhea and nausea taking hold. Though she was cold from the damp, dark basement, she sweated as if it were a hundred degrees.

He could have at least left her a mattress to lie on.

There was a bath mat on the floor in front of the toilet, so she curled up on it in a fetal position, hugging herself.

She thought of praying, but what good would it do? You didn't live your life like Lucifer until you drove your car into a ditch, then expect a holy God to pull you out. In fact, this was all probably God's doing. Like Jonah in the belly of the whale, God had zapped her into the hands of a killer.

She got to her knees and threw up again, then backed against the wall and set her elbows on her knees. Her hair was filthy. She couldn't remember the last time she'd washed it. Even before her mother's sneaky intervention, she'd let it go for days. Now that she hadn't had a cigarette in days, she could smell the scent of her dirty clothes and her dirty skin.

She supposed this dirty basement was just where she belonged.

She wiped the sweat out of her eyes and hugged herself against the shivering. As aware as she was of the consequences she was paying for her drug use, if someone came in right now and offered her a hit, she would throw herself at it. She would do almost anything to get it.

Just one hit.

Her mother was probably sitting in her pristine office, shaking her head and asking some pious friend for prayer for her wayward daughter who'd run away. She was probably using all those Al-Anon techniques and forcing herself to detach.

Lance was surely going through her journals and the posts of her deepest thoughts on Instagram.

They may never know that she wasn't here by her own choice. That, for once, things had spewed out of her control, and she'd been swept into something so big she couldn't sort it out to make sense of it.

If only they knew how it had all started. But the truth was, it was all such a blur that she wasn't sure herself. She remembered the day of the intervention clearly, and in the last forty-eight hours, had wished a million times that she had done things differently. If she could only go back and start over . . .

Emily had already felt a rising sense of panic when she got off the plane with Trish in Atlanta. Her life was about to change, and nothing familiar was going with her. She hated treatment centers, where people were irritable and angry, and the counselors and directors treated you like you couldn't be trusted, and didn't believe you no matter how sick you told them you were.

Yes, there were ways to work around the system. There were always doctors you could manipulate, who were more concerned with covering their tails than with getting someone sober. But would that work at this place? So far, Trish seemed cool. She was probably aware that Emily had used on the plane, but since they hadn't been sitting together, she'd gotten away with it. Then she'd let her use her cell phone as they walked through the airport.

Her mother had sounded relieved on the phone. She was probably throwing a party. *Ding dong, the junkie's gone . . .*

Emily's panic rose as they headed to baggage claim, but she tried not to show it. It didn't pay to be vulnerable when you went into rehab. Instead, you went in looking tough, trying to one-up the others. Her first time in rehab, she'd been strictly a marijuana user. She'd learned quickly not to tell the hard-core users that. They would think she was a lightweight. By the time she'd been there a week, she'd convinced them all she was a cocaine addict. When she came out, she became one, just to make her story true. The doctor gave her Xanax to help with her fake withdrawals, so she added that to her arsenal of favorites.

If her mother only knew.

As she followed Trish through the airport, Emily's mind raced with schemes. Even though she knew her way around rehabs, she couldn't stand the thought of going through it again. Her friend Paige was having a party tonight, and Caleb was getting a disability check that he was going to spend on everybody there. They were all going to score big. When would she get a chance like that again?

Emily waited at baggage claim, craving a cigarette, as Trish got her bag. Emily had to be reminded to get hers, but she dragged it off the conveyor belt, stacked her carry-on on it, then let Trish pull it behind her.

They both stopped and lit cigarettes as they left the airport. As they walked through the parking garage, Emily looked from side to side for an escape. If only she could have gotten the phone long enough to call one of her friends. There might be someone here who would come get her, someone she'd connected with online. But since she didn't usually notice their home cities, she didn't know who it might be.

She wanted to cry, but she didn't dare. She had to work up her toughness. She followed Trish through the garage as the woman chattered about how they would stop at the store and buy her a twelve-pack of soda before they headed north.

Like soda would calm her nerves and make this ninety-day detour in her life all right.

It was only an hour to the center, Trish said. They'd be there before she knew it.

Emily had little to say to Trish on the way to her car. A Lexus. Business must be good. The interventionist clicked open the trunk, and Emily didn't even help her put her suitcase in. Trish deserved to do the heavy lifting, after all. She was getting paid for it.

Trish closed the trunk and walked to the driver's side. "Come on, time to go. Put your cigarette out."

"Can't I smoke in the car?"

"No, it's brand new. I'm trying to protect it. It won't be a long ride."

"Then can I at least finish it?"

"All right. But hurry."

Trish got into the car, and Emily turned around and looked across the garage. There really wasn't a way out of this. She would have to go, bide her time, just to please her mother.

She took her last drag of the cigarette. Tears filled her eyes, and she swabbed at the corners of them with her knuckles. But they were coming too hard; there was no hiding. She wiped them and turned back to the car, dropped her cigarette on the ground and stomped it out. Then she opened the passenger door and slipped inside.

At first, she didn't realize that Trish was slumped over the steering wheel. Then a hand touched Emily's shoulder, and she swung around.

A man sat in the back seat, holding a syringe. Trish's state clicked in her mind then, like the chamber of a gun. She was unconscious . . . and this man . . .

Emily pushed out a scream and stumbled out of the car. He muttered curses behind her.

She sliced between parked cars, running for help, her screams echoing over the garage. She saw a car coming and ran out in front of it, making the driver slam on the brakes.

"Please, help!" she cried. "Call the police!"

But the driver only laid on her horn, blaring the shrill chord like a train. Emily moved to the side as the driver sped past her.

Emily turned and ran back the way they had come, toward the street between the garage and airport. Surely there were security guards, police . . . anyone . . . She saw cabs lined up, cars moving by.

Then suddenly, a black car pulled up beside her. "Do you need help, honey?"

She spun toward it, saw a man talking to her through his passenger window. "Yes," she cried. "My friend, she's back there in the car, and this man . . ."

"Get in." He leaned across the seat and threw open his door.

Grateful, she jumped inside and slammed the door. "Please, you've got to help me! I need to call the police. Do you have a phone?"

He pulled his phone out of his pocket. "I'll call," he said. "You're too upset." He punched 911, waited as he drove to the garage exit.

As he headed down the spiral ramp, she turned in her seat and looked through the back window.

"Yes," he said into the phone. "I'm just leaving the airport, and there was a girl screaming, and she says there was a guy in her car . . ."

Emily listened as he relayed what she'd told him. "Tell them it's a gold Lexus," she added. "It's in the second row of cars, whatever floor we were on. Tell them there's a man who injected her with something. Tell them to hurry."

His voice sounded way too calm as he spoke into the phone. Maybe he didn't understand Trish was hurt.

As he spoke, he drove out of the parking garage and got into the line at the payment booth. Finally, he hung up. "They're sending an ambulance and police to the scene."

She breathed relief. Maybe they'd get to Trish in time and catch the man.

"They told me to bring you to the police station to make a statement. Tell me what you saw."

She couldn't catch her breath. "This guy had a syringe. He must have injected her with something because she was passed out . . ."

He paid the woman in the booth, and the exit rail came up. "Was she breathing?" he asked as they drove out.

She looked back, wishing she'd told the woman. The police weren't here yet. Maybe she could have alerted security.

"I didn't stay around long enough to tell. How far to the police station?"

"Not far. Just calm down, honey. It's going to be okay. My name's Dr. Leigh. What's yours?"

"Emily." The word *doctor* snatched her thoughts away from the crisis. Cravings reared up in her like a flock of bats. "Do you have, like, medication?"

He frowned. "Some, why?"

"Because . . ." She touched her chest, gasping. "I have an anxiety disorder," she lied, "and I left my bag in her car. It had my Xanax. I'm having a panic attack."

"Don't you want to wait to take something until after you talk to the police?"

She made a show of hyperventilating. "No, I don't think I can talk to them until I have that. I feel like I'm having a heart attack."

He pulled over to the side of the road, touched her neck and took her pulse. "Your heart rate is fast, but you've been running. I can give you something to calm you down."

He reached into the back seat and she waited, almost forgetting the events at the garage. She couldn't see where he was reaching, but she hoped he was digging through his doctor bag, looking for Xanax.

A scent filled the air . . . the scent she remembered in Trish's car.

His hand came up with a rag, and before she could react, he pressed it to her mouth and nose, shoving her head back against the seat. She leaned back, fighting him. He was smothering her . . . killing her . . .

Her brain felt like it was melting out of her skull, running out her ears, her nostrils, her eyes . . .

And as she plunged into darkness, his face faded into the shadows of her consciousness.

When Emily woke, she was no longer in the car. She found herself in a room she'd never seen before.

Her vision was foggy as her eyes came open. The walls were painted apple green, with a big orange stripe slashing diagonally across the wall. A big teddy bear on a chest of drawers. A pair of ballet shoes hanging off the lamp. She was under a goose-down comforter, and the light of a lamp shone down on her.

As her eyes began to clear, she realized someone was sitting beside her. Mom? Her head gonged as she turned her face . . .

Not Mom. It was the man. Her rescuer, the doctor who was supposed to take her to the police station. But he hadn't taken her. He'd smothered her, instead.

"Where am I?"

"You're at my cabin," he said in a smooth, low voice. "How are you feeling?"

She tried to sit up, but her head exploded. "Terrible headache."

"You passed out."

"You . . . tried to kill me."

He laughed softly. "No. I gave you something to help you relax. You asked me for it, remember? I brought you here because the woman you were with is dead. I heard on the radio that they think you killed her."

Dead? Trish was dead? "I need to call the police and tell them what happened. I didn't do anything." She tried to slide out of bed, but her head was too heavy. "Please . . . get me a phone."

His voice was unnaturally calm. "I can't do that, Emily. You're an addict, and you need help to get sober. The drugs are going to kill you."

"No, you're going to kill me. Whatever you gave me made me like this. I have a high tolerance for drugs, so you had to give me some pretty powerful stuff to knock me out."

"If I'd taken you to the hospital, they would have locked you in the psych ward and put you on detox. They don't know how to do it properly. I do."

Was he crazy? She glanced from wall to wall. "Whose room is this?"

For a moment he was silent, then he looked around, his cold eyes softening. "It's my daughter Sara's. She died of a drug overdose, and I don't want it to happen to any other person, ever. I don't want it to happen to you."

"It won't! I was on my way to treatment. I want to call my mom." She tried to sit up, but he pushed her back down. "My mom is going to worry. She needs to know where I am."

His eyes grew glacial again. "You don't care about your mom.

How many times have you stayed out all night, never letting her know where you are? Not even a phone call?"

She twisted her mouth. "You don't know me."

"I know addicts. I knew my daughter."

"I'm not her!" She managed to sit up, and tried to gauge the distance to the door. Would he let her leave? "Listen, my mom's going to freak."

"I'm sure the police have called her by now. They've told her you're a killer."

"No!" She shook her head, trying to shake out the cobwebs. Would her mother believe them? Of course she would, after all the stuff she'd done.

"Are you hungry?"

She couldn't think of food. "No, I don't want to eat. I want to go home." She started to cry. He reached for her, and she recoiled . . . then he stroked her face, of all things. "What do you want from me?"

"Nothing but your sobriety. I'm not going to hurt you. You can trust me. I'm not that kind of man."

"But you're the kind who kidnaps a girl and holds her hostage?"

"I'm not holding you hostage. I'm helping you."

"You're not helping me! Trish was helping me."

"They weren't going to help you where she was taking you. The people at Road Back Recovery Center don't care anything about you. They just medicate you and let you run around town. You'd be right back where you started, maybe worse."

"Are you crazy? I was going willingly. I need help. I'm going to go through withdrawal, and I don't want to do it here."

"I'm a doctor. I'll monitor you closely."

"So, you're keeping me locked in here against my will, without telling my mother or anybody?"

"It's a risk. A sacrifice I'm willing to make to save a life."

"This is kidnapping. You could go to prison for this."

"You'll thank me one day." He got up and backed to the door. "I'm going to leave you in here to rest. You can't get out. The windows are barred. I've taken out everything you can hurt yourself with. There is a bathroom if you need it. If you get hungry, just knock on the door and I'll bring you something."

"But what are you gonna do about my withdrawals? I can't be here all panicked and sick."

"What were your addictions?"

"Everything. You name it."

He shook his head. "No, you name it."

"Xanax, opiates . . ."

"You'll be sick, have diarrhea, dilated pupils, tremors . . . You'll have trouble sleeping . . . but you won't die."

"You're not going to give me anything for it?"

"There are a couple of things I can give you to help you through it. But I won't dope you up with something as bad as what you were on. I won't be an accomplice to your getting high. There's not going to be anybody here who can teach you new tricks about how to work the system, or who will promise to leave with you on a pass and hook you up with dealers. That's not going to happen here."

She couldn't believe what she was hearing. Of all the cars to jump into, why had she chosen this one? "I don't even know what you're talking about!"

He closed and locked the door, and she sat on the bed, legs beneath her, trying to work through what she remembered of the events at the airport. Could Trish really be dead? That woman who had done nothing wrong? She wasn't someone who deserved to die.

Was the man in the car with the syringe a dealer? No, he hadn't had time to find a vein. He had injected her too quickly for a tourniquet. Had that injection killed her?

She lay back in bed, wondering if God had ordained this . . . that she would jump into the car with a stranger who promised to save her, only to find that he was crazy, and had some murderous desire to heal her. How could she wrap her mind around that? And why did her head hurt so bad?

Whatever was on that rag had knocked her out, so he could get her here without her protest. He wasn't the man in Trish's car. But was he working with the killer?

Her mother would assume she had taken off. Maybe she would even blame her for what happened to Trish. Would anybody care, or would they just imagine that another stupid addict had gotten herself into a mess?

God was probably laughing.

Emily slept fitfully that first night, so exhausted that she couldn't stay awake. But she woke as soon as the sun came up, lighting the curtains in the window. Panic shot through her. She had to make a run for it somehow, had to do something to get word to her mom. She stood on the bed and reached the window. It was nailed shut and had black wrought-iron bars on the outside. There was no way she could get through it.

Across the yard, she saw the doctor walking out to a pile of firewood. An ax blade was stuck into some large chunks of wood. He wrenched the ax out and began to split wood.

She slid off the bed and pulled open his daughter's drawers, rifled through them for anything she could use. There were barrettes and snapshots, a hairbrush. Beneath a scarf lay a school ID card. It was laminated, stiff. Perfect.

She went to the door and stuck the card between the door and its casing, and tried to slide the latch back. It didn't stick, just slid across the metal. She tried again, turning it sideways, hitting against the lock bar, pushing as hard as she could.

It took several tries and she almost gave up, but finally it began to move. This could work, she thought. It was actually possible. She tried again, this time applying as much pressure as she could while still sliding it back.

The doorknob clicked. Holding her breath, she turned it and pulled the door open. She looked into the house, didn't see him anywhere. He must still be outside. She tiptoed through, careful not to make a sound.

She followed the hall to a large room, richly decorated like a lodge, with a big stone fireplace. The kitchen was big and ruggedly decorated, something her mother might have done for a rich guy's hunting lodge. Her heart pounded and her hands trembled as she stole through the kitchen. She saw him through the window just outside the door, talking on his cell phone and walking toward the door. He was coming back in with an armload of firewood.

She thought of making a run for it, hoping the wood would slow him down. But she was too weak to outrun him. No, that wouldn't work.

She looked around for a place to hide, but the room was too open. She'd have to go back and wait.

Just as he reached the door, she stole back up the hall to the girl's room, locked the door from the outside and closed herself in. She slid the card into her jeans pocket and heard the outer door close as he came back in. She would wait and listen, and maybe she could tell when he went out again.

She heard the television in the great room, heard his footsteps as he walked around the house, but he didn't go back out.

Several times during the day he brought her food and water, checked her vital signs, offered her blankets. But he didn't go out again until the sky had grown dark. How would she have the courage to escape in the dark? All she could see around the place was forest.

When she heard the door close again, relief almost brought tears to her eyes. Determination revived her courage. She went to the window, peered out. She saw a light come on in the back of the yard. He had gone into a shed, then he came back out with a bag of charcoal.

Good. He was probably cooking on the grill, which would give her some time. She slipped the ID card out of her pocket and worked on the door again. The lock bar moved more quickly this time.

She ran back to the great room, saw him through the window under the porch light, pouring the charcoal into a grill. She searched for another door, but that was the only one, and he was just outside it.

Then she saw his cell phone, lying on the table. She dove for it, ducked behind the table so he couldn't see her. She flipped it open, then keeping her eyes on the door, made her way to the text screen and punched in her mother's number. She texted:

mom help me

She heard the grill close outside, saw him wadding up the charcoal bag. The phone rang, and she almost dropped it. It had to be her mother. She clicked and held the power button, until the phone turned off. As he came toward the door, she abandoned it, ran back to her room, and closed herself in, locking it from the outside.

She would keep that card close to her so she could get out again when she had the opportunity. As soon as she heard his car pull away she would go. But now her mother at least had a phone number to trace. The immediate call back told her that her text had gone through. Maybe the police would come soon.

But as day turned into night, and night into morning . . .

. . . No one ever came.

On the third day of her captivity, Emily's sobriety ebbed like the flu, aching through her, racking every joint and wrecking every bodily function. Fatigue ate into her bones, marrying itself to her nausea and the cold that chilled her no matter how many blankets the doctor brought her. She longed for comfort, but it evaded her.

Emily gave up on anyone coming. She would die here. As the toxins fought their way out of her body, she wished death would finish its work.

When her captor unlocked her door that morning, he held a plate of scrambled eggs.

"Are you hungry now?" he asked.

She sat up. "No, I'm sick. But I'll try. It might make me feel better."

"Good. That's progress." He brought her the plate and she smelled the food. He had scrambled it with bell peppers, onions, and cheese, even little bits of bacon, much the same as her father used to do. She hadn't had scrambled eggs like that since before her dad got sick.

Her stomach growled. Hoping the food wouldn't go right through her, she took the plate and sat down on the bed. He stood over her, watching as she ate.

"Are we still in Atlanta, or some other town?" she asked.

"You don't need to know that."

Why did he watch her like that? Was he looking for his daughter in her face? "My mom is probably losing her mind."

"I've been watching the coverage on the news," he said. "I think you like to keep your mother worried sick."

She shook her head. "No, I don't."

"The reporters have started to dig up your history."

"Why?"

"I told you. They think you killed Trish Massey. They're digging up piles of dirt on you."

She was doomed. They'd never believe she was innocent. Nausea rolled through her. She handed the dish back. "I'm not hungry."

"I was going to call your mom and tell her you were okay, that I had you here, but I can't let them find you now. They'll put you in prison. You don't want that, do you?"

"No! I can't go back to jail."

"So you've been there before?"

"Just for three weeks. In juvie."

"What for?"

"Possession, DUI . . . Nothing big." She thought about her terrible mess. Even if she got away, what would she do if they thought she'd killed Trish? "I'll clean up my act, and explain what happened. I can describe the man in the car." The moment she said that, she wondered if it was wise. What if they were partners? It couldn't be a coincidence that he'd come along when he had. "My mom will know what to do."

"Your mom is the one who chose to send you to Road Back. What does she know?" He took her plate and went back to the door. "I'll leave the water for you in case you want more. What do you like to drink? I'll go to the store and get it for you."

She thought of telling him to get her a bottle of Jim Beam, but it might send him over the edge. "I like Coke and cranberry juice."

"Anything you like to munch on?"

"No." She could already feel the eggs turning in her stomach. She felt feverish, and she was getting another headache. Why hadn't her mother come? "What are you gonna do with me when I'm detoxed? Let me go?"

He stared at her for a moment. "I don't know. I can't let you go back out there to the streets, can I? You need significant time sober before your brain can heal."

"Significant time? Like how long?"

"However long it takes." A soft smile came to his lips. "But I'm glad you're here. You remind me of my Sara."

She was silent as he walked out and closed the door. She sat back on the bed, looking around at the things that had belonged to his daughter. She wondered how long the girl had been dead, and how she'd died. She had to get him to talk about it. Maybe he was just a grieving father doing the wrong thing. Maybe she could help him see that he had to do the right thing.

But her withdrawals robbed her of all energy and initiative, and despite her efforts to stay awake and wait for her opportunity to escape, she kept drifting into semi-sleep, plagued by vivid dreams of predators chasing her.

When she woke, it was dark again. She'd missed a whole day, and still her mother hadn't come with the police. Maybe she didn't believe the text was from Emily. Or maybe she'd sent it to the wrong number.

Emily tried to shake her brain clear and think. Somehow she had to get out of this room. Maybe if she acted friendly, engaged the doctor in conversation, he'd think of her more as his daughter and less as his victim.

When he unlocked the door to bring her dinner, she gave it her best shot. "I'm feeling really claustrophobic. I'm hungry, but I don't think I can eat. Can I please come out and sit at the table?"

A frown pleated his forehead, and he slid his hands into his pockets and seemed to consider it for a moment. "No, I don't think so."

"Please? I'm afraid I'll spill something on your daughter's bed. I can see you've kept it nice. How long since she died?"

He rubbed his mouth, cleared his throat. "Two years."

Recognizing the emotion in his eyes, she softened her voice. "How did it happen?"

His reply came out raspy. "She was with some of her newfound drug addict friends on a pass from Road Back."

"A pass? They give passes?"

He breathed a bitter laugh. "It's a deadly practice, but what have they got to lose? They attract more addicts that way. If they're court-ordered to go somewhere, they'll choose the place with the most freedom. Trish Massey only cared about money. She didn't really care about people getting better."

It didn't sound like a bad place, Emily thought. Maybe if she got out of here, she'd really go there. "Did you ever do this with her? Lock her in a room and try to get her sober yourself?"

"No, but I should have. She'd be alive today." His voice hitched. "It's my biggest regret in life."

Silence hung between them for a long moment, and she saw a sheen in his eyes. He was softening . . . weakening.

"That must have been awful for you," she said, working up some tears of her own. "I know a little about what it's like to lose someone you love. I lost my dad when I was fourteen."

His eyebrows lifted. "So that's what happened. I've been wondering if your mother was divorced, ever since I saw her on the news."

"You saw my mom?"

"Yes. She was asking people to look for you."

Of course her mother was looking. She wondered if her mom had mentioned the text. No, if she had, he would have gone ballistic. "Was she really upset?"

"She seemed like a strong lady."

She hoped her mother was strong enough to find her. "Well, you can imagine how she feels," she whispered. "The way you felt when you lost your daughter. My mom feels just that way." She looked down at her feet and almost whispered, "She probably thinks I'm dead too."

There was a long moment of silence. She tried to wedge herself through it. "It was hard for her to bury Dad. It was hard for all of us." She dabbed her eyes. "I really miss him. I thought I'd be over it by now, but you don't get over death, do you? Not when it's someone you love."

"No, you don't." He stood there for a moment, looking down at her with soft eyes. "Tell you what. Come on out here, and you can sit at the table."

Her heart jolted, but she tried to look even weaker than she was. Slowly, she got up and pulled on her shoes. She reached out to steady herself on the dresser as she crossed the room.

He probably thought she was too weak to run, but as she went to the table, her blurred gaze went to the windows, the door. The porch light was on. Maybe it would give her enough light to see her way to the road.

"You're breathing hard," he noted as he took her food from her tray and set it in front of her. "Do you feel congested?"

She nodded and took a bite of the chicken potpie. Strength. She would need it to get away.

"When you go off painkillers, it often makes the phlegm in your chest thicker. Flu-like symptoms are normal. The Xanax withdrawal makes it a little dicier, though. That causes some neurological symptoms. You may feel like your skin is crawling."

His textbook knowledge didn't come close.

"But you'll be all right. I won't let you die."

She took another bite, trying to steady herself.

He ate, then set his fork down. "Sara and I used to eat together, right here, like this. She loved chicken potpie—the frozen kind. My wife tried making one from scratch, but Sara said it just wasn't the same. Do you like it?"

She tasted nothing, but she nodded. "It's good."

"I know you don't feel much like eating, but it'll make you feel better if you do."

She took another bite and glanced at the door. It had a simple dead bolt.

"I don't want you to think of me as some horrible person who's holding you against your will. I want you to think of me as someone who has your best interests at heart. Like your father would."

She almost choked.

"You haven't been drinking enough," he noted. "I don't want you to get dehydrated."

Her grasp was so weak that she didn't know if she could lift the glass. Shaking, she took it, drank some of the water. Maybe if she finished it off, sent him to the refrigerator for more, she'd have the chance to run.

She chugged it, hoping her churning stomach wouldn't rebel. When she emptied it, she set the glass down. "Could I have more? I didn't know how thirsty I was."

"Of course." Looking pleased, he got up and went around the counter into the kitchen.

Emily sprang up and shot across the room.

"Emily!"

She hit the door, threw back the dead bolt and pulled it open. Cool, fresh air blasted her face.

"Stop!"

She took off toward the gravel driveway, framed with trees. She couldn't see the street yet. She heard him yelling, running behind her. Her legs wouldn't move fast enough. She gasped for breath. The driveway snaked down an incline. She heard cars passing below. Birds flapped out of a tree.

"Help me!" she screamed. "Somebody, help me!"

He tackled her before she could even see the street, knocking her into the gravel. Flesh scraped from her chin, her hands, her knees. He was strong, and she was so weak. Despite how hard she bit and kicked and twisted and squealed, he got one hand over her mouth and lifted her off the ground with his other arm.

She was sweating when he got her inside. Her dirty, tangled hair stuck to her perspiring face.

He was sweating too. "You whining, manipulating little junkie," he said through his teeth. "I should have known." He took her back into Sara's room, pushed her onto the floor, and locked it.

She got up and threw herself against it. "Let me out!" she screamed. She kicked it but didn't even leave a mark.

She couldn't believe she had failed. Now what would she do?

Why hadn't they come? There was no excuse. Her mother had failed her . . . again.

But worse, Emily had failed herself.

The scrapes on her chin, her hands, and her knees stung, and she was so tired she wanted to collapse. But she couldn't. She had to think. There had to be something she could use as a weapon. She went to the curtains, looked at the rod that held them. It was too flimsy . . . useless. She turned to the closet. There was a heavy metal rod holding Sara's clothes.

She took the clothes hangers off, dropped them in a pile on the floor. Was it possible to take the rod out? Her dad had once built her mom a new closet, and Emily had helped him with the rod. In the wooden casing, there was a slot where the rod could be inserted. She found it, lifted it out. It was heavy, long . . . just what she needed. The next time he came in, she'd be ready. Why hadn't she thought of it before?

She began to break things to make him come back. As she'd done in her own room the day of the intervention, she pulled drawers out of the nightstand, flung them against the wall, toppled the bed table, knocked Sara's things off the dresser . . .

Adrenaline strengthened her. He would come back to save his daughter's things. He had to.

She heard his footsteps bounding down the hallway, and she grabbed the rod and moved to the hinged side of the door so that she'd be behind it when it opened.

The door cracked open, but he didn't come right in. He looked toward the bed and saw she wasn't there. Then, too cautiously, he stepped inside, looking toward the bathroom on the opposite side of the room.

She came around the door and swung, but the rod was too long, and instead of hitting him, it punched through the sheetrock. She reared back and tried again, but this time he caught it in his hand, and used it to hurl her back.

Then he fell on top of her, held her down, and put a rag against her mouth. The same stuff he'd used in the car took her breath again.

Again, her brain seemed to seep out through her nose, her consciousness fading away . . .

When Emily woke up, she was no longer in Sara's room. Instead, she was in this damp, concrete basement, a room with four cement walls and a fluorescent light overhead. She was lying on the cold floor. A small blanket lay wadded beside her, as though her kidnapper had tossed it there. She sat up and saw stairs that must lead into the house. Emily forced herself to her feet. Wobbling, she made her way to the stairs, pulled herself up each step. She tried to open the door at the top of them, but of course it was locked. She banged on it, kicked it, and screamed to be let out.

Her voice reverberated against the walls, bouncing against the ceiling.

Where was her mother? Hadn't she gotten the text? If she was really looking for her, she would have taken it seriously, wouldn't she? The police could trace the number, find out where this doctor lived. Why hadn't they come?

When she'd beaten her fists bloody, she went back down the stairs and looked around. There was a sink, a toilet, and a water heater in a small, concrete bathroom.

There were no windows, so she couldn't tell if it was day or night. How long had she been out? Maybe it was still daylight.

She hunkered down on the floor, wrapped the blanket around herself. Her head was killing her. She didn't know what was in that rag that had knocked her out. Combined with her dope-sickness, it made her even weaker.

Had she finally hit bottom? She and her friends used to laugh at that term. When they blew a vein or broke a needle, they'd say, "Okay, this is it. This is the bottom." And they'd all crack up. Such comedians.

She remembered the day Corie didn't wake up. She'd OD'd after a three-day high. That day, they talked about Corie hitting bottom, and no one laughed. But soon they forgot.

In treatment the first time, Emily's counselors talked about "raising the bottom," using logic and facts to convince the group of addicts to stop their descent. She and the others had gotten a weeping laugh out of that one. For days, they talked about raising their saggy bottoms, mocking the concept and the counselor.

Now she was on a free fall, waiting to splat.

Her brain screamed out for a fix or company, anything to ease the pain. She lay there for hours, staring at the four gray walls, the ceiling, the stairs, the door . . . all the while hating God for the things that led her to this . . . the things he could have prevented.

The only hero in her life was her dad, and God had taken him. He'd let him die a long, slow, miserable death. He'd snuffed out his life while they prayed. She'd sworn that day never to pray again.

And despite all this, she was going to keep that promise.

thirty-six

Kent Harlan stared at the phone number that had clicked into place like a key puzzle piece—Greg Leigh's number.

The one from which Emily's text had come.

His heart pounded as he got the words out. "I don't believe this."

Andy glanced over. "What?"

"The phone number Emily texted from? You'll never guess."

Andy looked at Kent's computer screen. "You've got to be kidding."

"The phone belongs to our illustrious doctor."

Andy stared at him, mouth agape. "Un. Stinking. Believable."

"He had access to the drug injected into Trish Massey."

"Yeah, but so did Tredwell. Are you sure about this?"

"Positive. It's the same number, registered to the alias Ethan Horne. Leigh's receptionist told me he'd been out of the office all week. That should have been a waving red flag to me. Of course he's been out. He's holding a hostage, lying low after a murder. He and Tredwell must have been working together. Tredwell in Trish's car with the syringe, Leigh in the Infiniti."

Andy headed back to his desk. "All right, let's get busy."

Kent turned back to his computer, adrenaline pumping. He pulled up everything he could find in his database about Dr. Greg Leigh. No arrests. He'd lived a squeaky clean life—not even a malpractice suit.

Straying off the database, he pulled up the archives for the local newspaper and typed in Dr. Leigh's name. Any wedding announcements, obituaries, or articles about his practice would come up.

He waited as the search engine did its work. Finally, an article appeared:

Local Girl Found Dead of Overdose

Kent frowned and leaned in. Leigh's daughter had been found dead of a drug overdose two years ago. Kent remembered the case. The girl, Sara, ended up OD'ing in an alley. At the time, she was on an afternoon pass from her rehab center.

Which one?

He went to the next match and found a picture of the girl. She was blonde, with homecoming queen potential, but she had that tired, worn-out, hungry look that so many addicts have. Too much makeup, not enough shampoo.

The reporter had interviewed Leigh and his wife, Joan. "We did everything we knew to do for her," Leigh said. "We sank a fortune into drug rehab, and what did they do? Let her out on a pass, way too soon. She bought drugs, of course, then overdosed. I blame the idiots running the rehab. I plan to file a lawsuit."

He printed out the article, ready to show it to Andy. But Andy was already crossing the room. "Guess where his daughter went to drug treatment?"

Kent didn't have to hear the words. "Road Back Recovery Center."

"You got it," Andy said. "So our Dr. Leigh has a beef against

Trish Massey. Lost a lawsuit he filed against Road Back a few months ago. Must have decided to get his revenge another way."

Kent went back to his computer, pulled up Leigh's driver's license again. He studied his picture. Then he ran through a list of the doctor's connections.

A home in Buckhead, an upper-class area of Atlanta.

A medical practice here in town.

His motor vehicle tag.

He zoomed in on the model of car he owned.

"Well, you don't say." He enlarged the registration for a black Infiniti. Yes, he felt it in his gut. Dr. Leigh was the man who'd given Emily the ride. The pieces were finally falling into place. "Andy, I think we've got our man. Leigh knows where Emily is."

"Probably. Dead or alive. His only motivation for abducting her would be to keep her from talking. So he'd have to kill her."

Kent's stomach took a nosedive. He couldn't stand the thought of telling Barbara that Emily was dead. "Maybe the fact that he's a grieving father would keep him from hurting someone else's child."

"What planet are you from? The guy could be a sicko. Maybe Leigh's daughter was an addict because of him. And even if he wasn't mental before her death, that could have pushed him over the edge. After he lost the suit, maybe he felt murder was the only justice Trish Massey was going to get."

Kent Harlan didn't believe in prayer, but as he drove to Leigh's address, he found himself pleading with the God he hadn't spoken to in years. Emily had to be okay.

When they got to Leigh's house, they found no one but a housekeeper who said that Dr. Leigh had been out of town for the last few days. She didn't know where he was.

They would have to get a search warrant, which might prove tricky, because all of their evidence was circumstantial. The phone number was the strongest thing they had. It was the sum total of all of the parts that added up to murder, but judges weren't big on granting warrants against prominent members of society, unless the evidence was unequivocal.

No, their best bet would be to convince Leigh to volunteer to a search of his home. Or get him to come in and make a statement against Tredwell, and try to catch him in a lie.

"Whatever we do, Andy, we can't let this leak to the press. This is just between you and me right now, okay? Nobody else in the department."

Andy nodded. "Yeah, we sure don't want to tip him off."

thirty-seven

Dr. Leigh was surprisingly cooperative the next morning when Kent reached him. He told Kent he'd discovered that sample packs of drugs and a vial of Tubarine were indeed missing. He agreed to come in and sign the affidavit.

It took Leigh two hours to get there, during which time Kent was able to convince the judge to give him a search warrant for Leigh's home. While Kent interviewed Leigh, Andy would go to his house and try to find Emily.

When he showed up, Dr. Leigh looked more like a doctor than a kidnapper or killer. He was about 5'10", well-dressed, and he looked like the kind of guy Kent would trust with his health.

Yet Leigh seemed a little nervous as Kent took him into the interview room. "I don't have a lot of time," he said. "If I could just sign the affidavit . . ."

Kent closed the door and motioned to the metal folding chair. "Sure. Have a seat. We can talk a little while the form is being prepared."

Leigh sat down stiffly. "I've already told you all I know."

"Yeah, just a few more questions." Kent took the chair across the small table from Leigh. It was a small room, not meant for comfort. But Kent struck a relaxed pose. They were just two pals talking. "Dr. Leigh, I appreciate your coming in," he said. "You mind if I record our conversation?"

"No, I guess not."

"I just want to get everything we say here on the record."

Leigh hesitated. "I thought we were just talking about the missing drugs."

"Sure, that's pretty much it. I just need information about this guy Tredwell. He's a heavy drug user, so I'm confused as to why you hired him to work in your office."

Leigh rubbed his chin. "As I told you, he was sober when he applied for the job, and his drug test was clean. I wanted to give him a break. A chance to start over and prove himself."

"But he didn't stay clean, right?"

"No. About three weeks ago he started missing work. When he came in, he looked rough. I suspected then that he was using again."

"Did you test him?"

"No. I gave him a stern warning, hoping he'd pull himself together."

"Your receptionist says he's a bad employee. She didn't know why you hadn't fired him."

"Yes, the other employees resent him."

"You've been out this week, right?"

He cleared his throat and shifted in his seat. "Yeah, doing a little fishing. The business side of my office is still open, though."

"Where do you fish?"

"I sometimes go to Lake Lora."

Kent smiled. "You got a boat?"

"No. I fish off the bank. Actually, I do more thinking than fishing."

"Catch anything?"

"Nothing to speak of." He hesitated. "I just needed a few days off. I've been working really hard and dealing with a divorce. I also lost my daughter two years ago, and that's been difficult. She died of an overdose."

"I'm sorry."

Pain dragged at Leigh's face, and he looked down at his hands. "So you understand why I'd have compassion for a guy who had addictions."

Kent checked his recorder, made sure it was running. "An overdose, huh? I sometimes work those cases. Was it here in Atlanta?"

"No, it was in Emerson."

He sat up, as if surprised. "Oh, yeah. Sara Leigh, right? Like the cupcake lady."

He nodded.

"Wasn't she the one who was in treatment, and went out on a pass?"

"That's right."

"That was Road Back Recovery Center, wasn't it?"

Leigh swallowed. "Yes."

Kent sighed and tried to soften his voice. "I remember that case. Didn't I hear that you filed a lawsuit?"

Sudden awareness flickered in Leigh's eyes. Clearly, he knew the interview was taking a dangerous turn. "Can I just sign the affidavit? I have some things I need to do."

Kent got up, leaned out the door. He retrieved the paper he'd left on a file cabinet beside the door. "Great, it's ready," he said, coming back in. He handed it to the doctor. As Leigh read over it, Kent kept talking. "Yeah, this case looks pretty cut-and-dried. When did you first hear about it?"

Leigh swallowed. "I don't know. The day after it happened, maybe . . . on the news. Do I sign here?"

Kent leaned forward. "Yes, right there. So where were you that day?"

"What day?"

"The day of the murder, October 2nd. Were you at work?"

Leigh's face came up, and Kent noticed beads of sweat forming over his lip. "I was at home. Piddling around the house . . . Detective, do I need a lawyer?"

The last thing Kent wanted to do was put an attorney between him and the truth. "Hey, you're not under arrest. I basically ask the same question of everyone involved with the case."

Leigh signed the paper, then got up. "Then I'll leave now."

He held Kent's gaze for a moment. "Look, Detective. I realize that my lawsuit against Road Back Recovery Center might implicate me somehow in your case. But that's absurd."

Kent felt his phone vibrating and glanced down. He had missed calls from Barbara, and a text from Andy.

We searched the house. She's not there.

His heart sank. Now he'd have to let Leigh walk out of here. Kent slid the phone back into his pocket.

"Did you hear me?" Leigh asked. "I'm not a killer. I pursued justice through the courts. Now, Tredwell could have done it, thinking he was helping me out. If he was thinking through a haze of drugs . . ."

"Did you two talk about it?"

Leigh seemed to think too hard. "About the lawsuit, yes. He probably realized I've been depressed since the verdict. Who knows what goes through an active drug user's mind? Maybe he thought I'd helped him out, and he owed me or something."

"Did you give him any reason to think he owed you a debt? One you expected to have paid?"

"Absolutely not." The color flushed back into his face. "You know, I think I'll contact a lawyer. If you have any more questions, you can contact him."

"No problem. Let us know who you retain."

Leigh got up, and Kent followed him out of the interview room. Leigh said good-bye and hurried toward the front doors. As he watched him go, Kent saw Barbara and Lance standing at the sergeant's desk across the room. She spotted him, pushed through the desks, and came toward him.

"Kent, I've been trying to call you ever since the news broke about an arrest." She stopped and followed his gaze to Dr. Leigh. "Who is that?" she whispered.

He frowned. "Shhh. Let's not talk right here."

"But you were interviewing him, right? Were you working on our case?"

"Not now." He left her standing there and got Andy on the phone, asked him where he was. He was just pulling up out front. "Dr. Leigh's on his way out. He has on a yellow polo shirt, khaki pants. Follow him."

"I'm on it," Andy said.

Kent hung up, keeping his eyes on the door.

"Who was that?" Barbara demanded on a whisper. "Why do you want Andy to follow him?"

He sighed. "He's the doctor who employs Tredwell."

"And Tredwell is the one you've arrested?"

"That's right."

"What's the doctor's name?"

"I can't share that with you, Barbara."

"I'll find out." She looked at the affidavit in his hand. "Is that his signature? Dr. Greg Leigh?"

Kent rolled his eyes. Why did Leigh have to be the one doctor who wrote legibly? "Barbara, leave it alone. We're making progress here. Things are very delicate. If you get in the way, you could blow the whole case. Now, I've got to go. I have my hands full."

Kent left her and ran up the stairs to his office to call Andy. "Are you on him?"

"Yeah. He's in the black Infiniti. Tag's still covered so you can't read it. Looks like mud, but my guess is it's brown paint. I'm putting you on speaker."

Kent heard the sudden hiss of the speakerphone.

"He must realize he's being tailed. He's trying to lose me."

"Stay with him!"

"I'm trying. Did you get anything out of him?"

"Not enough," Kent said. "What about the search?"

"Nobody was there. We went in and did a quick search of every room. No sign of Emily. I don't think he's been holding her there."

"Where are you?"

"On 401. He's flying. Maybe I should pull him over for speeding."

"No, then we'd never find her."

"Aw, no!" He heard Andy curse. "Unbelievable! He pulled off at the Pine Street exit at the last possible second. I couldn't get over. I've lost him."

Kent groaned. "Can you get off at Spring Street? Maybe you can find him."

"I'm doing it now. But if he knew he was followed, he's not going to be easy to find."

Kent wanted to throw something. "I could put out an APB. Get some uniforms on it. But we can't arrest him yet."

"I'll keep looking," Andy said. "Maybe I can double back and intercept him."

"Meanwhile, I'll go talk to Tredwell again. Make him think Leigh exposed him. Maybe that'll make him talk."

thirty-eight

Fuming, Barbara drove Lance back to the hotel so she could look up Dr. Greg Leigh. As Lance surfed the TV for reports of Emily, she Googled Leigh, hoping to find a phone number and the location of his office where Tredwell worked. Several hits came up. Fascinated, she read newspaper articles about his daughter Sara dying of a drug overdose, and the lawsuit he'd filed on behalf of several other parents against Road Back Recovery Center. Her chest tightened.

If he had such a strong connection to Trish Massey, why had Kent let him walk away?

She wrote down the names of the other parents involved in the lawsuit, then Googled each of them. It was basically the same story. They had paid Road Back's high fees with hopes of curing their addicted children, only to have them return to the streets. None of the others had died, but their family members all felt that malpractice had been committed at the rehab center, and that there had been false advertising to get them to send their children there.

In one of them she found a link to a Facebook profile, and she went there and read a woman's account of her own trials with her addicted child. Barbara could have written it herself. The woman's struggles with her son had brought her to the brink of suicide at least three times. Barbara had never entertained the idea of suicide, because she didn't want to heap more baggage on her children. But she certainly understood why some people did. The woman had found a support group that helped her through it. There was a link to the group. Barbara clicked on it, and the welcome page came up.

Welcome to Parents of Prodigals. Post here about your experiences with bad rehabs, and the ones that actually work.

Quickly, Barbara created a username that didn't identify her as Barbara Covington—SavvyMom—and joined the group. Within minutes, she got a welcome email. She was in.

The email told her she could go to the website and view the archives.

"What are you working so hard on, Mom?" Lance asked.

She clicked the link. "Just trying to get into the head of the man Kent was interviewing."

"Is he involved in the case?"

"Could be."

She got into the archives and typed in Leigh. Two dozen posts came up, from the man himself.

"Something has to be done," he wrote.

Places like this shouldn't continue getting away with the racket they call rehab. My daughter overdosed while she was on an afternoon pass. Those morons, who didn't care whether she got sober or not, gave their residents afternoon passes to go wherever they wanted. Plus, the whole time she was there she was doped up on benzos. Genius doctors got them addicted to more stuff than they were on when they came in. One time, she claimed she sprained her ankle, and they gave her pain meds. It was the most asinine way to treat addictions. It's just a money-making enterprise, with no concern for changing people's lives. You send them there, pay a fortune for them to go, hoping that they'll get sober and clear, that their brains will heal. That when they get out, they'll make the right decisions. But how can that happen when they're giving them passes before they've even made up their minds to stay clean? My daughter might be alive if I had chosen more wisely. I don't intend to sit by and let other people get caught in this trap.

Barbara stared at the words. So *she* had chosen foolishly too. The rehab she'd put so much hope in wouldn't have been Emily's answer, after all. She had simply Googled "drug rehab" and "Christian," and Road Back was the first to pop up. From these parents' accounts, she saw that the Christian part of it was minimal. There was a Christian workbook the residents could go through if they chose, and one of the counselors went to church. That was the niche that got them the hits on the website. And the phone calls. And the fortunes people invested in the program for their children or loved ones.

She didn't blame Dr. Leigh for being so angry, but what did he have to do with Trish's death? Was he angry enough to kill her? And what did that mean for Emily?

She read back through each of his messages, some of them written during the time when he was working on the malpractice suit. Then she finally came to the one after the judge had ruled that Road Back was not at fault for Sara's death, or the failure of any of the other residents to recover.

"I'm flabbergasted," he wrote.

Absolutely flabbergasted. I thought I could depend on the justice system to do something about this. Now more and more addicts are going to die, if not quickly, over a period of years. A long, slow, cruel death through addiction. No one is going to be helped there. They have to be stopped.

Someone had commented in reply,

Because of the opioid crisis, we have the opportunity to educate people about it. Set up a clearinghouse for this information, and figure out a way to have our site come up first when people Google "Christian rehab."

There wasn't a reply from Dr. Leigh. He hadn't posted again. Had he chosen another course of action to deal with his desire for vengeance? She decided to try to connect with him privately. She went to the Contact page and quickly drafted a message.

Dear Dr. Leigh,
I'm so thankful for this email group. I was about to send my son to Road Back until I saw all these messages. I'm sorry for your daughter's death.

She hit Send, doubting she would get a reply. At least not today. The man was probably back at work, seeing patients.

She turned to Lance. The news channel was doing a story on the economy. "Nothing about Emily," he said.

Not good. She had to keep Emily's face in front of people as much as possible. "Maybe we'd better do another press conference," she said. "Do you think anybody would come?"

Lance rolled his eyes. "Mom. They won't stop calling and leaving messages. You know they want to talk to you. I think we should go back on."

"We?"

"Yes. I'm part of this family."

"Lance, this isn't about us."

"No, it's about Emily. But I have stuff to say."

She sighed and glanced back at the computer. Her email showed that she had one message in her Inbox. Already? She clicked on it and saw that the reply was from Dr. Greg Leigh. Her heart jolted.

"It's from him! The doctor Kent was interviewing!"

Lance sprang up, and Barbara opened the email.

He stood over her, reading over her shoulder.

Dear SavvyMom . . .

"SavvyMom?" Lance asked.

"I didn't use my real name." She started to read.

Thank you for writing with condolences about our daughter. I'm not Greg. I'm his ex-wife, Joan. He doesn't moderate this group anymore, so I took over his account. I recommend that you go to Sonya Minn's clearing-house for information on the rehabs that might work for your son.

"Your son?" Lance bit out. "What did you tell her?"

"I didn't want him to figure out it was me."

"Thanks a lot. His ex-wife, huh? That figures."

"No, this could be good. She could give us information about him. Maybe even more than the police got out of him."

His eyebrows shot up. "So ask her some questions. Tell her who you are."

"No, that's not a good idea. What if she's still friendly with her ex-husband? If she mentions my name and he has anything to do with all this . . ."

"Right," Lance said.

She didn't want to blow this chance. She hit Reply and typed:

I know you're busy and probably don't want to do this
with a stranger like me, but I could use a listening ear. I
see that you're here in Atlanta. Any way we could get
together for coffee and talk?

She sent it off and waited for a reply—almost holding her breath. Within five minutes, one came back.

I have an appointment in a few minutes, but there's
a Starbucks in the Buckhead Barnes & Noble, where I
could meet you in a couple of hours. Say, two o'clock?

Barbara wrote back,

Perfect. See you then.

As she sent it off, she jumped out of her chair and hugged Lance.

"Way to go, Mom. But she's gonna recognize you as soon as you walk in, you know."

"Maybe. If she does, I'll confess. But at least she won't have time to tell her ex before we talk."

thirty-nine

Barbara pulled her hair up into a ponytail and wore sunglasses to the bookstore, hoping that people wouldn't recognize her and get in her way.

She and Lance got there before Joan and picked out tables in the Starbucks area. Barbara bought Lance a caramel latte and let him sit alone in the corner, playing on the laptop. He'd be so hopped up with caffeine that he probably wouldn't sleep at all tonight. Why hadn't she ordered him a decaf?

She took a table across the room, watching the door for any sign of someone who might be looking for her. Finally, a woman came in alone, and Barbara lifted her hand in a wave. The woman had short brown hair and was very thin. It was the kind of thin that came from grief, not vanity.

"SavvyMom?" she asked.

"Yeah, it's me." She stood up and shook Joan's hand. "I'm Barbara. Thank you for coming."

Joan studied Barbara as they sat down. "Do I know you? You look familiar."

"No, I don't think so."

"No, I do."

Finally, Barbara lowered her sunglasses. "You may have seen me on TV. I'm looking for my daughter."

Her eyes rounded. "Yes, the Covington girl. Emily, right?"

"That's right."

"Why didn't you tell me that in your email? I thought you wanted to talk about rehab . . . for your son."

"Yeah, I lied. I have a lot of press people tracking my every move."

"I understand," Joan said. "I know what you're going through."

Somehow, Barbara felt that she did.

"I'll do whatever I can to help you. Would you like a coffee?"

Barbara still had some. "No, thanks."

"I'll get one. Be right back."

As Joan went up to the bar to order, Barbara met Lance's eyes. He mouthed, "Did she recognize you?"

Barbara nodded.

After a moment, Joan got her coffee and came back. "So, are you any closer to finding your daughter?" she asked as she sat down.

"No, not at all. I'm just grasping at straws, basically. I guess I felt a common spirit on that email loop, and I . . . I don't know. I just wanted to talk to you."

"I'm glad you did. I can't imagine going through it alone. At least I was still married when we were looking for Sara."

"When did you get divorced?"

"Six months ago. After my husband lost the lawsuit, I knew we couldn't go on."

"Why not?"

Joan took a long sip, as if it gave her strength to talk about this. "He changed. He became completely obsessed with getting revenge on Road Back. After we lost the suit, it was like everything fell apart. He was a bitter, angry man, and he was impossible to live with."

"I guess that happens a lot when people lose a child."

"Yeah," she said. "I never would have thought it before." She took the lid off her coffee and poured in some sugar, began to stir. "He started blaming me for the overdose."

"Blaming you? How?"

"He said I was too lenient with her, that I allowed her to get on drugs, that if I'd been doing my job as a mother, she wouldn't have turned out like that and none of this would have happened. And then I blamed him for being too strict and making her rebel. You know how it goes. One blame leads to another, until finally you realize you dislike each other more than you ever loved each other."

"Where's your ex-husband now?"

"Still here in Atlanta. He's a general surgeon. But ever since Sara's death, he takes a lot of time off and spends a good bit of time at our cabin."

Barbara's heart jolted. "Where's your cabin?"

Joan put the top back on. "It's up in Dalton. We bought it a few years ago. It was a great little escape for us, in the mountains. We used to go up there a lot with Sara." Her voice broke off. "I let him have it in the divorce. It brought back too many memories."

"So he spends a lot of time there now?"

"Yes, every weekend." She reached into her purse, pulled out her wallet, and showed Barbara a picture of a young woman with long blonde hair. "I cried when I saw your press conference, because Emily reminds me a little of Sara."

Barbara took the picture, looked down at the girl. There were similarities. She prayed Emily hadn't met the same fate. "How old was she?"

"Twenty. Just starting her life." Her voice broke again.

"She's beautiful."

Joan took the picture back, looked wistfully down at it. "She was my life. I never dreamed I would lose her so young. Especially to drugs. I used to think that kids who got on drugs must have terrible parents. That those of us who were involved and modeled good behavior, those of us who expected things of our children, wouldn't ever go through that. But be careful who you judge, right? The Bible says, 'In the way that you judge, you will be judged.' I discovered the truth in that."

"So you're a Christian? Me too."

"Probably why you chose Road Back, right? It was the first one to come up in your Google search."

"Bingo."

Joan gently put the picture back in her purse. "I started a support group at my church and found out how many other families are suffering because of drugs. Our culture is killing our kids."

"Yes, it is."

"The group has been a godsend. If you'd like to come, we meet tonight. It's for anyone who has a prodigal."

Barbara smiled. "I might take you up on that."

"I wasn't a Christian when Sara died," she said. "But it was the church that comforted me and ministered to me, and later helped me through the divorce. And one day I was talking to another mother who had a child on drugs. Her daughter had just been arrested, and she didn't know what to do. I said we should start a support group so we could pray for our children together. She reminded me that I didn't need to pray for Sara anymore." She looked down at her coffee. "But I don't know, I thought maybe I could help pray for all the other kids, and all the poor parents out there going through the same stuff. So we put out the word. The first night we had ten people show up. We've been meeting once a week ever since, talking and encouraging each other, advising each other . . . but mostly praying. And we lift each other up during the week."

Barbara blinked back tears, thinking that she should start a group like that when she got back to Missouri. "I'd appreciate it if you'd pray for Emily."

"I already have been, since I saw the story on TV. And you," she said. "I've been praying for you."

Barbara liked Joan, and wondered why any man would ever cut her loose. "Tell me about your ex-husband," she said. "What kind of man is he?"

"He used to be a good man, but he needs Christ. He's the only one who could get that bitterness out of his heart."

Barbara glanced at Lance before speaking again. "Do you think he would have done anything to Trish Massey? Maybe for revenge?"

Joan didn't seem offended by the question. "The thought crossed my mind when I first heard about it, but no, he's not the malicious sort. He's just in a lot of pain."

"Do the two of you communicate at all?"

"Occasionally, but not much. It's a strange thing, to cut ties with someone after you've lived with them for twenty-five years. But this life is full of surprises, isn't it? You never know what's coming around the corner. But God does. And he knows where your Emily is right now."

forty

When Kent got Tredwell out of his holding cell again, Tredwell looked hopeful. "Are you letting me go?" he asked.

Kent shook his head. "No, I'm not letting you go. See, you're in a real mess, but I wanted to give you the benefit of the doubt. I'm aware that people don't always tell the truth, and Dr. Leigh's account might not be truthful."

Fear passed across Tredwell's face. "Dr. Leigh? You're talking to him?"

Kent turned the recorder on. "I'm recording this, by the way. If you want to wait for your attorney, that's fine, but then you'll have to wait to hear what Leigh told me about you. I just had a conversation with him a few minutes ago. And I gotta tell you, his testimony isn't doing you any good. He signed an affidavit and everything."

Tredwell sprang out of his seat, indignation all over his face. "He put the heat on me? When he's the one who's been blackmailing—" He cut off the sentence, let it hang in the air.

Kent tipped his head. "Blackmailing . . . ?"

The man kicked his chair, then lowered himself back into it.

Kent leaned forward, elbows on his knees, trying to look sympathetic. "Look, Tredwell. I know you've been abused."

"You bet I have."

"And Dr. Leigh has a few secrets of his own. Why don't you tell me what they are?"

Tredwell rubbed his face. "I can't."

"You're willing to cover for him, while he implicates you?"

Tredwell seemed frozen, then looked up as if he'd come to a decision. "He asked me to do it, okay? But I said no."

Kent's heart beat faster. "He asked you to kill Trish Massey?"

"No, he asked me to inject her, not kill her." Tredwell lifted his chin. "Give me a deal, and I'll tell you everything."

"No deal, Tredwell. We've got Leigh's testimony. It's not looking good for you. You don't have any negotiating power here. But if there's something we need to know, I highly recommend you tell us. Otherwise, you're going down for first-degree murder."

"He caught me doing something, okay? He found out I took some prescription pads. I didn't use them, I just took them."

Of course. "Go on."

"He was holding it over my head, threatening to ruin everything if I didn't do what he said. He was determined Trish Massey was going to pay for what happened to his daughter. He said if I helped him, he'd let me keep my job. He'd treat it like it never happened. He didn't tell me that he wanted me to kill her. I was just supposed to use chloroform on a rag to knock her out, then inject her with some drugs and take off. Told me he was just trying to get her into trouble. If she woke up and drove under the influence, it would ruin her reputation. It might close her down."

Kent sat straighter. "What drug?"

"He didn't say. I figured it was morphine or something."

"Try Tubarine."

He frowned. "What's that?"

"It's a paralytic drug used in surgery."

He shrugged. "I've never worked with it before. I don't assist in surgery."

Kent stared at him, looking for a sign of guile. "So you agreed to do it?"

"No, I told him I wouldn't. I have enough legal problems without doing something like that."

"So you showed up at the airport to watch him do it? Because we've already established that you were there."

"No. I stayed at baggage claim."

"Your girlfriend says you left."

He slammed his hand on the table. "She lied!" He got up. "I'm not answering any more questions. You might as well just put me back in my cell."

That was fine with Kent. He stepped out and told the guard to put Tredwell in with the most intimidating prisoners they had. Maybe soon he'd be ready to tell them everything.

forty-one

As Barbara and Lance left the bookstore, she called Kent and told him what she'd just learned about the cabin in Dalton.

"Dalton?" he said. "Did she give you an address?"

"No. Kent, do you think Dr. Leigh could be involved in the murder?"

His pause was the answer she needed.

"Kent, so help me, if you don't tell me what you know, I'm going to find that cabin myself."

"All right." He hesitated, then went on. "You can't say this to anyone. Not even Lance. We can't take the chance of it getting leaked before we make an arrest."

"What?"

"The text you got from Emily? It came from Leigh's phone. And it pinged off of a Dalton cell tower."

The blood drained from Barbara's face. Her lungs tightened, and she couldn't catch a breath. She pulled off the road.

"What is it?" Lance asked.

She shook her head and raised her hand to quiet him. "Kent, he must be holding Emily in that cabin!"

"If he is, we'll find out."

"I'm going to Dalton," she said. "I can look it up in public records."

"I have a database here. If there's a title in his name, I can find that information quickly."

"Yeah, but you won't give it to me."

"Why would I? Do you really plan to barge into his yard and bang on his door, demanding that he turn over your daughter?"

"I might."

"Barbara, this is a good lead. The best we've gotten. Now I'm asking you to back off and let us work. If Emily's there, we don't want to get her killed."

Barbara was going to be sick. "All right, but you need to go *now*."

"Trust me, Barbara. What I need is for you to stay at the hotel and wait. Can you do that?"

"I don't know."

"Barbara?"

"Kent, hurry. She's in trouble. She could be hurt. He could be doing horrible things to her."

"I'm on it, Barbara," he said more gently. "Please trust me."

Barbara had never felt more helpless. As she clicked the phone off, she looked at her son. Lance stared back at her.

"We're close to finding Emily," she said. "So close I can almost feel her."

"So what do we do?" Lance asked.

She couldn't just sit here and wait. Despite Kent's warnings, she would go to Dalton and get as close to that house as she could without going there. But it could get dangerous. She couldn't take Lance with her again.

She pulled back onto the road and headed toward the hotel. "Lance. It's time for you to go back home."

"What? No, I don't want to!"

"You've missed enough school. You can stay with Jacob and his family. I had a message from them saying they'd do anything they can to help, and they suggested you stay with them. I can get you on the next flight, and they'll pick you up at the airport."

"Mom, please. I didn't do anything wrong. I've been helping, haven't I?"

"You've been a big help, honey. This is not a punishment. But this is going to take me into some dark places. Last night it was stupid of me to take you to that motel."

"Mom, I'm fourteen."

"Honey, I've made my decision. You're going back and that's that."

"Who's going to watch over you while you're chasing killers? You'll be in danger—"

"Don't start that stuff again. I'm not listening this time."

"Mom, I'm serious!" he yelled. "I'm gonna lose my sister and my mother. I already lost my dad."

"Lance, I'm trying to keep you from losing anyone else. I won't do anything dangerous."

"Yes, you will. You know you will."

She pulled around to the back of the hotel, and they both hurried in. Inside their room, she said, "Lance, this is what I have to do. I don't want to hear any more about it. You're going home and that's final. You can be mad at me if you want, but I'd prefer you spent your time praying for me and getting everyone else to pray. You can be our ambassador back at home."

She thrust his duffel bag at him, but he flung it across the room. "Mom, chill. I'm not Emily, okay? I haven't shot up anything. I haven't run away, or disappeared, or gotten kicked out of institutions. I haven't murdered anybody."

"Your sister didn't murder anybody, either!" she shot back.

"We don't even know that for sure, but you're treating me like

I'm the one who's disappointed you, like I've ruined your life and sucked all the joy out of it. I'm not the one who did that, okay?"

He knew which buttons to push, but Barbara resolved to follow through. He grabbed her purse and got her phone out, headed for the bathroom.

"What are you doing?"

"Going to the bathroom," he said.

She sat at the computer and pulled up the travel site to reserve his ticket. Then she heard Lance's voice. "Detective Harlan?"

She went to the open bathroom doorway. "Lance, what are you—"

He held out a hand to keep her from snatching it away. "This is Lance Covington. I wanted to tell you that my mom is freaking out and making me go back to Jefferson City."

"Lance, give me that phone!"

She could hear Kent's voice. "I'm sorry to hear that, Lance."

"Yeah, we're headed for the airport in a few minutes, and I wanted to tell you because I know why she's doing this. She thinks without me she can do stupid stuff that'll get her killed."

Barbara lunged and got the phone away. "Kent, I'm sorry—"

"Barbara, is he right? Are you going to do something stupid?"

"No, I'm not!"

"Yes, she will!" Lance yelled. "She's as stubborn as Emily. That's where Emily gets it."

"Okay, that's enough," she said. "He's way over the line."

"What time is his flight?"

"Four thirty," she said. "We're leaving now, whether he likes it or not."

She clicked off the phone and snatched up Lance's bag. "Why can't you respect me?"

"I do respect you. That's why I don't want you dead."

"Go get in the car, Lance."

She took deep breaths as they made their way down the hall, and prayed the press wouldn't be waiting outside. If they were, Lance would use that forum to try to sway her. She was certain of it.

Thankfully, the reporters weren't there. They got into the car with no fanfare. But Lance protested all the way to the airport, even while she called his best friend's family to ask them to pick him up and keep him for a few days. When they arrived, she got his ticket and an escort pass to walk with him through security to his gate, since he was underage. There wasn't much time at the gate before he boarded, which meant less time to listen to his pleas not to send him home.

"Mom, please don't make me go." Lance's anger had deflated now, and his plea came in a soft, low voice. Even so, she felt the eyes of everyone at the gate. She longed for anonymity.

The gate attendant announced that it was time for first class to board.

She looked at his ticket. "This is you, honey."

He rolled his eyes and picked up his backpack, shrugged it on. Grabbing his duffel, he said, "This is wrong. You'll be sorry about this."

"Probably," Barbara said. "I'm sorry about everything. Just go, have fun, go to school, be a kid."

"I can't be a kid. My sister is missing and wanted for murder."

"Do your best." She took his face in her hands and kissed him on the cheek. "Please, Lance. I need you to be strong for me. Ask everyone to pray. Go to church and tell them all that Emily didn't do it. Make sure they're not just dismissing her as the kid who keeps getting into trouble."

His eyes filled with tears. "It's just . . . I don't know when I'll see you again. How long will you stay if you don't find her?"

She shook her head. "I can't even think about that, Lance. I will find her. We're so close."

"But it could be weeks. Months."

"It won't be. Now, go."

Slumping, he pulled away from her, and started for the ticket agent.

"And Lance?"

He turned back.

"Please don't get into any trouble."

He shrugged, as if refusing to commit. She knew it was just a way to twist the knife a little.

Her eyes stung as he walked onto the jet bridge, out of her sight. She wished he would at least turn back, give her half a smile, lift his hand in a wave. But he was angry, and he wasn't going to.

Touching her mouth, she turned and headed back up the concourse, back through security and out to the parking lot. She thought about waiting to see if his plane had taken off, but people were staring at her, whispering, and she needed to be alone.

She went back to the garage where the murder had taken place and crossed to the side for short-term parking. She got into her car, careful to check the back seat. No one was there, so she slipped in, locked the door . . .

And then she lost it.

It was a terrible thing, being separated from the one child she had left. She closed her eyes, hating her tears.

How had she come to this? Here she was, a single mom, trying her best to raise her children, doing all the right things. The Bible said that you reaped what you sowed. But she hadn't sown this, had she? All the time she'd been caring for her sick husband, was she sowing the seeds of drug abuse? Was she sowing disobedience, wickedness, murder?

She opened her eyes and looked toward the long-term parking area. She imagined Emily walking out to the car with Trish, probably trembling because she needed a fix, smoking a cigarette, wondering where this car was going to take her and what her life would be like for the next several months. She probably felt like she'd been punched in the gut, much like Barbara felt now.

She'd gotten into the car and encountered the killer. Then she'd run the other way and jumped into the car of a stranger.

Was it Greg Leigh's car? Had he been Tredwell's accomplice? Did they kill Emily to keep her from identifying them?

Oh, God, please don't let that be. Take care of Emily, and take care of Lance . . .

The phone rang, startling her. She checked the screen. It was Kent. Suddenly a sure, swift knowledge slammed through her body. He was calling to tell her Emily was dead. A tremor started at her feet, made its way to her knees, to her heart, out to her hands and fingers.

Swallowing the dry knot in her throat, she answered. "Hello?"

"Barbara, where are you?"

"At the airport. What is it? Do you . . . have some news?"

"No." The word brought such relief that she almost collapsed. "I wanted to make sure you were okay. Obviously, you're not. I'm on my way to the judge's office to try to convince him to give me search and arrest warrants. Andy's already on his way up to brief the police in Dalton. I was calling to see if Lance got off all right."

"Yes, he's on the plane. He wasn't happy about it."

"And you're not too happy, either."

She shook her head and her face twisted as she tried to hold back her emotions. "I thought it was the right thing when I bought the ticket."

"And now you're not so sure?"

"No." She wiped her cheeks. "You must think I'm a basket case. I'm usually not like this. I'm usually strong."

"I know. I can see that."

"My daughter's being held by some crazy person, and I'm a wreck because my son didn't wave good-bye to me."

"That's not why you're crying, Barbara." His voice was soft, intimate. "You're crying because you've been through so much. I'm sure Lance would have waved if he'd known you'd be this upset."

She stared toward the area where the murder had occurred. "You know now that she didn't kill Trish, don't you?"

"Yes, we know."

"That she was abducted?"

"Yes. We think that's what happened."

"Oh, dear God." She pressed her hand against her forehead. "My husband would be so disappointed if he knew the mess I've made of things."

"You didn't do this, Barbara. You can't blame yourself for the kidnapping any more than you can blame yourself for her addictions."

"Then who can I blame? It's not John's fault. He did everything right."

"And so did you."

"No, I must have done everything wrong. When he got sick, I was totally consumed with him. Right at the end I couldn't think of anything except helping him through his pain. For the last couple of weeks I stayed up all the time so I could work his morphine pump every twelve minutes just to keep him from suffering. That time is such a blur. There's a whole year of our lives that has practically vanished from my memory. And now I put all my energy and focus on Emily . . . and Lance gets pushed to the side."

Kent was silent for a moment. "My mother used to be more focused on my brother," he said. "The Emily of our family. One time I told her that it felt like she didn't even realize I was there. You know what she said?"

"What?"

"She said that you give your time to the one who needs you the most. That's what you've done."

"Yeah. But my children needed me too, and I wasn't there for them."

"So who took care of them?"

"I guess they pretty much fended for themselves. They ate a lot of ravioli and macaroni and cheese during those days. Friends helped me get them to school and back. We suspended all our activities for a few months."

"Barbara, what else could you have done?"

"I don't know," she said. "I was put in that position of making tough choices. I did the only thing I felt I could do. You prioritize, you make decisions, you respond, you react. Maybe I left them out. Maybe if I'd made them a part of it . . . let them pump the morphine to ease their dad's suffering. But I was trying to keep them away from him, trying to keep them from suffering too. And I just failed at all of it. He still died, and I didn't ease my children's pain."

"You were there for them after he died," he said into the phone. "You know you were. I can't imagine a scenario where you wouldn't be. Look at you now. I don't know what keeps you going, but you keep trying. You've been terrible places, and I can tell from knowing you just a few days that there's nothing in this world that would stop you from trying to rescue your child in distress. You're a good mother, Barbara. You need to know that."

Kent drove with his phone to his ear, wishing he could turn his car around and go to her. It had been a long time since he'd wanted to comfort a crying woman. His wife had gotten so cold and hard toward the end of their marriage, before she left him for another man. Holding her had been the last thing on his mind.

But Barbara's weeping turned him inside out. Finding Emily was the only comfort he could give.

"I have to believe there was a purpose in all this," she said. "I believe God took John when he did because he was building something in us. I have to believe that even the drug abuse has a purpose. God's weaving something into Emily's character, something he'll need to use someday."

Baffled by that kind of faith, Kent didn't answer.

Barbara went on. "Maybe someday she'll have a testimony about how God broke her free of her chains, and she'll help people who are going through the same things."

He didn't know what to say. He'd never seen that much purpose in anything in his life. His brother was now in prison, his mother was clinically depressed, his ex-wife was now on her third marriage. But he admired it in Barbara.

"You keep your faith, okay?" he said into the phone. "Don't let it waver. Keep believing there's a purpose, because there probably is one. I'm going to find her as soon as I can. Do you believe that?"

"Yes."

That one word of affirmation tugged at his heart. Maybe she was right. Maybe all this did have a purpose. "I'll call you as soon as I know something."

"Thanks, Kent. I didn't mean to fall apart on you. I wanted you to think I was stronger than this."

"You are stronger than this," he said. "You didn't fall apart. You just opened the pressure valve and let a little stress out."

He heard a long sigh. "Be careful, okay?"

No one had told him that in years. "You too. You go back to the hotel and wait until I call you."

She didn't commit to that, and he had the sick feeling that she wouldn't. He hung up, glad Andy hadn't been with him to hear any of that. His response to her was unprofessional. He couldn't let his mind dwell on her again until he found Emily.

Please, God, help us find her.

The words were out before he realized he was praying again. What did that mean? That he believed there was someone up there who heard him? For the first time in years, he actually considered the possibility that the creator of the universe might have a purpose for him, and that he might hear him. Maybe he hadn't forgotten him, after all.

forty-two

Barbara's widowhood had never been more cruel. Driving back from the airport, she battled the mocking voices whispering despair into her ear. She was alone in this fight, and she lacked the courage to defeat her enemies. But she would take them on anyway.

She got back to her hotel room and sat down on the bed. She had to go to Dalton, to be there if they found Emily. But details waylaid her. Should she leave her things, planning to return? Or should she pack and check out?

The big decision to send Lance home had rendered her unable to make the small ones.

Why hadn't God allowed John to be here, to hold her up when she suffered? Why was there no one to walk alongside her? Kent's phone call had only reminded her of her loneliness.

She turned on her television to chase away the shadows as she packed her things. Up came a football game. For a moment, she closed her eyes and listened to those familiar sounds, trying to imagine that her husband was close to her, watching the game while she busied herself with household chores.

She had no interest in football, but those had been the sounds of her home when John was still alive. It melted her into tears.

"Where are you, John? Why aren't you here with me?" She looked at the ceiling. "God, I don't understand it. What have I done?"

Did she dare call it injustice, this condition of her life? She longed for someone older, wiser . . . someone with more courage to walk her through this.

Suddenly, she missed her mother. She picked up the phone, dialed her number. It rang six times, and she almost gave up. Then there was a feeble voice.

"Hello?"

"Mama? It's Barbara."

"Barbara, you were supposed to be home hours ago."

Barbara's thin hopes vaporized. Her mother's dementia still held her in its clutches. "Mama, I need to talk to you. I'm going through something, and I just need you to be clear for a minute."

"They steal from me."

"Who does?"

"The people who broke into my house."

Her mother lived in an assisted living home. The "thieves" were the staff who helped care for her. There would be no clarity today.

She heard a click, then the phone cut off. As she often did, her mother had forgotten she was talking and hung up.

Rage shuddered through Barbara, threatening to explode her skull.

The phone rang in her hand. Had her mother called back? Without checking the caller ID, she clicked it on. "Mama?"

"Barbara, it's Fran."

She thought of hanging up, but Fran forged on.

"I got permission to use an antique secretary's desk and some memorabilia from David Francis's collection. I can go by and take a picture of it for the presentation if you want. And I found all sorts of great stuff on your other design boards—"

"Not now," Barbara bit out.

"Barbara, we have to get this done if we're going to meet our deadline."

"Then we won't meet it. I have to go."

"Barbara, what about the Francis stuff?"

She stood up and screamed into the phone, "I said, it's over! I can't meet the deadline! Find another job! I can't deal with this now."

She cut off the phone and heard cheers and applause rising from the television. Snapping, she grabbed the desk chair, lifted it, and crashed it into the screen. The game died.

Smoke and the smell of burning wires puffed out from the set.

What had she done?

She collapsed onto the bed, screaming things at God that she'd never thought she'd say.

Get up.

Whether it was God's still small voice or her own, she wasn't sure, but as her fury drained, a calm replaced it.

You're not alone.

She sat up, blew her nose again, and stared at the casualty of her rage. The broken TV would have to be replaced.

I'll walk with you. You don't have to do this by yourself.

She held her knees for a moment, wondering why the smoke hadn't set off the alarm system. Water pouring down on her head would have been a fitting end to this moment. That there was none was evidence that God was still there.

That, and the whisper, coaching her along.

Pack. Go.

She threw the rest of her things into her suitcase, then picked up the glass on the carpet in front of the TV. Thank God she hadn't done this in Lance's presence.

She picked up the hotel phone, dialed the front desk.

"Front desk. May I help you?"

She cleared her throat. "Um . . . this is Barbara Covington in 403."

"Yes, Mrs. Covington, what can I do for you?"

Her voice was shaky. "Uh, these televisions that are in the room? I was wondering how much they cost."

"I'm not sure. Why do you ask?"

"Because . . . I need to pay for one."

"Ma'am, you can buy one at Walmart . . . I can give you directions."

"No, I need this one." She shoved back her hair. "See . . . I kind of broke it."

A pause. "Would you like me to send a maintenance man up to repair it?"

"No, I don't think it can be repaired."

"Oh? What's wrong with it?"

She surveyed the broken glass, the chair lying on the floor. "I sort of dropped something . . . against it."

"I'm sorry . . . you dropped something against it?"

Hearing it repeated back to her was too painful. "I lost my temper, okay? I've been a little upset."

A beat of silence. "And rightfully so, ma'am."

"Anyway, I broke the blasted TV, and I need to pay for it. If you could, just find out the cost and add it to my bill."

"Yes, ma'am. Would you like us to replace it?"

"Not for me. I'm checking out. Do I need to come to the desk?"

"No, ma'am. It's okay. I'll check you out and add the cost to your credit card. I hope you . . . enjoyed your stay."

She hung up, then ran around the room, throwing her things into her suitcase. It was time to change locations anyway. Maybe then she wouldn't have to worry about the reporters every time she stepped outside.

Feeling like a coward and an idiot, she rolled her suitcase into the hall, out the side door. A cluster of reporters had gotten wise to her covert exits, and they descended on her now.

"Barbara, where are you going?"

"Are you returning to Missouri?"

"Have you gotten word on your daughter's whereabouts?"

She pushed through them, trying to dodge the cameramen who blocked her way. She got to the car, popped the lock. She opened the driver's door, pushed her suitcase across to the passenger side, and slid in beside it.

"Barbara, do you have anything to say to your daughter if she's listening?"

A reporter blocked her from closing the door. "Excuse me." She reached for the handle, threatening to close it on her. The woman stepped back.

"Where's your son, Mrs. Covington?"

Barbara closed the door and started the car, checked her rear-view mirror. There were cameramen behind her. She backed out slowly, forcing them to move.

Finally, she put the car in Drive, and the crowd parted enough for her to get through. She let out a long breath as she pulled out of the parking lot, knowing that they'd be following her. Somehow, she'd have to lose them before she could head toward Dalton.

It took a few twists, turns, and lane changes, and a dangerous U-turn on the four-lane highway, before Barbara felt certain she'd lost them.

Finally, she put Dalton in her phone's map app and headed north.

forty-three

Greg Leigh knew he was in trouble. It was bad enough that they'd connected him to this case through Tredwell, but now they were probing around as if he were a suspect. He needed to call a lawyer, but he didn't have one. He'd burned bridges with the attorney who'd handled his lawsuit, blaming him for losing the case. Now he'd have to start over with someone else.

When he got back to Dalton, he would get on the phone and find someone to represent him. This was all getting out of hand. Why hadn't he thought more about what could go wrong?

It had seemed like a great plan. He'd been watching Trish Massey's Instagram for weeks. He'd "friended" her under a fake name so he could read her posts, looking for an opportunity for revenge. When she stupidly posted information about this trip and her return time, leaving out the fact that she'd have a girl with her, the idea had blossomed to life in his mind. Theoretically, he wouldn't even have to be nearby.

His drug-addicted nurse, Gerald Tredwell, was the perfect one for the job. He should have been thrown out on the street after Leigh caught him taking prescription pads. In fact, he should be in jail. Leigh had threatened to press charges unless Tredwell did him this favor, and if Tredwell pulled it off, Leigh had promised him a huge payday at the end.

To prepare for the big event, he'd bought a prepaid cell phone under a fake name. In case Tredwell got caught, phone calls he exchanged with him before and after the confrontation couldn't be traced back to him.

All Tredwell had to do was wait in Trish's car for her to return, knock her out with the chloroform, then inject her with the Tubarine which would paralyze, then kill her, and be on his way. The night Trish was away, Leigh had gone to the airport to find her car, and had even checked the location of the security cameras, so that Tredwell could get in on the side of the car where he wouldn't be as visible, then easily slip out the same way. He'd hoped hours might pass before anyone noticed the woman slumped over her steering wheel and called for help. By then, Tredwell would be long gone.

Leigh should have just waited at home for the call that it had all been done. But no, he was so uneasy about the whole thing that he'd decided to go to the airport himself, and watch from his car across the garage.

They hadn't counted on the girl being with her. On her blog, Trish had left that part out, probably due to confidentiality laws. Tredwell had seen Trish walking to the car, but if he saw the girl with her, the moron didn't realize they were together. From his vantage point, Leigh hadn't seen the girl, either. She must have been walking behind Trish.

It had gone just as planned, until the girl appeared . . . When she ran off screaming, Leigh knew he had to do something to stop her. He started his car and pulled out of his space, and as Tredwell made a panicked phone call to tell him what had happened, Leigh drove up beside her.

Getting her into the car had been easy. He pretended to call the police, which had calmed her. He still had the bottle of chloroform in his car, so when he'd pulled over, he used it to knock her out.

He realized quickly that he couldn't keep her for long in his Dalton cabin. If by any chance they connected him to the case, it was too easy to look it up. But there was a small house For Sale By Owner that he'd driven past a hundred times on his way to his cabin, so he called about buying it. It had been vacant for months, and needed a lot of work. But it had a basement built like a bunker. He'd bought it with cash under the name Ethan Horne—the name he'd put his phone in. He had taken immediate possession, then with a few modifications, made it into the perfect place to hold Emily. He'd planned to furnish the basement before moving her, but when she tried her escape, he decided to take her there sooner, and let her sleep on the cold floor for a while.

The whole plan was insane. He saw that clearly now. He should have killed her and dumped the body somewhere remote, where it wouldn't be found for months, even years. But he couldn't make himself do it. She was just a kid, like his own daughter. Trish had deserved death, but this girl was just an innocent victim . . . a girl with problems like Sara's. A girl he could save.

After all, his whole career had been about saving lives, not taking them. Even with Trish, he'd been one step removed from the actual murder.

But now the police were asking too many questions, and he couldn't be sure Tredwell wouldn't talk. If they decided to search Leigh's Atlanta house and his Dalton cabin, they wouldn't find anything. He was sure he'd removed all traces of her. Still, she was a liability.

He had to get a grip on reality. Emily wasn't Sara, and she wasn't going to turn into a replacement daughter and let him nurture her to sobriety. He couldn't rewrite that horrible chapter of his life, no matter how he tried.

It was time to kill Emily and put this whole nightmare behind him. It was the only way he could save himself.

forty-four

Emily retched into the toilet, flushed, and pulled herself up. She steadied herself as she stood over the sink. Cupping her hands, she washed her mouth out. As she straightened, she considered her reflection in the mirror. She had never looked worse. Her hair was greasy, stringing into her eyes, and her face was dirty. She needed to brush her teeth. How long had it been since she'd even thought of that?

Now, they looked brown and decaying around the edges . . . and they ached.

Funny, when she was high she hadn't looked at herself that much. She didn't really care how she looked then. But sobriety made things painfully clear.

How many days had it been since this nightmare began? She'd been kidnapped Tuesday . . . and three nights had passed. It must be Friday.

Anger at herself and the drugs and the situation curled up inside her like toxic smoke, and she wanted to jerk that mirror off the wall and throw it across the room.

The mirror. She could break the mirror!

Turning, she stepped into the bathroom doorway and looked across the basement, up the steps to the door. She turned back to the mirror. If she were careful, she could break it without the doctor hearing. He had left a couple of towels for her hanging on the towel rack, as though she were a guest who happened to like damp, concrete basements. She slid one of the towels off the rack and laid it on the floor. The mirror was hung on the wall like a picture, so she lifted it off its hook. She laid the mirror facedown on the towel. Kneeling, she hit the back of it with the heel of her hand, hard enough to crack it. She did it again twice more, hoping that somewhere in the fragments she would find a piece long enough to use as a weapon.

Satisfied that she had enough pieces, she carefully lifted the mirror. Dozens of fragments, large and small, lay on the towel. She knelt beside it and separated the pieces, careful not to cut herself. She found one that made an isosceles triangle, long, with a sharp point. It would be tricky to hold it without cutting her hand. She needed something to wrap around it so she could get a grip and surprise the doctor the next time he came close enough to strike.

She got the other towel hanging on the rack and ripped off a strip. Then she wrapped it around the broken glass, pulled a piece through to knot it off. Glancing back at the door, she gathered up the pieces of glass from the towel and stuck them down into the toilet tank, where she hoped he'd never look. She took the broken mirror frame and slipped it behind the hot water heater in the corner of the basement. Maybe he wouldn't notice it was gone.

Then she went up the stairs and sat near the door, waiting for her chance.

At least an hour passed, and he didn't come. Finally, she went back down and curled up in the blanket, clutching that piece of mirror. He would come eventually, and when he did, she'd be ready.

She waited, shivering, her head racked with pain. Finally, she heard footsteps across a wooden floor above her, then a fumbling of the lock. Her hands shook as she positioned the glass between her fingers, the blunt, cloth-covered end pressed against her palm.

The doctor opened the door, looked down into the room. "Are you ready to eat?" All compassion was gone from his voice.

"Can't," she said, lying still. "I'm having chest pains. What did you do to me? I'm dying."

"You're not dying. It was just chloroform. You're all right. Now, do you want food or not?"

She gasped a breath, wheezing like an asthmatic. "Can't breathe."

She heard him step down, one creaky step after another. "F-fever," she said, shivering. "Heart's pounding." He moved faster, crossed the floor, bent down to feel her forehead . . .

She swung up with the glass.

The blade gashed his chin, his lips, his nose, his cheek, his eye . . .

He yelled and fell back, clutching his face, blood drenching his fingers.

Emily sprang from the floor and burst up the stairs into the house. She closed and locked the door, heard him bounding up the steps.

She scanned the room, surprised. It was a different house. Where was the door?

He pounded, kicking, cursing.

She ran through the small, unfurnished house, found a side door.

She unbolted it just as she heard the basement door crashing open.

"I'll kill you!" he screamed.

She tore out of the house and down the gravel driveway, racing toward the street.

As she reached the asphalt, a car whizzed by. She ran along the road, searching for somewhere to hide. A bridge was up ahead, where a narrow river snaked across the road. She crossed it, then heard him coming closer. She veered off into trees. Maybe she could hide there, in the forest. Her feet slid in mud. She leaped over a stump and fell, got back up. Her breath came in gasps, and dizziness made her stagger. She had to go faster. She ran through someone's yard, saw the river winding behind it, and decided that she would follow it downstream. There were more places to hide, fewer easy trails where he could follow her.

She ran along the bank, legs burning. Glancing back, she didn't see him. She went through the trees, up over a hill, and made her way down the far slope. She could hear traffic just below—it sounded like a main road. She crossed a creek bed, getting her feet wet. Plodding onward, she pushed through bushes and brambles and branches reaching out to slow her, but finally she burst through the trees and onto the road.

Cars flew by. She waited for a break in traffic, then dashed across the street. There was a strip mall a block up ahead. A big sign heralded Boutique Square. She ran behind it, checking back doors for one that was unlocked. None of them were. She dashed up to the far corner of the shopping strip, peered around to the front. She didn't see him anywhere. Maybe she had lost him.

The store nearest to her was a dress shop, so she slipped in the front door. The welcoming bell chimed. The clerk was busy helping another customer, so Emily grabbed an outfit off the closest rack and headed for the dressing room. She went in and sat down on the bench, trying to catch her breath.

If he reached the strip mall and went through the stores looking for her, this would be the last one he'd come to. That would buy her a little time. She could go out there right now and get the clerk's attention, ask her to call the police. But if the doctor had told her the truth, she was wanted for murder. She didn't want to go from one prison to another. No, she had to call her mother first.

She heard the clerk coming toward the dressing room. "If I can get you anything, let me know. My name's Marianne."

Emily stood up and called through the door. "I love this outfit. Do you have a phone so I can call my mom? She's a few doors down. I'll get her to come pay for it."

"Sure," the voice said. "I'll get it for you."

More footsteps, then she heard the bell as the front door opened. Someone stepped inside.

"I'll be right with you," the clerk said to the new customer. She came back to the dressing room door. "Here's the phone, honey."

Emily cracked the door open and took the store's cordless phone. "Thanks," she whispered, not showing herself. Her hands trembled as she dialed her mother's cell phone. It rang once, twice, three times . . .

The number showing up on her mom's caller ID would be this dress shop. What if she thought it was a telemarketer and didn't answer?

It went to voice mail. "Hi, you've reached Barbara Covington of Covington Design Studio. Please leave a message and I'll call you back."

She heard a man's voice in the front room. Emily's heart slammed against her chest as the voice mail beeped.

She whispered, "Mom, I was kidnapped and held in a basement, but I got away. I'm at the Boutique Square shopping center. I don't know where that is." She paused, listened for the voices.

". . . paper towels. You're bleeding. Should I call an ambulance?"

The man gave a muffled response. ". . . mugged me. Got my wallet. Blonde hair . . ."

Dr. Leigh!

She heard the words *dressing room*. She had to get out of here.

Still clutching the phone, she slipped out the door and headed for the stockroom. It was a mess, full of boxes and shelves and empty racks. She wove through them to the back door, unlocked it, and slipped outside. Dumpsters sat behind each back door. If she hid in one, would he look in them?

Of course he would.

She looked both ways up the alley, then put the phone back to her ear. "Mom, please come!" she said as she ran, not certain how far the phone's range would extend. "Dr. Leigh's after me. He'll kill me."

Then she heard the line cut off. She tossed the phone into one of the dumpsters and climbed over a half wall, ran up another alley. How would her mother know where to look for her? She'd never find her now.

She couldn't worry about that. First, she had to shake off her kidnapper. Then she could find another way to call her mother.

forty-five

On her way to Dalton, Barbara's phone rang. She saw Cabaret Dress Boutique on the caller ID, and let it ring through to her voice mail. As soon as she did, she regretted it. What if it was someone with information about Emily? She waited a few seconds for the message to show up, then tapped it.

"Mom, I was kidnapped and held in a basement, but I got away." Barbara's heart almost stopped. She turned up the volume. *"I'm at the Boutique Square shopping center. I don't know where that is."*

Her mouth fell open. "Dear God . . ."

There was a long pause. *"Mom, please come! Dr. Leigh's after me. He'll kill me."*

The message ended, and the recorded voice said, "There are no more messages." Barbara clicked it off and tried to return the call. All she got was a busy signal. Maybe Emily was calling back.

She waited, but no call came. Finally, she called Information, suffered through the robotic operator. "Georgia," she said. "Cabaret Dress Boutique. I don't know what town."

The computer system got confused, and asked her to repeat the city and state. "I need a human," she yelled, hoping that someone, somewhere, heard it.

"May I help you?" It was a living, breathing woman.

"Yes," she said, breathless. "I have a number and I need the address."

"What city and state, please?"

"I don't know!" She pulled off the road and held the phone down, turned on the speaker, then tapped back to the list of missed calls. "Can you look up this number, and you tell me? It's 555-943-8878."

There was a pause that took way too long. "That's in Dalton, Georgia. Cabaret Dress Shop, 3213 Benson Boulevard."

"Thank you." She clicked it off, and tried the number again. Still busy. She pressed Kent on her speed dial. It rang to voice mail. She hated voice mail! Where was he? She quickly left a message with the address, then called back and asked for Andy. They routed her to his voice mail too.

As soon as she finished, she punched the address into her app. It showed her the route, but she couldn't see how long it would take to get there. She pulled back into traffic, headed north. Somehow, she had to reach the police. She willed her hands to stop shaking as she dialed the emergency number.

"911, may I help you?"

"Yes, this is Barbara Covington. My daughter Emily Covington, who's been missing, just called me from the Cabaret Dress Shop in Dalton, and I need police to go there and get her."

"Dalton? Where is that?"

"North of Atlanta somewhere! In the mountains."

"Atlanta? Where are you calling from?"

She looked around, trying to see a sign. "I'm half an hour north of Atlanta."

"I'm sorry, ma'am, but we're in Missouri."

She sucked in a breath. Of course. Her phone number originated in Jefferson City. She'd gotten that dispatcher. "Listen to me! I need the 911 for the Dalton, Georgia, area. Please, can you transfer me or something?"

"I'll try to patch you through."

She waited, holding her breath, but after a moment, realized the connection had been lost. She looked down at the phone. There were no bars. She'd lost the signal.

Now what?

Slamming her hand on the steering wheel, she stomped the accelerator and flew north. If she got stopped, at least she'd have the police's attention. If she didn't, she might get there in time to find Emily herself.

forty-six

Lance had messed up, big-time. His mother was going to kill him.

He hadn't planned to ditch the plane. He'd really meant to fly home when he boarded and found his seat next to a fat, hairy man who smelled of vinegar. He tried to get comfortable in half of his seat, and leaned his head back. He stuck his earbuds in and closed his eyes, listening to music on his iPod. The brain-rattling volume didn't chase away his thoughts that he'd failed his mother, his sister, his dad.

They sat on the tarmac for way too long, and when he opened his eyes and looked up, the door was still open. The jet bridge hadn't even been removed. He checked his watch. It was four thirty. The plane was supposed to have left at four. If he had his phone, he'd call his mom, or Jacob's parents, to let them know they hadn't taken off yet. But he didn't have it. He closed his eyes again, waited.

What was his mother doing? Was she waiting there for the plane to leave? Or was she on her way up to Dalton to bang on the door of a killer and offer herself as a sacrifice?

How could he leave her alone, even if she'd demanded it?

Another hour passed. He hated himself. He was supposed to be the man of the family. Dad had told him to take care of his mom, but he wasn't doing it.

Finally, at five o'clock, the flight attendant came on and told them that the plane was having technical problems. They would have to disembark and change aircraft.

It was a sign, he thought. A sign that he couldn't go. He had to go back and help his mom, whether she liked it or not.

He got his bag from the overhead bin and waited for his turn to file off the plane. By the time he got into the terminal, it was filled with irritated people. He heard an announcement that the new plane would be at the next gate over and they would board in twenty minutes.

Since he was over twelve, no one with the airline had taken charge of him. If he just left the airport, no one would care.

As the passengers headed for the new gate, Lance hurried down the concourse, wishing he had money for a cab, or a cell phone, at least. But it was no problem. The hotel was only a couple of miles away. He could walk.

He followed the signs to baggage claim, found the exit, and stepped out of the airport. It had started to rain.

It took a while to get to the hotel, because it wasn't a straight shot. The road that took him out of the airport was a maze. A couple of people slowed and offered him a ride, but remembering his sister's fate, he refused.

The sky opened and rain poured down, slanting sheets pounding him. When he finally got to the hotel, he was soaking wet. The press people were gone. The rain must have sent them back to their vehicles. He went in, thankful for shelter, and dripped across the lobby. He got on the elevator and went to his floor. When he reached his room, he stuck his key card in. The green light didn't come on. Now what?

He knocked and heard someone clicking the dead bolt.

The door opened, and a strange man looked out. "Yes?"

He frowned. "Where's my mom?"

"Son, you must have the wrong room."

"No, this is my room. Who are you?"

"I just checked in. Why don't you go down to the desk and tell them you forgot your room number?"

The door closed, and Lance stood there, dripping on the carpet.

He headed back to the elevator, and went to the desk. There was a line, and only one clerk. He stepped to the front of it, raising his voice. "Where's my mother?" he asked. "Barbara Covington? There's some guy in our room."

The woman looked troubled. "Your mother checked out a little while ago. She didn't tell you?"

"What? Where did she go?"

"She didn't say."

What was he going to do now? "Could I use your phone?"

"Of course."

He took the phone, dialed his mother's cell phone, and prayed she would answer.

Barbara's phone started to ring, and she looked down at it, hoping it was Emily again.

It wasn't. Instead, it was the hotel she'd just checked out of. Probably the manager calling to make her explain the broken television. He'd probably told the reporters, and her fit of rage would be all over the news.

She couldn't deal with it now.

When it quit ringing, she tried Kent's number again while she had a signal. She only got voice mail. Quickly, she blurted out what had happened and told him where Emily was. As she drove through the storm that had overtaken her, she hoped Kent would call back soon.

forty-seven

Lance stood at the hotel desk, shivering as his wet clothes clung to his body. He hung up and tried to think. What would his mother want him to do now?

Duh. She wanted him on that plane to Jeff City. She wanted him staying at Jacob's house.

But if she knew that he'd bucked her orders, and wound up stranded with no money or phone . . . she would totally freak out. And now he couldn't reach her. What did that mean?

He should call Detective Harlan.

He turned back to the desk clerk who was clicking on her computer. "Do you have a phone book?"

"Sure." She pulled it out from under her counter, slid it to him.

He opened it and flipped to the yellow pages. No police department there. Despite his chill, his face burned. He flipped back to the white pages. There were only names. "Where the heck is the police department?" he asked.

"You could call 911."

"No, it's not an emergency. I just need to talk to a guy I know."

Huffing out a sigh, the desk clerk turned the book around and flipped to the blue government pages. "You know the precinct?"

"It's the head one."

She showed him the number.

"Score," he whispered, and dialed the number. Someone answered, and he asked for Kent Harlan.

"He's not in. You want his voice mail?"

He wanted to hit something. "When will he be back? This is really important."

"I don't know. Can I help you?"

He hesitated a moment. "Um . . . this is Lance Covington. Emily Covington's brother? I'm sort of stranded and I need to reach him."

He told the officer what he'd done, and expected him to yell. Instead, he said, "Wait there. I'm sending a car to pick you up."

"Pick me up?" he asked. "I didn't do anything."

"Calm down, kid. I'll have them bring you here. Can't have you wandering around Atlanta alone. One missing Covington kid is enough."

"Okay . . . thanks."

His heart was pounding as though he'd committed a crime and now had to face the music. He thanked the desk clerk and went to stand by the door. Shivering and longing for dry clothes, he watched the rain and wondered where his mother was.

forty-eight

Kent was just leaving the judge's office, warrants in hand, when the front-desk sergeant called.

"Kent, there's a kid here. Says he needs to talk to you."

He turned on his windshield wipers and tried to see where he was going. "What kid?"

"Lance Covington."

"What? What's he doing there?"

"Says he missed his plane or something, can't reach his mother."

He sighed. "Okay, I'll call her. Just keep him there."

"I'm not a babysitter."

"All right, I'll get there quick. Just . . . don't let him leave."

Kent tried calling Barbara, but she didn't answer. Where was she? He parked in front of the department and ran through the rain, into the station. Lance stood near the front desk, soaking wet and clearly out of his element. "I thought you were on a plane home," Kent said.

"I kind of messed up." Lance told him what he'd done. "Now Mom's checked out of the hotel, and I have no idea where she is. She's not answering her phone, so I don't know what to do."

"She's not answering your calls? Lance, she thinks you're in

Jefferson City. She's going to be a wreck when she finds out you never got there."

He threw up his hands. "I know, but what am I supposed to do?"

"You should have stayed on the plane like she told you."

"But I didn't, so now what?"

Kent stared at him for a moment. What was he going to do with him? "Come on up to my office."

They got on the elevator, rode up, and Kent hurried across the floor of his office to the phone. "I'll call your mom right now."

"She might answer," Lance said. "I was calling from the hotel phone. She probably ignored it when she saw the caller ID."

Kent dialed her number again, put the phone to his ear. "I didn't know she was checking out. She should have told me."

"Well, you're not exactly answering your calls, either."

"I was with a judge, trying to get a warrant." This was ridiculous. Was he really explaining himself to a kid? A voice answered: "We're sorry. The number you are trying to reach is out of range at this time. Please try again later." He slammed the phone down. "Out of range."

"Out of range, where? Isn't Atlanta in range?"

Maybe there was a message from her. Kent checked. He sucked in a breath when he heard Barbara's voice, rushed and panicked. *"Kent, I just got a call from Emily. She escaped from Dr. Leigh, but he's after her. She was calling from the Cabaret Dress Shop at the Boutique Square in Dalton. I'm heading there now."*

His heart skipped a beat, and he grabbed a pad and took down the shop name, then hung up and ripped off the page. "Okay," he said to Lance. "I have to leave. You're going to stay here until your mother gets back."

"I heard her voice mail," Lance said. "She's going to get Emily. You can't leave me here. I won't stay."

"Lance, this is police business. I'm not going to argue with you."

"But I saw the shop you wrote down. I'll go there myself."

He pointed at him. "Don't threaten me. You're staying here. That's final."

Lance's cheeks were flaming. "If you don't take me, I'll get a cab."

"You don't have money, Lance. How are you going to do that?"

"The driver won't know I don't have money until I get there. My mom can pay him."

Kent had no doubt the kid would do it. He was that determined. What were his options? Kent could lock him in a holding cell, but putting a minor in an adult jail without a proper reason would cause too much trouble. He couldn't just leave him here unguarded; the kid would follow. He grabbed his jacket, shrugged it on.

Surely there was someone around who could watch Lance until Kent came back. Someone who could put the fear of God into him if he tried to leave. But the kid was resourceful.

Kent had no choice. "All right, Lance. You can ride with me to Dalton. Andy's already up there, briefing the Dalton police. When we get there, I'll drop you at the police department where you'll stay until your mother can come and get you. Have you got that?"

The kid's eyebrows shot up. "Yes. Why is Detective Joiner there? Does he know Emily called?"

"No. He's gone to make an arrest."

"Did you find that doctor guy?"

"Stop asking questions, Lance." Kent grabbed an umbrella from a stand near the door, and pushed the door open. Lance followed quietly as they hurried out to the car.

forty-nine

Rain burst from the sky, soaking Emily. It was cold, and all she had on was the T-shirt and jeans she'd worn for the last few days. She didn't know how far she'd gone from the shopping center where she'd called her mother. She ran down a quiet street, making her way between buildings, looking for a place to hide.

Maybe by now Dr. Leigh had stopped searching and gone to the hospital to get stitches. She hoped she'd done a lot of damage . . . enough to slow him down for a while, enough to scar him for life.

It was getting dark. Rain poured down. Her clothes were plastered against her skin. She may be out here all night, so she had to find shelter.

There was a dumpster up ahead. She hated the thought of sleeping in a giant garbage can, but what else could she do? She approached it cautiously, looked in the square opening, saw that it held only cardboard boxes. Maybe it didn't have rotting food or rats. It didn't reek like some did. She could tolerate it.

She climbed in, her head touching the slimy, mold-covered top. Wincing, she ducked and stomped down some of the boxes, making a clean place for herself to sit.

Thunder cracked, and the rain came harder, pounding down

on the metal lid. The last vestiges of daylight showed her just how dismal her shelter was. She moved the box next to her, bracing herself for a rat to come running out. Nothing did. She hugged her knees, shivering against the cold. How long would she have to hide here?

She needed to call her mother again, to let her know where she was. But if she ventured out of the dumpster, the doctor would find her, drag her back, and throw her back in the basement. There was a simmering, bubbling insanity inside him.

He wouldn't stop until he found her, unless someone stopped him first.

So she sat among the boxes, quietly biding her time as the rain hammered around her. It was a strange protector, a wall of rain that slowed down her enemy. She supposed she should be thankful for it.

fifty

Barbara tried calling Kent again, but there was no signal. Maybe as she got closer to Dalton, it would pick up again. She drove eighty miles an hour in silence, broken only by her prayers and the sound of the pelting rain.

Finally, she reached Dalton and zoomed out on the map, so she could see how far she was from Boutique Square. The electronic voice spoke. "At the next intersection, turn left."

She followed the voice's directions to the shopping center. The parking lot was lit up, and the stores were still open. Her heart raced as she drove past each shop, looking for Cabaret Dress Shop, where Emily's call had originated. It was the store at the very end. She scanned the parking lot, searching for her daughter. She could be here now, ready to run into her arms. She stopped at the curb and hurried in.

A bell chimed as she crossed the threshold. The store clerk spoke to her across the room. "Hi, can I help you?"

"Yes." She went to the counter as her words tumbled out. "I got a call from here an hour and a half ago. My daughter was frantic. Do you know where she is?"

The woman's smile collapsed. "A girl with blonde hair?"

"Yes, that's her."

The clerk grunted. "She ran away and took my phone, stole it right out of the store. Went out the back way and never brought it back. A man comes in all bloody, says she mugged him. I called the police on her but they didn't catch her."

Bloody? The thought of Emily fighting herself out of captivity made Barbara's chest hurt. She touched it, trying to breathe. "The man. Did he talk to police?"

"No. He lit out looking for her. He needed an ambulance if you ask me. Face was all cut . . ."

Barbara hoped Emily had disabled him. But what if he'd found her?

She steadied herself on the counter. "The police . . . Did they know who she was?"

"What do you mean, who she was?"

"She's Emily Covington! The girl who's been missing."

The clerk looked confused now. "The one who killed that woman at the Atlanta airport?"

"She didn't kill anyone!" Barbara gritted out. "What did the police say?"

"Just that they were going to keep looking. I saw their cars again a minute ago." She looked out the front window. "I don't see them anymore."

"Look, I need to use your phone. My cell phone can't get a signal, and I really need to call the police in Atlanta, the ones working on her case."

"I told you, I don't have a phone. Your daughter took it."

Giving up on the hostile clerk, she pushed through the glass door and went to the next shop. Two women were decorating a display window. They greeted her as she went in. "Excuse me, do you have a phone I can use? I need to call the police."

"Is it about that girl who mugged that guy?"

"She didn't mug him. He's a kidnapper!" She tried to calm her voice. "Have you seen her?"

"No, but I heard about it. Marianne, next door, was pretty upset. She said the girl cut his face."

"She was fighting for her life! The guy is a killer, not a victim!" She went to their counter, grabbed their phone. Just let them try and stop her.

She dialed Kent's cell phone number. Finally, it rang through. "Kent Harlan."

She almost burst into tears. "Kent, I can't believe I finally got you!"

"Barbara, where are you?"

She told him where she was, and what they'd said about Emily. "Now she's gone. I can't find her anywhere. She fled for her life, and that man is still out there. God help her, he may have found her already."

"Barbara, we're on our way—about half an hour away. But I need to tell you something. I've got Lance with me."

"*What?*"

"He got off the plane. He went to the hotel, but you had checked out."

She shook her head. "Is he okay?"

"Yes."

Barbara's head was beginning to split. "Put him on the phone!"

She heard the transfer of the phone, and Lance's sheepish voice. "Mom?"

"Why can't I have just one child who obeys me?" she screamed into the phone.

The store clerks stared.

"What got into you, not going on that plane?"

"Mom, I just felt like you needed my help."

"I do need your help. I need you to help me by going back to

Jefferson City and going to school and being safe. That was the help I needed!"

"But I didn't do that, okay?" he yelled back. "There was something wrong with the plane and they were moving us to a different one, so I left."

She ground her teeth and shot a look at her captive audience. Turning away from them, she said, "I don't even know what to say. This is a nightmare! Put Kent back on the phone."

Kent took the phone back. "Barbara, I need you to sit and wait until we get there."

"No, I can't! Emily's here somewhere, waiting for me to come. I have to find her."

"Barbara, we'll be there soon. I asked the Dalton PD to send some cars to the shopping center. Do you see them?"

She looked out the window. "No. The clerk said they came and went. Kent, I'm going to look for her. I have to go. My cell signal is really weak, but I'll find a way to call you when I find Emily." She hung up, put the phone back on the counter.

"Is there anything we can do?" one of the girls asked.

"Just . . . when the police get here, tell them everything you just heard, and tell them about the man who came looking for her." She rubbed her temple and went back to the door. "Thank you for the phone."

fifty-one

From the back of the parking lot at the Boutique Square—lost among the employees' cars—Greg saw Barbara Covington arrive. He recognized her from the news.

He watched as she went into the dress store, saw her come out and go into the one next door. He waited, looking in the rear-view mirror to see just how freakish he looked with this diagonal gash down his face. Whatever the girl had used as a weapon had slashed one eyelid, part of his nose, his lips, and the opposite side of his chin. He hadn't wanted to go to the hospital. It would call too much attention to him. So he'd used the things in his own medical bag to clean and dress the wound. Twenty Steri-Strips held the gash together. At least the edges were clean, but the cut in some places was half an inch deep. It was beginning to swell and bruise. His eye was swollen shut, and if he didn't get the right kind of stitches soon, he'd wind up with a permanent scar. He'd have Emily to thank for that.

He'd driven around, searching for her on all the roads behind the shopping center, going up alleys and searching in doorways and dumpsters. She could have gone into any of the buildings she saw, but he couldn't keep showing his bloody face to people without talking to police.

As he'd searched, he tried to anticipate what Emily would do. She had stolen the phone from that dress shop. She'd probably called her mother and the police. Already, the police had been to the shopping center twice, but their stay had been brief. Were they looking for her . . . or him?

After they left, he'd pulled into the back lot and parked. If he couldn't find Emily, he would wait for her mother. Unless Emily had given her another meeting place—and he doubted that since she didn't know where she was—her only marker would be this shopping center. The phone belonged to Cabaret Dress Shop.

And now his logical thinking had paid off. That was exactly what had happened.

He turned his car on and flicked on the windshield wipers, so that he could see clearly when Barbara came out of the store. The lights in the parking lot were on, but the rain made it difficult to see. If he pulled closer, he could see better, but he couldn't take the chance of being seen. So he sat, waiting for Barbara to come back out so she could lead him to Emily.

Then he would kill them both.

fifty-two

Lightning flashed as Barbara stepped out of the store, back into the rain. Of all nights for the sky to burst.

She went around the shopping center, to the drive that ran behind the shops. She was going to have to think like Emily. There was a dumpster outside each shop, so she ran from one to another, looking in each and calling for Emily. Rain soaked her clothes, plastered her hair against her head. It couldn't be more than forty degrees, and she didn't have a coat. Emily probably didn't, either.

Emily wasn't in any of the waste bins, so Barbara stood there, trying to think like her daughter. She saw an alley, cutting behind an adjacent strip of stores, and ran in that direction, calling. Finally, she came to a fork. If Greg Leigh was chasing Emily, which way might she have turned? There were more places to hide toward the right, so she ran that way, calling her daughter.

Wouldn't Emily still be around here somewhere, waiting for Barbara? Maybe she hadn't gone far. But as she ran, looking in every doorway and dumpster she came to, Barbara's heart filled with terror at the possibility that Leigh had found Emily already.

fifty-three

Emily curled up and lay down on one of the cardboard boxes she had flattened in the dumpster. Rain fell so hard that, even though there was a lid over her head, mist sprayed inside the opening. She was cold and wet. It was going to be a long night.

She tore some boxes and unfolded them into a cardboard blanket. It helped a little with the cold, but the boxes were too damp to provide much comfort. She balled up in a fetal position, holding her knees close to her chest and shivering.

Bitter tears assaulted her. She was miserable, and had no one to blame but herself. If she hadn't started using, she wouldn't be an addict. If she hadn't been an addict, she wouldn't have been sent to rehab. If she hadn't been sent to rehab, she wouldn't have been kidnapped. She wouldn't be lying here, scared, sick, and absolutely alone, holed up in a dumpster in who-knew-what town, hiding from a man who wanted her dead. In her glamorous quest for the darkest light and the lowest high, she now found herself wallowing on the bottom of a filthy garbage bin.

So this was it. The "bottom" she'd mocked. It wasn't an ambulance ride to the hospital where everyone gathered around, and you looked up at them with some glorious epiphany and announced that you had seen the light. No, it was damp darkness in a green metal box, with no one to tell . . . and fear crushing like a trash compactor as she came to the end.

In her loneliness and desperation, she looked up to God, the one person she'd been taught was always there with his eye on her. In her rebellion, she'd hated that thought. But now it brought her a thin, transparent sliver of hope.

"If you're still there, God, I have a few things to say."

She wept as she waited for a slice of lightning, an angry rumble of thunder.

"I wouldn't blame you for turning your back on me, or leaving me here with the garbage."

Suddenly she saw the absurdity of her life. Her mother had told her again and again that she was her own worst enemy. For the first time, she saw it too. It was as though she'd taken the razors of torture and destruction out of the devil's hand, and begun slashing herself with them. That's what the drugs had been. Torture turned on herself.

As she wept over her foolish self-destruction, she felt the pain of God's weeping too. He didn't hate her. He grieved like a devastated father.

A Scripture verse she'd learned as a child began to whisper through her mind.

"Then you will call upon me and come and pray to me, and I will listen to you. You will seek me and find me when you seek me with all your heart."

She wept so hard that she felt herself melting into a puddle that would drain through the cracks of the dumpster. In her despair, she finally called out. "I'm so sorry, Jesus. Please forgive me."

An image came into her mind of the cross—that image she'd once thought was so overused. But now she saw it with new eyes. She saw it with a man hanging on it, suffering and bleeding, weeping the way she wept now. And from the top of that cross, she heard a voice.

"Emily, I took this for you."

"I know you did," she cried. "But it's too late for me."

"No." He shook his bloody head. *"It's not too late. Not yet."*

She felt the sweet, warm cleansing pour through her heart. The blood of Jesus, which she had thought was another one of the church's clichés, seemed to boil through her, blistering off all the sin, all the evil, all the hate and anger, and replacing it with the warm, sweet stream of life.

"Follow me, Emily. Follow me."

Her strength renewed, she felt herself rising out of her pit. God had not turned his back on her. Maybe now he would answer her prayers. Whether he led her to freedom or to prison, she would trust him. She would finally do what her dad had admonished before he died . . . what her Savior invited.

She would follow him.

She looked out the opening in the dumpster. It was completely dark now, and there were no lights in the alley. The rain still fell. She didn't see anyone around. The buildings around her didn't appear to be open. But if she walked far enough, maybe she could find a convenience store that would let her use their phone.

"God, please help me reach my mom." She climbed out of the box and walked through the rain with a renewed sense of courage, and a warmth that burned deeper than the cold rain could reach. For the first time since her terror began, she didn't feel alone.

fifty-four

"Do you have a siren in this thing?"

Kent glanced at Lance. "Yeah, of course."

"Sweet. Can I turn it on?"

"No."

"Why? We could go faster."

"The police light is flashing. It's clearing the way for us already. If I need for someone to move, I'll turn the siren on." He checked his clock. Andy was on his way over to Leigh's cabin with a crew of Dalton police. He hoped they'd find him there.

Lance looked out the window, brooding. "If we chase the kidnapper guy, can I turn it on then?"

"If we chase the kidnapper guy, you're not going to be with me."

"What'll you do, just dump me out on the side of the road?"

"Hopefully, I'll have time to be a little more discriminating than that." He saw a sign for Dalton, Georgia. Twenty more miles.

"I'm thinking about being a detective when I grow up. I'm pretty good at it. I helped my mom find a lot of clues about Emily."

Kent wished the kid would be quiet so he could think. But Lance was clearly nervous. "Yes, you did."

Lance looked at him, oncoming headlights passing over his face. "What made you want to be a cop?"

Kent thought about that for a moment. "Anger, I guess."

"Anger? At what?"

He checked his rearview mirror and changed lanes. "I think I had some delusion that I would be able to clean up the streets, run the drug dealers out of town, so my brother couldn't get high."

"Your brother?"

"That's right. He was an addict too."

Lance seemed to run that through his mind for a moment. "So you were in the same boat I'm in."

"That's right."

"What happened to your brother?"

Kent wished he hadn't brought it up. He didn't want to talk about it. Sighing, he said, "Almost died a few times, close calls. Wound up going to prison for armed robbery."

"Armed robbery? Who did he hold up?"

"Convenience store. Tried to get cash with a gun to somebody's head. He was high as a kite and wanted to make sure he stayed that way."

Lance shook his head. "I don't get why they call it high, when it makes you do such low-down things." He looked away, staring through the passenger-side window. "I hope I never have a sister in prison."

"I know what you mean. I tried my best to keep my brother out. By the time he committed armed robbery, I was a cop already. Pulled every string I had, but I couldn't save him."

"And the drug dealers are still out there," Lance muttered.

"Yes, they are. Business is booming."

"So don't you have that feeling anymore? That you're supposed to get them off the streets?"

"Let's just say that I'm more specialized now. When they start killing people, I go after them. There are others on the force who deal with the narcotics end."

"Do you think most crimes are committed because of drugs?"

"I know it for a fact."

"So how's your brother now?"

"Prison changed him. He had a religious experience, and now every time I visit him, he tries to preach to me."

Lance smiled. "But that's good, right? You believe in God, don't you?"

Kent hesitated. If he told the truth, he knew he would confuse Lance. Why challenge the boy's faith if it was something that anchored him?

But Lance wouldn't leave it alone. "Well, do you?"

"Sometimes." Hoping to turn the conversation, he said, "So what do you think happened with your sister? Why did she turn to drugs?"

Lance gave him a long look. "She's not a suspect anymore, right?"

"Right."

"You're sure about that? Because I can't talk to you about her if you're gonna use it against her."

"I understand. We know who the killer is."

Lance rubbed his chin. "Well, I don't really know what she's thinking most of the time. But when my dad was sick, she and I got pretty close. She used to do everything for me. Then when dad died . . . she just got kind of mean."

"Mean? In what way?"

"I don't know. She was just mad all the time, and grumpy. I couldn't blame her, because I was pretty upset too."

Kent saw Lance's Adam's apple move, and he wondered if he should have taken the boy down this path.

Lance traced one of the raindrops on his window. "That's when Emily started going psycho. She didn't want me around her . . .

didn't want anybody around her. She even stopped hanging out with the friends she'd grown up with and started hanging with losers. The ones who smoked weed and popped pills. I think she found other people who had sorry lives, and when she started drinking and using drugs, it made her feel a little better for a while."

"For a while," Kent said. "It never lasts. If you wanted to sign people up for a club, you wouldn't advertise by saying, 'Want dark circles under your eyes? Sores on your face? Want to go days without eating or sleeping? Weeks without bathing? We'll help you spend every cent you have on dope and steal to get more, and you'll never be able to hold a job . . .' Who would join a club like that?"

"I don't know," Lance said, "but lots of people do." His voice lowered. "Sometimes, when your friends get real in-your-face, begging you to do what they're doing, you almost, for a minute, think that maybe you should try it just once, just to make yourself feel better after all the junk in your life . . ."

Kent frowned. "That would be a terrible idea."

"Yeah, I know. When I get like that, I remind myself what a crock it all is. That it's a big lie. I was always sneaking in Emily's room, reading her journals and stuff, trying to figure out what needed to be done to fix her. And then I would talk to her about it and tell her not to hang out with losers, that they were bad news, that she was gonna wind up being a loser like them. She just said I was judgmental. Then I told her, 'Okay, so if it's so great and everything, why don't I start doing it too?' "

"You asked her that? What did she say?"

He could see the pain on the boy's face. "She didn't even care. To her it was the best thing ever. Wallowing in a pigpen with her brain all fried. She would have been glad to have me join her."

"Wow. That must have been hard."

"Yeah, and I was mad enough at her to do it, just to show her.

But I'm smarter than her. So I prayed that God would keep me from it. And he took away those stupid thoughts."

"Sounds like a good prayer."

Lance glanced over at him. "Does God answer your prayers?"

Kent didn't want to tell him that the first prayers he'd prayed in twenty years were this very afternoon. "I guess I wouldn't pray if I didn't think God would answer. But I don't think he's sitting around, waiting to do my bidding."

Lance seemed to mull that over. "I hope he's answering my prayers now."

Kent's throat tightened. "I don't know God as well as you do, Lance, but somehow I think he will."

fifty-five

Barbara couldn't find her daughter. She'd never felt more help-less. She stood in an alley, dark shadows jutting in the moonlight, luring her. But she'd already searched them, and Emily wasn't there.

Had Greg Leigh already found Emily? Had he gotten revenge for the injury she'd inflicted on him?

She reached a dead end, turned, and ran back the way she'd come. Darkness hung like a curtain, working with the rain against her. As she ran back up the alley, she saw a cluster of people hun-kered in a doorway, but none of them was Emily. Up ahead, two men slogged toward her. Bolstering her courage, she didn't turn away. She kept running right past them, almost daring them to get in her way.

She got back to the crossroads and went the other way, ran all the way to the other end of the alley, calling out for Emily.

Where was she?

Finally, soaked to the bone, she went into a doorway and fell to her knees. "God, please. I'm lost here." She hugged herself as she knelt, and lowered her forehead to the cement floor. "I don't know where to find her. I can't do this by myself. But you can look down and see her. You know right where she is. Please, God, you've got to point me to her. You helped her escape and brought me this far. She's around here somewhere. Please!"

Her pleading voice was muffled by the pounding rain.

Emily walked in the rain until she saw an Exxon up ahead. Feeling like she'd just reached the Promised Land, she sloshed through the parking lot. Stepping inside the brightly lit store, she looked cautiously around. There were several customers in line, and a stressed-out woman behind the counter, who looked as if she'd rather be shot than ring up another sale.

"Excuse me," she said, shivering. "Can I use your phone?"

"It ain't for public use," the woman muttered.

"But it's an emergency. Please . . . just one phone call."

"Go find a pay phone."

"I will, if you'll tell me where one is. Please!" When the clerk ignored her, Emily turned to the people in line. "Can't somebody let me use their cell phone?"

The woman who'd just paid turned to her. "You can use mine, darlin'. Come on out. It's in my car."

Emily eyed her suspiciously, afraid to get into any stranger's car again. "Uh . . . could I use it inside? I'm really freezing."

The lady got her bag and came toward her. "Sure, I'll go get it. Look at you, sweetie. You're drenched." She pointed to a table where people could sit while snacking. "Go wait there, and I'll be right back in."

Emily went over and slipped into the yellow booth, watching through the window as the woman got her phone out of the car. She looked harmless . . . kind, even. Emily scanned the parking lot, the gas pumps, searching for the black car that had gotten her into this mess.

The lady came back in. "Here, honey. Take all the time you need."

Relief swarmed through her. Emily's hands trembled as she dialed her mother's phone. She waited. Please, God. It began to ring, then went straight to voice mail. "No!" She hung up, then clicked it back on and pressed redial. "Why won't she answer? It's not even ringing through."

Again, voice mail. Her mother must have a weak signal. How would she ever connect? She tried Lance's number. It was a different cell phone service, so maybe it had some bars.

An operator's recorded voice said, "This Inbox is full. Please try again later."

"The Inbox is full?" she cried. "What does that mean?"

"Honey, calm down," the woman said. "Keep trying. Why don't you try texting her?"

Yes, maybe a text would get through. She navigated her way to the text window, typed in her mother's number. She could give her the address, tell her to come here. "Where is this place?" she asked.

"It's the Exxon right after the Second Street exit." The woman lifted her voice. "Excuse me, what's the address here?"

The desk clerk barked out the address, and Emily typed it in with a message that said:

mom im at Exxon 2nd ave please come

"Are you hungry, honey?" the woman asked. "Can I get you anything to eat?"

She was too distracted. "No. I have to keep trying my mom."

"You're shivering. How about some coffee, at least?"

"Okay." She kept trying to call while the woman got her some coffee. When she came back, she had bought her a sweatshirt too.

She handed it to her. "It's not much, but you can at least change out of your wet top. Might warm you up a little."

"Thank you." Emily took the coffee, but wouldn't go into the bathroom to change, for fear of missing her mother. She sipped the coffee, grateful for the warmth.

As she dialed again, she looked up at the woman. "God sent you," Emily whispered. "My mom must be praying."

As Barbara prayed in that cold, wet doorway, her phone chimed. She stopped praying and flipped it open, saw a text from an unknown number.

mom im at Exxon 2nd ave please come

Barbara's heart almost lunged out of her chest. She tried to call the number back, but again, it didn't connect. There were no bars. She felt like throwing the phone, but didn't dare. Sporadic service was better than no service at all.

She scrambled to her feet and sprinted back to her car.

fifty-six

Barbara had been gone too long, and her Navigator still sat in front of the Cabaret Dress Shop. Leigh began to wonder whether she would come back to her car. Fatigue and thirst was pulling him down, and the pain from his facial cut was killing him. He needed something for the pain, but if he took anything, he might fall asleep and miss her.

Then it hit him. The best way to get to Emily was to wait in Barbara's SUV. Had she taken the time to lock the doors?

He looked around the parking lot. A couple walked out to their car on the other side of the lot, but they were paying no attention to him. Hoping the darkness would be adequate cover, he got out. Shielding his face, he crossed the lot and reached her car. As he'd hoped, the door was unlocked. He slipped into the back seat, then climbed over and crouched in the space behind the seats.

All he had to do was be still and quiet, and she'd never even know he was there.

He waited for a while as the rain beat down, and finally, he heard the door opening.

Someone slid in and started the car. He heard little clicks as Barbara typed. A voice told her to pull out of the parking lot and turn left. Yes, she knew where Emily was. Soon he would have them both right where he wanted them.

fifty-seven

On the way to the Exxon, Barbara tried to call Kent. Her phone showed that she had a slight signal—only half a bar—but maybe it was enough.

He answered quickly. "Barbara!"

"She called from the Exxon station on Second Avenue. I'm on my way there!" she said.

"Barbara, we're minutes away. I'll have the Dalton police dispatch cars right now."

"Hurry!" She cut the phone off and saw the Exxon sign looming ahead. Her heart jolted. As she pulled in, Barbara flashed her lights and laid on her horn. Through the window she saw her daughter!

Emily stood up, wet, dirty—the most lovely sight Barbara had ever beheld. Before Barbara could pull into a space, Emily bolted out the doors. Barbara stopped where she was and opened her driver's side door.

Emily flung herself at her. "Mom!"

Barbara held her, weeping, not wanting to loosen her hold or move away from her child. But after a moment she pulled back and looked at her. "Are you okay?"

"Yes, just get me out of here."

"No, we have to stay here. The police are on their way. Get in the car, honey."

She let Emily go, and her daughter went around the car and got in on the passenger side. As she closed her door, a voice came from behind her. "I should have killed you while I had you."

Barbara jumped, and Emily turned and screamed.

"Shut up, Emily," Leigh said, leaning over the back seat and aiming a revolver at her head.

Barbara looked out the window, hoping someone saw. The woman who'd been sitting with Emily was getting into her car. She smiled and waved, oblivious. The back windows were tinted, so no one could see the killer.

Leigh looked like something out of a horror movie—his eye cut and swollen shut, tiny bandages across a gash on his face, one side of his mouth thick and split. Holding the gun fixed on Emily, he clambered over the back seat and sat just behind them, the revolver inches from Emily's head. "I want you to do exactly as I say."

Barbara gritted her teeth. "You are not getting my daughter."

"Drive or I'll blow her head off."

Barbara turned back around. Blue lights signaled the arrival of the police. Slowly, she began to drive.

"Don't even think about it," he said. "You flash your lights or blow the horn, and Emily's gone. I'll get caught, but it'll mean two life sentences instead of one, which doesn't make any difference to me."

She had no doubt that he meant it. Trembling, she stepped on the accelerator and looked over at her daughter. Emily stared out the windshield . . . petrified.

"Drive, Barbara. Let's go."

She pulled out of the parking lot, knowing that the gun was trained on the back of Emily's skull, and that with one bump or jostle, he could squeeze the trigger.

fifty-eight

Kent saw four police cars when he pulled into the Exxon parking lot, but he didn't see Barbara's SUV.

"Where are they?" Lance asked. "Where are Mom and Emily?"

He hadn't taken time to drop Lance off at the police station. When he'd gotten Barbara's call, he decided instead to take him right to his mother. "I don't know. Maybe she parked in the back. Wait here. I'm going in."

His voice brooked no debate, so Lance sat quietly as Kent got out.

He went inside. Andy was standing with the Dalton officers, talking to a lady who must be a witness.

"Where are they?" Kent asked.

Andy turned to him, frustration drawing his face. "You're not gonna believe this. They drove off. This lady says Emily and her mother were together in Barbara's vehicle, and that they left."

"Left? I told her I was coming!" He turned to the officers. "Were they here when you got here?"

"No sir," one of them said. "She was already gone."

Something was wrong. Kent dialed Barbara's number, waited.

It rang four times, then went to her voice mail. "Barbara, where are you? I need you to call me back. I told you to wait at the Exxon station."

As he clicked the phone off, a sick certainty hit him. They were in trouble. "She's driving a white Navigator. Didn't any of you see it?"

"I did," one of the Dalton cops said. "That car was driving off when I drove up. I didn't know it was her." He went to the window, looked out. "She can't have gone far."

Kent couldn't believe it. "We need to set a fifteen-mile perimeter and put up roadblocks."

"Maybe she was headed to the closest precinct," Andy said.

Kent walked outside and looked up the street, as far as he could see, both ways. *Please, God . . .* He turned back, saw that Andy and the police had followed him out. "Could you guys check to see if she is at the precinct?"

While they radioed in, Kent tried her phone again. Still no answer.

"We have people watching Leigh's cabin. They were waiting for you to get here with the warrant. If by some chance he has them . . ."

The cop got off the radio and shook his head. "They're not at the precinct. They said they'd let us know if she shows up."

"All right," Kent said. "We need to go search Greg Leigh's cabin."

"We'll meet you there," one of the officers said.

Kent looked at Lance through the windshield of his car. The kid sat there with a perplexed look on his face. He hated to tell him that his mother and Emily were gone.

"I need one of you guys to take the boy to the police station. Have someone there keep an eye on him until I can get back for him."

One of the cops agreed, and Kent went to Lance's door. He opened it and leaned down. "Lance, your mother and Emily were here, but they left. I'm sure they're all right, probably just heading to the police department. So this officer is going to take you there."

"They left?" Lance cried. "No! You told them we were coming."

"Well, she's not here, so maybe she just misunderstood."

Lance looked at the cop, then regarded Kent again. "Why can't I go with you?"

"Because I'm going to Greg Leigh's cabin with a search warrant, and I can't have you tagging along."

The corners of Lance's mouth pulled. "Is that where you think they are?"

"No. But I still have to search it. Now come on, you're slowing me down."

Reluctantly, Lance got out of Kent's car and into the cruiser where the uniformed officer waited. When the cop had closed the door, Kent stepped toward him. "He's a good kid. Go easy on him. He's been through a lot."

Andy left his car there, and he and the crime scene investigators he'd brought with him got into Kent's car. They headed toward the cabin. Kent had a bad feeling that Barbara was now in as much trouble as Emily had been. His stomach burned.

As they drove to the cabin, he saw the Boutique Square. That was where Emily's original call had come from. He pulled in quickly, to see if he could find Barbara's car.

He saw no trace of the Navigator, but a dark Infiniti sat at the back of the parking lot. No one was in it. He pulled behind it . . .

"The same muddy tag," Andy said. "Greg Leigh's car."

"So where is he? Lurking somewhere nearby, or does he have Barbara and Emily?"

He called for more police, and in moments the place was swarming with squad cars. He left them to search for Leigh while they headed for the cabin.

They made their way up the hill to the address Andy'd gotten earlier—the cabin Leigh's ex-wife had mentioned to Barbara. There wasn't a vehicle in the driveway, and the lights were all off, as if the place was empty. They went to the door and knocked hard, heard nothing. Kent kicked the door in.

Inside, they turned on the light and fanned out around the house. There must have been forty pictures of Leigh's daughter Sara. Some of her artwork as a child was matted and hung in frames.

The house was an open floor plan, kitchen and den together. Kent hurried up the hall, leading with his gun, and looked in the master bedroom. Everything was neat and in its place. He looked in the first bedroom that also functioned as an office, then across the hall.

An apple-green room, probably Sara's. Kent stepped in and studied it. There was nothing out of place here either, except the comforter looked a little off, not quite even on both ends. He stepped into the room, looked around.

From this side of the door, he could see that things weren't quite right. There was a hole in the sheetrock near the door. The closet was open, and clothes on their hangers were piled on the floor, the rod leaning against the corner.

There had definitely been a struggle here.

A vague, familiar scent hung in the air. Kent's gaze flew to the trash can under the desk where a rag had been discarded. He pulled on his gloves and picked up the rag. It was the same scent he'd found on the rag in Trish Massey's car. Chloroform.

On the dresser lay some of Leigh's daughter's things—pictures, ribbons, and certificates, all lying under a piece of acrylic. He went back through the house, as the crime scene investigators began to rope off the place.

"Trash can in his daughter's room," he told Andy. "A rag of chloroform."

"You sure?" Andy asked.

"Yeah, I'm sure. All we have to do is find a bottle, and that's exhibit A."

"This place have a basement?"

"Nope, no basement. But Emily told her mother she was held in a basement. He must have moved her. If he's got them, that's where he's holding them." He strode to the door and into the night. "This dude's about to make me mad."

fifty-nine

"No, not there!" Emily's sobs filled the car as the doctor instructed Barbara to drive back toward the house she'd escaped from.

"Emily, shut up! I'm fed up with you," he said. "Give me enough reason, and I'll make your little brother an orphan."

Barbara bit her lip, hoping Emily would heed his warning. Barbara's heart pounded, and she prayed ferociously as she followed his directions.

"Here," he said. "Turn in here."

Barbara pulled down the dirt road, memorizing every landmark in case they made their way out later. It was dark, so she couldn't see much, but she scanned left and right, looking for anything that might help. She tried to choreograph an escape. If he got close enough as they got out of the car, could she knock the gun out of his hands? No, he was too close to Emily, and she couldn't risk it.

"Drive around back. There. Stop the car." Barbara didn't pull all the way behind the house. She left the tail visible.

"Hands up. Over your heads. Now."

They raised their hands, removing any possibility of their grabbing something. "The police are everywhere," she said. "They're going to find you. They're going to come after us."

"They won't find this place," he said calmly. "I didn't use my real name when I bought it. They have no idea it even exists."

"I told them," Emily bit out.

"If you'd told them, they'd be here by now." Misty moonlight gave his disfigured face a macabre look as he jerked her out of the car.

He gave Emily the key. Keeping the gun on her, he told her to open the door.

She did, and hesitated at the threshold. "What if someone did this to your daughter?"

"Inside, Emily. You've lost my sympathy."

"They know you're the killer," Barbara tried. "Your face is probably plastered all over the news."

Emily picked up on that. "The people who sold you the house will remember."

If it moved him, he didn't show it. "In the house!" he said through gritted teeth.

They stepped inside. A lamp shone in the corner of the small den. The room was empty of furniture, dimly lit, dusty. He walked them to the basement door. It had swung closed, but was splintered and broken where he'd kicked it open. "Emily, open the door."

She hesitated.

"Emily, I said now!"

She opened the door, turned on the dim light, took a step down. "Hurry up. All the way down."

Barbara followed her, her hands on Emily's shoulders. He made them sit on the rug. Gun still on them, he backed into the bathroom.

Barbara eyed the stairs. If they ran, he would shoot.

Emily held Barbara's hand, squeezing tight.

Barbara saw Leigh glance in the toilet tank. "Nice try, Emily." He dipped his hand in, pulled out the glass shards she'd hidden there, dropped them onto a towel on the floor. "I ought to make you eat it."

Then clutching the wadded towel, he backed his way up the stairs and closed the door.

Barbara got up and went back up the creaky wooden steps. The door was broken and wouldn't shut right. She doubted it would lock.

Then she heard hammering . . . pounding.

The splintered hole at the edge of the door was quickly covered. More hammering . . .

She turned the knob, and it gave easily, but the door wouldn't budge. He'd caged them in with a hammer and nails.

sixty

"We're okay," Barbara said, trying to sound calm as she went back to her daughter. "We're going to be all right."

Emily was crying. "Mom, it was so hard to get out of here the first time, and now I'm back?"

"We'll get out. Let me think."

She walked into the bathroom. The toilet tank was open, and there was no lid. There was a metal bar inside the mechanism. It might be possible to disengage that and use it as a tool or weapon. But it wasn't strong or sturdy enough, and it certainly wasn't sharp. Besides, they would need the commode to work if they were going to be down here long.

She walked out of the bathroom. There were beams in the ceiling, along the wall. If she had the right tools, she could pry them loose over the stairs. She knew how they were hung. Maybe she could use the bar in the toilet as a screwdriver. It was a possibility.

Another option was the light fixture. If she could hold Emily on her shoulders, show her how to take it down, maybe they could use it. Even a fluorescent bulb could be useful for fighting their way out. If they hit him in the face where he was already wounded . . .

She went up the staircase that led to the door, tried to move the hand rail. She could use it like a bat.

And then it hit her. She knew what might work.

"Come help me, Emily."

"What?"

"We're going to get ready for the doctor. And when he comes back, we'll have a nice surprise."

sixty-one

Minutes ticked by . . . one after another . . . after another. Maybe he wasn't going to come tonight. Barbara sat on the floor at the bottom of the stairs, Emily leaning against her. Irony razored through Barbara like asbestos, cutting her from the inside. How could it be that she was with Emily now, while Lance was out of her grasp? At least he was with Kent. She prayed nothing would happen to him.

"Mom, is Trish really dead?"

Barbara kissed the top of her head. "Yes, honey, she is."

Her voice squeaked. "I'm so sorry."

"Me too."

"We could die here."

"But we won't," Barbara said. "We have to be okay for Lance." She looked at her daughter fully for the first time since she'd found her. She looked awful. Her skin was gray, her eyes sunken. Her lips were dried like raisins, and she'd lost weight.

Emily wiped her face. "When I was sitting in that dumpster waiting for you, I talked to God for the first time in a long time. I told him I was sorry . . . for this whole mess I've made."

Barbara had heard Emily's repentance before—just empty

words. Foxhole faith wasn't necessarily enduring. But it was a beginning. Something God could work with. Maybe this time . . .

"If we ever get out of here, I won't use drugs again, Mom. I mean it. I'm sick of them. I'll go to any rehab you pick. I'll do whatever I have to do."

It was all Barbara had ever wanted to hear. The ultimate goal of so many of her prayers. She looked up the steps to that door. "We have to make sure you get that chance."

Emily's face twisted. "Dad would be so ashamed."

Barbara drew in a deep breath and turned her daughter's face up to hers. Drying the tears on Emily's face, she said, "By the time you see your dad again, he's going to be very proud of you, because you'll have overcome all this."

What if they died here? She knew their death would give them an immediate reunion with John . . . But what about Lance?

What must he be thinking, if he'd found out that his mother and Emily were together, captives of a crazed doctor? If anything happened to them, he would be left alone. There would be no one for him.

It was too cruel.

Aloud, she began to pray for Lance, for his peace, for his safety. She prayed for Greg Leigh, her enemy, that he'd be flooded with compassion, that his evil motives would be foiled, that her plot would work, and that they could escape.

When she finished praying, her face was wet with tears, like Emily's. But she saw new strength on her daughter's face.

"He'll answer your prayers, Mom. I know he will."

Barbara looked at the stairs again, wishing Leigh would come . . . They were ready. She hoped he wasn't.

"He's probably going nuts up there," Emily whispered, "trying to decide what the police know. He thinks of himself as this kind, noble person, doing the right thing."

Maybe Leigh wasn't as rabid as he seemed. Before his daughter died, he may have been a rational man. Barbara closed her eyes and tried to imagine her own bitterness if Emily had died the way Sara did. Maybe she would be insane with rage too. The smashed TV would have been the tip of the iceberg. Maybe she would have been the one to kill Trish Massey.

After all, she was plotting Leigh's death now.

Maybe they weren't so different, after all.

sixty-two

The Dalton PD found no properties owned by Greg Leigh in the entire state of Georgia, other than the one in Atlanta and the vacation cabin here in Dalton. Maybe Leigh had bought another property in the last few days. Kent searched his database for the homes near the shopping center that had sold recently. It would have had to be filed with the tax office, and legal papers would have had to be signed, even if he'd bought it under some alias. On the other hand, there might be some lag time between the purchase and the filing. The tax office was closed, so he couldn't check to see if they had the paperwork and hadn't yet made the entry into the computer.

There was also the possibility that Leigh was renting something, or even that he had broken into a vacant house or building and was using it.

He had to locate it quickly. Emily's and Barbara's lives depended on it.

"Since his Infiniti's at the shopping center, he must have moved them in Barbara's car," Andy said.

How had he let that happen? The police should have intercepted Barbara long before Leigh could get to her.

He drove slowly along the road near the shopping center, the one Emily must have run down to get to the Boutique Square. "Look for a For Sale sign or a neglected yard, anything that says it might have been vacant for a while. And keep an eye out for her car."

The thought that Leigh had probably ridden away with Barbara in her own car meant that he was getting desperate, taking risks. At first, Leigh's only motive for murder seemed to be getting revenge on the person he blamed for his daughter's death. Even Emily's kidnapping had a strange logic. But things had turned now, gotten darker, more erratic.

According to the store clerk, Leigh had been injured. That, along with Emily's escape and the fact that he was about to be exposed as a murderer and kidnapper, might prompt him to do something drastic.

As he drove, Kent found himself praying again—that God would keep Leigh from getting rid of his two major problems.

They followed the road leading up the mountain. How far had Emily run before reaching the shopping center? Some of the houses for sale weren't visible from the street, but most were close to the road, and they could see the cars in the driveway, the condition of their yards.

"There. That one," Andy said. "The yard's grown up."

But there were two cars in the driveway, a bike toppled over. Kent kept driving.

"Up here, three houses out, there was a house sold two days ago," Andy said, glancing at his notes. "Slow down."

Kent slowed as they passed the house. A U-Haul moving van sat in the driveway, and there were plenty of lights on. "Doubt it's that one."

They drove farther, wishing it were daylight, but they didn't have the luxury of waiting until then. They went by several more houses, then crossed a small bridge. A small house came into view, sitting back from the street, almost invisible because of the trees. A light was on somewhere inside.

"This might be it," Andy said. "Grass is tall."

Kent cut off their lights and pulled in, rolled a few yards up the gravel drive. In the moonlight, they could see the tail end of an SUV behind the house.

"Nail on the head," Andy said. "Barbara's rental car."

sixty-three

Greg Leigh thought he heard a car door. He went to the window, cut on the outside light. It only lit the area on the side of his house, and he saw nothing out of the ordinary. Maybe it had been a branch cracking, dropping to the ground . . . or a deer walking through the yard.

Or maybe it was the police.

He had screwed everything up. He should have known better than to leave his car at the shopping center. What had he been thinking? He'd been so determined to get Barbara and Emily back in his grasp that he hadn't thought things through.

He turned the porch light back off and strode through the house to the bathroom. He looked in the mirror, startled by his disfigurement. What had he become? He wasn't a man who committed murder, at least not before his daughter's death. He was sworn to do no harm . . . to save lives, not to take them. Hatred, anger, and bitterness had done its terrible work in him, and now it oozed on his face. He thought of his ex-wife, who managed to live on without that sour, fermenting hatred. When he saw her now, her face reflected peace, though grief had not left her eyes.

But bitterness was eating him from the inside like a slow poison, manifesting in bleeding ulcers, chronic headaches, trembling hands.

Killing Trish Massey had been intended as an act of justice. An eye for an eye. He'd entrusted his daughter to her, and Sara died. It was only fitting that Trish pay with her life.

But one murder led to another. Now he had no choice but to kill them both, mother and daughter, to save himself. Then he could start over somewhere in another state, or another country. Maybe Costa Rica or Cabo San Lucas. The waters were especially blue there, and the climate was good. He could buy a boat, and sail up the Mexican coast.

He heard another sound outside. Was that wind rustling against his house, or people rustling through his yard? He looked out again, saw nothing. He went around to one of the other windows, looked around the dark edges of his unkempt lawn. Trees and bushes swayed in the wind and rain. No one seemed to be there. Not yet.

The sooner he did this, the better. He got his hammer and went to the basement door, pried off the board he'd nailed across the door's casing. Then he picked up his revolver. It was heavy in his hand. Cold.

Maybe he shouldn't kill both of them yet. Maybe, instead, he should keep one of them alive to use as a shield if the police came. Killing Barbara made sense. Emily was weak, easier to control. If the police came and surrounded him, he could load her into his car at gunpoint, and they'd have to let him go. He could arrange for a chartered plane and kill Emily once they were in the air.

He would go down into the basement, feigning kindness, asking Barbara and Emily what they wanted to eat, setting them up, putting them off guard.

He could do this. He had to.

He opened the door, looked down into the basement room.

Emily sat on the floor, her back against the wall. She looked up at him. Lifting the gun, he said, "Where's your mother?"

"In the bathroom," she muttered.

His gaze went to the bathroom. He'd have to wait until she came out. He took a step down . . .

But the stair was gone. His foot went through, and he cursed and dropped the gun, trying to catch himself as loose boards tumbled. He bumped and scraped through the opening and hit the concrete beneath it.

Barbara was waiting there, a plank in her hands poised like a baseball bat. He threw up his arms, blocking her swing. The board rammed into bone, crushing his elbow. He roared in agony.

Teeth bared, she swung again, hitting the side of his head. "Emily, get the gun!"

Emily slid behind the staircase and dove for the gun, but Greg flipped over and grabbed it with his left hand. Wincing with pain, he slid back against the wall. "Get back," he yelled. "Put the board down."

Determination glinted in Barbara's eyes, as she held the board in her hands. "Emily, get behind me."

"I said, drop it!" he yelled. "Emily, don't move or I'll kill her first."

Emily froze, looked at her mother. "Put it down, Mom," she whispered.

Biting her lip, Barbara bent, lay the board near her feet, and slowly stood back up.

"Wouldn't Sara be proud of you?" Emily dared to say.

His rage mushroomed. "Don't talk to me about my daughter."

For a moment, there was silence. He told himself to pull the trigger . . . just squeeze it and be done with it.

Emily cut the silence. "You're not a killer. You were just a dad trying to do the right thing."

Yes, just a dad . . . a grieving dad . . . trying to get justice for his precious daughter. Righting wrongs.

Barbara's voice was hoarse. "If you stand trial, the jury will understand that. But if you shoot us, they'll just see you as a killer with no regard for life."

"I've always had regard for life," he bit out. "I've spent my entire career saving people's lives. But no one was there to save Sara!"

Anguish drew him tight, and he brought the gun up, held the cool barrel of it against his own forehead.

Barbara moved closer. "They shouldn't have let Sara go out alone. They should have watched her, kept her safe."

He knew she was going to take the gun . . . and for a moment he didn't care. It was all such a waste. The murder, the kidnapping . . . his life.

She reached out and he didn't stop her. She closed her hand over his hand, tried to slip the gun from his fingers.

He caught himself and jerked the gun away. "Get back," he said. "Both of you."

Barbara backed away.

"Sit down." His good eye was swelling where she'd hit him, and he could barely see. "Sit down, I said!"

Barbara and Emily sat slowly down. Barbara pulled Emily's head against her, shielding her with both arms.

He thought of himself shielding Sara when she was small, before life had fallen out from under them. He didn't want to kill anymore. Sara was dead, and nothing he'd arranged, nothing he'd schemed, nothing he'd hoped had turned out. It was all just a terrible mess.

He had nothing else to live for.

He put the gun to his head.

"Don't do it." Barbara's voice wobbled. "Please. It'll just bring more pain to your wife. I met her. She still loves you. She prays for you."

He began to weep, hating himself and the circumstances that had brought him here.

"And please . . . don't do that in front of Emily."

He cocked the gun and looked at the girl. Her eyes were squeezed shut, and her mother was protecting her, holding her face against her shoulder, keeping her from seeing the bloodshed that would come.

His bloodshed.

So much death.

But it was the only noble thing to do. The only thing that would set things right. He thought of his ex-wife's way out of the crippling grief. She had turned to God. She told him it was never too late for him to turn too.

But it wasn't forgiveness he was seeking. It was retribution. And there could never be retribution for Sara's death.

He tried to squeeze the trigger . . . His heart hammered, kicking against his chest. Sweat dripped into his eyes.

Something crashed upstairs, and he jumped. Footsteps bounded across the floor overhead. They had come for him.

He'd known they would.

Suddenly, he wanted to live. He had to save himself. He'd kill Barbara, shield himself with Emily . . .

He turned the gun on the mother.

sixty-four

Kent reached the basement threshold, saw the broken steps, heard the voices. Through the hole in the staircase, he saw Leigh below him, raising the gun to Barbara.

Kent lowered his weapon and fired twice. Each bullet hit home, convulsing Leigh's body. The gun slid to the floor.

The room echoed with screams.

"It's okay," Kent yelled down, stepping over the broken stairs. "Barbara, it's me."

Racked with terror and clutching her daughter, Barbara looked up. "Oh, dear God, I thought we were going to die."

Kent stepped over the broken steps and hurried down, reached the floor, and came around the staircase. Leigh lay dead in a pool of blood.

"Don't look, honey," Barbara was whispering to Emily. "Let's just go upstairs."

Still shielding Emily, Barbara looked at Leigh's lifeless face as she and her daughter got to their feet.

So this was Emily. Kent stepped toward her, touched her damp hair, gazed into her terrified face. "Emily, are you all right?" he asked. "Did he hurt you?"

Trembling, she shook her head. "No . . . I'm okay. Let's get out of here, Mom."

Barbara held her daughter as they made their way up the stairs together, into the group of police who waited.

sixty-five

When they got to the end of the driveway, Barbara saw a dozen or more police cars with blue lights flashing, blocking the road.

Ambulances were waiting, and while two of the paramedics ran to the dead man, the others surrounded Emily. Barbara's heart still raced as she stood just outside the vehicle.

That gun . . . she'd been sure the discharge had been from Greg's weapon, that bullets would end hers and Emily's lives.

Kent's appearance had been a miracle.

She saw him emerge from the house and went toward him. "Thank you, Kent. God used you to save us."

Kent met her eyes and smiled. "Imagine that. I've never been used by God before."

"Where's Lance?"

"At the police station. I'll call and have someone bring him here."

"Thank you. Have them tell him we're all right. I know he's worried."

"I will. He'll be okay. He's a good kid. Real strong."

She was grateful for that. Kent looked at the ground, then back up. His eyes were soft as they swept across her face. He touched her shoulder and whispered, "So are you."

Tenderness for the man who'd come for her calmed her heart. She hoped he wouldn't just close the case, let her go back to Jefferson City, and forget he ever knew her.

She wasn't ready to say good-bye.

Kent made the call and went back to work inside the house, sorting through the things going through his mind—gratitude that his own prayers had been answered . . . that he'd gotten there in time . . . that Barbara was safe . . . that Emily had been found . . .

As he let the CSIs gather the evidence, he watched Barbara through the windows, talking gently with Emily. After a few minutes, a squad car pulled up and Lance jumped out of the back seat. "Mom! Emily!"

He ran to them, tears on his face, and threw his arms around them. They hugged ferociously.

Kent walked outside, drawn to the warmth of a family reunited.

When the hugs were done, Emily sat back in the ambulance. Barbara turned back to Kent and reached up to hug him. He held her longer than he should, but she didn't push him away.

She felt so small, so fragile. He wanted to make it his business to protect her, even when she wasn't in danger. As her cheek touched his, he hoped he would have that chance. Silently, he gave God thanks.

In the ambulance, he heard Emily talking to the paramedic. "What's in that IV?"

"You're dehydrated. We're starting some fluids and some medications."

"Fluids, yes," she said, "but no meds."

Kent let Barbara go, and they both looked at the girl sitting on the gurney with her brother.

"Are you sure?" the medic asked.

"Positive," Emily said. "I'm a recovering addict, four days sober. I want to stay that way."

Lance took her hand. "Go, Sis."

Kent watched the smile make its way to Barbara's moist eyes. As she joined her children in the ambulance, he wondered if there might be any openings for detectives in the Jefferson City Police Department. He dared another silent prayer.

He hoped God was still listening.

A Note from the Author

Years ago, Bob Dylan recorded a song that said, "It may be the devil or it may be the Lord, but you're gonna have to serve somebody." I would never realize how true those words were until I got involved in prison ministry and became personally involved with women who were in bondage to chemical substances, alcohol, men, and the government, and that bondage had robbed them of healthy, happy, productive lives of liberty.

Later, when I learned of a family member's bondage to drugs, I embarked on a journey to help her find freedom. In His gentle way, God had prepared me for this fight. My participation in jail ministry had given me many tools and a unique perspective that I wouldn't have had otherwise. Often, I was reminded that even in the darkness of prison I had seen much light. Some of those women shone with the grace of a redemptive God who had intervened in their lives, and they saw their incarceration as a time for God to get their attention, so that He could speak words of life to them. God sent Christian groups to come in and love them and teach them the Word of God. Some of them saw jail or prison as the best thing that had ever happened to them because it woke them up from their lives of death and gave them a rebirth. They wound up transferring their bondage to all those false idols in their lives to Christ, who'd saved them.

All through the New Testament, the apostle Paul refers to himself as a bondservant of Christ. A bondservant was someone who had served as a slave for a family, but when he was set free, he chose to remain and continue serving. This only happened if his master was kind, and if the life the servant lived there was better than it would be somewhere else. To demonstrate his allegiance to that master, he would take part in a ceremony. An awl would be driven through the lobe of his ear, and it would leave a large hole. When people saw that hole in his ear, they would understand that he was a bondservant. They would know that his master must be kind and generous and that even though this person had been given his freedom, he'd voluntarily chosen to serve that man.

Paul used that to describe his bondage to Jesus. Christ had set him free from his own bondage to things that would destroy him, and as a free man, he'd chosen to become a voluntary bondservant of the Lord. In that bondage to Christ, he found the truest freedom he'd ever experienced, and he spent the rest of his life telling people about it, even when it resulted in his own imprisonment and execution.

But I'm constantly amazed at the number of Christians who don't live as bondservants of Christ. Some of them, once they've tasted His freedom, even sell themselves back into bondage to darkness. God is a jealous God, and like a loving husband, he's hurt when we turn away.

In Ezekiel 6:9, He says: "Then those of you who escape will remember Me . . . how I have been hurt by their adulterous hearts which turned away from Me, and by their eyes which played the harlot after their idols."

It breaks my heart to think of hurting the God who saved me.

It literally brings tears to my eyes. And going back into slavery after knowing the freedom of Christ is an absurdity that I cannot fathom.

"When the Son makes you free, you will be free indeed" (John 8:36).

Embrace that, and live life free!

Terri Blackstock

Resources

Boundaries, by Dr. Henry Cloud and Dr. John Townsend, Zondervan, 2001.

Hit by a Ton of Bricks, by John Vawter, Family Life Publishing, 2003.

Moments for Families with Prodigals, by Dr. Robert J. Morgan, NavPress Publishing Group, 2003.

Praying Prodigals Home, by Quin Sherer and Ruthanne Garlock, Regal Books, 2009.

Prodigals and Those Who Love Them, by Ruth Bell Graham, Baker Books, 1999.

Red Sea Rules, by Robert J. Morgan, Thomas Nelson, 2001.

Setting Boundaries with Your Adult Children: Six Steps to Hope and Healing for Struggling Parents, by Allison Bottke, Harvest House Publishers, 2008.

You're Not Alone website (for families dealing with addicted loved ones), www.notalone.org.

Acknowledgments

This book was a special labor of love, because I firmly believe that our culture is killing our kids. The story is fictional, but unfortunately, its truths apply to many families across the world today. For that reason, I'd like to say to all of those who are fighting for the lives of their addicted loved ones, that you are not alone. This is your story, and I hope it brings you some comfort and hope.

To those of you trapped in the bondage of addiction, it's your story too. The hill you're climbing may look insurmountable, and your prison bars (whether spiritual or literal), may seem impenetrable.

But Jesus came to set the captives free.

To all those treatment centers and recovery homes that aren't motivated by money—the ones that truly strive to repair shattered lives—I salute you. May God give you many victories and empower you in multiple ways. You do make a difference.

Discussion Questions

1. Did *Intervention* give you any insight into what families endure with addicted loved ones? What moved you the most about Barbara's situation? What would you do in her situation?

2. According to her journals, how does Emily view her mother? Does she blame her for her addiction? Do others judge Barbara's parenting because of her daughter's behavior?

3. What characters in the story suffer because of Emily's addiction, and how are they impacted? Would you call addiction a family illness?

4. After finding out about what happened to Sara Leigh at Road Back, Barbara realizes she made a mistake by choosing a rehab too quickly. What could she have done differently? How does Road Back's method of dealing with drug addiction differ from Greg Leigh's? What are the downsides of each approach?

5. Barbara believes that our culture sows addiction into its young. Do you agree with her? What beliefs and attitudes does society instill in its children that could

contribute to addiction? Can Christians minimize the negative effects of these beliefs and attitudes in their children? If so, how?

6. How did Emily's previous visits to rehab only make her addictions worse? What causes her to finally decide that she wants to get better? Do you think true healing from addiction requires more than rehab can offer?

7. Greg's ex-wife Joan deals with the death of their daughter very differently than he does. What does Joan do to cope with her grief? How does this guard her against the bitterness that plagues Greg? What does this say about the importance of faith and support groups?

8. Barbara tells Kent that she hopes good will eventually result from Emily's hardship. Do you think Emily's life will have a more defined purpose because of her suffering and addiction? Have you or someone you know ever experienced good as a direct result from pain?

About the Author

Photo by Deryll Stegall

Terri Blackstock has sold over seven million books worldwide and is a *New York Times* and *USA TODAY* bestselling author. She is the award-winning author of *Intervention, Vicious Cycle,* and *Downfall,* as well as such series as Cape Refuge, Newpointe 911, the SunCoast Chronicles, and the Restoration series.

TerriBlackstock.com
Facebook: tblackstock
Twitter: @terriblackstock